the perfect people

(a jessie hunt psychological suspense—book 27)

blake pierce

Blake Pierce

Blake Pierce is the USA Today bestselling author of the RILEY PAGE mystery series, which includes seventeen books. Blake Pierce is also the author of the MACKENZIE WHITE mystery series, comprising fourteen books; of the AVERY BLACK mystery series, comprising six books; of the KERI LOCKE mystery series, comprising five books; of the MAKING OF RILEY PAIGE mystery series, comprising six books; of the KATE WISE mystery series, comprising seven books; of the CHLOE FINE psychological suspense mystery, comprising six books; of the JESSIE HUNT psychological suspense thriller series, comprising twenty-eight books; of the AU PAIR psychological suspense thriller series, comprising three books; of the ZOE PRIME mystery series, comprising six books; of the ADELE SHARP mystery series, comprising sixteen books, of the EUROPEAN VOYAGE cozy mystery series, comprising six books; of the LAURA FROST FBI suspense thriller, comprising eleven books; of the ELLA DARK FBI suspense thriller, comprising fourteen books (and counting); of the A YEAR IN EUROPE cozy mystery series, comprising nine books, of the AVA GOLD mystery series, comprising six books; of the RACHEL GIFT mystery series, comprising ten books (and counting); of the VALERIE LAW mystery series, comprising nine books (and counting); of the PAIGE KING mystery series, comprising eight books (and counting); of the MAY MOORE mystery series, comprising eleven books; of the CORA SHIELDS mystery series, comprising eight books (and counting); of the NICKY LYONS mystery series, comprising eight books (and counting), of the CAMI LARK mystery series, comprising eight books (and counting), of the AMBER YOUNG mystery series, comprising five books (and counting), of the DAISY FORTUNE mystery series, comprising five books (and counting), of the FIONA RED mystery series, comprising eight books (and counting), of the FAITH BOLD mystery series, comprising eight books (and counting), of the JULIETTE HART mystery series, comprising five books (and counting), of the MORGAN CROSS mystery series, comprising five books (and counting), and of the new FINN WRIGHT mystery series, comprising five books (and counting).

An avid reader and lifelong fan of the mystery and thriller genres, Blake loves to hear from you, so please feel free to visit www.blakepierceauthor.com to learn more and stay in touch.

ISBN: 978-1-0943-8213-5

BOOKS BY BLAKE PIERCE

FINN WRIGHT MYSTERY SERIES
WHEN YOU'RE MINE (Book #1)
WHEN YOU'RE SAFE (Book #2)
WHEN YOU'RE CLOSE (Book #3)
WHEN YOU'RE SLEEPING (Book #4)
WHEN YOU'RE SANE (Book #5)

MORGAN CROSS MYSTERY SERIES
FOR YOU (Book #1)
FOR RAGE (Book #2)
FOR LUST (Book #3)
FOR WRATH (Book #4)
FOREVER (Book #5)

JULIETTE HART MYSTERY SERIES
NOTHING TO FEAR (Book #1)
NOTHING THERE (Book #2)
NOTHING WATCHING (Book #3)
NOTHING HIDING (Book #4)
NOTHING LEFT (Book #5)

FAITH BOLD MYSTERY SERIES
SO LONG (Book #1)
SO COLD (Book #2)
SO SCARED (Book #3)
SO NORMAL (Book #4)
SO FAR GONE (Book #5)
SO LOST (Book #6)
SO ALONE (Book #7)
SO FORGOTTEN (Book #8)

FIONA RED MYSTERY SERIES
LET HER GO (Book #1)
LET HER BE (Book #2)
LET HER HOPE (Book #3)
LET HER WISH (Book #4)
LET HER LIVE (Book #5)

LET HER RUN (Book #6)
LET HER HIDE (Book #7)
LET HER BELIEVE (Book #8)

DAISY FORTUNE MYSTERY SERIES
NEED YOU (Book #1)
CLAIM YOU (Book #2)
CRAVE YOU (Book #3)
CHOOSE YOU (Book #4)
CHASE YOU (Book #5)

AMBER YOUNG MYSTERY SERIES
ABSENT PITY (Book #1)
ABSENT REMORSE (Book #2)
ABSENT FEELING (Book #3)
ABSENT MERCY (Book #4)
ABSENT REASON (Book #5)

CAMI LARK MYSTERY SERIES
JUST ME (Book #1)
JUST OUTSIDE (Book #2)
JUST RIGHT (Book #3)
JUST FORGET (Book #4)
JUST ONCE (Book #5)
JUST HIDE (Book #6)
JUST NOW (Book #7)
JUST HOPE (Book #8)

NICKY LYONS MYSTERY SERIES
ALL MINE (Book #1)
ALL HIS (Book #2)
ALL HE SEES (Book #3)
ALL ALONE (Book #4)
ALL FOR ONE (Book #5)
ALL HE TAKES (Book #6)
ALL FOR ME (Book #7)
ALL IN (Book #8)

CORA SHIELDS MYSTERY SERIES
UNDONE (Book #1)
UNWANTED (Book #2)

UNHINGED (Book #3)
UNSAID (Book #4)
UNGLUED (Book #5)
UNSTABLE (Book #6)
UNKNOWN (Book #7)
UNAWARE (Book #8)

MAY MOORE SUSPENSE THRILLER
NEVER RUN (Book #1)
NEVER TELL (Book #2)
NEVER LIVE (Book #3)
NEVER HIDE (Book #4)
NEVER FORGIVE (Book #5)
NEVER AGAIN (Book #6)
NEVER LOOK BACK (Book #7)
NEVER FORGET (Book #8)
NEVER LET GO (Book #9)
NEVER PRETEND (Book #10)
NEVER HESITATE (Book #11)

PAIGE KING MYSTERY SERIES
THE GIRL HE PINED (Book #1)
THE GIRL HE CHOSE (Book #2)
THE GIRL HE TOOK (Book #3)
THE GIRL HE WISHED (Book #4)
THE GIRL HE CROWNED (Book #5)
THE GIRL HE WATCHED (Book #6)
THE GIRL HE WANTED (Book #7)
THE GIRL HE CLAIMED (Book #8)

VALERIE LAW MYSTERY SERIES
NO MERCY (Book #1)
NO PITY (Book #2)
NO FEAR (Book #3)
NO SLEEP (Book #4)
NO QUARTER (Book #5)
NO CHANCE (Book #6)
NO REFUGE (Book #7)
NO GRACE (Book #8)
NO ESCAPE (Book #9)

RACHEL GIFT MYSTERY SERIES
HER LAST WISH (Book #1)
HER LAST CHANCE (Book #2)
HER LAST HOPE (Book #3)
HER LAST FEAR (Book #4)
HER LAST CHOICE (Book #5)
HER LAST BREATH (Book #6)
HER LAST MISTAKE (Book #7)
HER LAST DESIRE (Book #8)
HER LAST REGRET (Book #9)
HER LAST HOUR (Book #10)

AVA GOLD MYSTERY SERIES
CITY OF PREY (Book #1)
CITY OF FEAR (Book #2)
CITY OF BONES (Book #3)
CITY OF GHOSTS (Book #4)
CITY OF DEATH (Book #5)
CITY OF VICE (Book #6)

A YEAR IN EUROPE
A MURDER IN PARIS (Book #1)
DEATH IN FLORENCE (Book #2)
VENGEANCE IN VIENNA (Book #3)
A FATALITY IN SPAIN (Book #4)

ELLA DARK FBI SUSPENSE THRILLER
GIRL, ALONE (Book #1)
GIRL, TAKEN (Book #2)
GIRL, HUNTED (Book #3)
GIRL, SILENCED (Book #4)
GIRL, VANISHED (Book 5)
GIRL ERASED (Book #6)
GIRL, FORSAKEN (Book #7)
GIRL, TRAPPED (Book #8)
GIRL, EXPENDABLE (Book #9)
GIRL, ESCAPED (Book #10)
GIRL, HIS (Book #11)
GIRL, LURED (Book #12)
GIRL, MISSING (Book #13)
GIRL, UNKNOWN (Book #14)

LAURA FROST FBI SUSPENSE THRILLER
ALREADY GONE (Book #1)
ALREADY SEEN (Book #2)
ALREADY TRAPPED (Book #3)
ALREADY MISSING (Book #4)
ALREADY DEAD (Book #5)
ALREADY TAKEN (Book #6)
ALREADY CHOSEN (Book #7)
ALREADY LOST (Book #8)
ALREADY HIS (Book #9)
ALREADY LURED (Book #10)
ALREADY COLD (Book #11)

EUROPEAN VOYAGE COZY MYSTERY SERIES
MURDER (AND BAKLAVA) (Book #1)
DEATH (AND APPLE STRUDEL) (Book #2)
CRIME (AND LAGER) (Book #3)
MISFORTUNE (AND GOUDA) (Book #4)
CALAMITY (AND A DANISH) (Book #5)
MAYHEM (AND HERRING) (Book #6)

ADELE SHARP MYSTERY SERIES
LEFT TO DIE (Book #1)
LEFT TO RUN (Book #2)
LEFT TO HIDE (Book #3)
LEFT TO KILL (Book #4)
LEFT TO MURDER (Book #5)
LEFT TO ENVY (Book #6)
LEFT TO LAPSE (Book #7)
LEFT TO VANISH (Book #8)
LEFT TO HUNT (Book #9)
LEFT TO FEAR (Book #10)
LEFT TO PREY (Book #11)
LEFT TO LURE (Book #12)
LEFT TO CRAVE (Book #13)
LEFT TO LOATHE (Book #14)
LEFT TO HARM (Book #15)
LEFT TO RUIN (Book #16)

THE AU PAIR SERIES

ALMOST GONE (Book#1)
ALMOST LOST (Book #2)
ALMOST DEAD (Book #3)

ZOE PRIME MYSTERY SERIES
FACE OF DEATH (Book#1)
FACE OF MURDER (Book #2)
FACE OF FEAR (Book #3)
FACE OF MADNESS (Book #4)
FACE OF FURY (Book #5)
FACE OF DARKNESS (Book #6)

A JESSIE HUNT PSYCHOLOGICAL SUSPENSE SERIES
THE PERFECT WIFE (Book #1)
THE PERFECT BLOCK (Book #2)
THE PERFECT HOUSE (Book #3)
THE PERFECT SMILE (Book #4)
THE PERFECT LIE (Book #5)
THE PERFECT LOOK (Book #6)
THE PERFECT AFFAIR (Book #7)
THE PERFECT ALIBI (Book #8)
THE PERFECT NEIGHBOR (Book #9)
THE PERFECT DISGUISE (Book #10)
THE PERFECT SECRET (Book #11)
THE PERFECT FAÇADE (Book #12)
THE PERFECT IMPRESSION (Book #13)
THE PERFECT DECEIT (Book #14)
THE PERFECT MISTRESS (Book #15)
THE PERFECT IMAGE (Book #16)
THE PERFECT VEIL (Book #17)
THE PERFECT INDISCRETION (Book #18)
THE PERFECT RUMOR (Book #19)
THE PERFECT COUPLE (Book #20)
THE PERFECT MURDER (Book #21)
THE PERFECT HUSBAND (Book #22)
THE PERFECT SCANDAL (Book #23)
THE PERFECT MASK (Book #24)
THE PERFECT RUSE (Book #25)
THE PERFECT VENEER (Book #26)
THE PERFECT PEOPLE (Book #27)
THE PERFECT WITNESS (Book #28)

CHLOE FINE PSYCHOLOGICAL SUSPENSE SERIES
NEXT DOOR (Book #1)
A NEIGHBOR'S LIE (Book #2)
CUL DE SAC (Book #3)
SILENT NEIGHBOR (Book #4)
HOMECOMING (Book #5)
TINTED WINDOWS (Book #6)

KATE WISE MYSTERY SERIES
IF SHE KNEW (Book #1)
IF SHE SAW (Book #2)
IF SHE RAN (Book #3)
IF SHE HID (Book #4)
IF SHE FLED (Book #5)
IF SHE FEARED (Book #6)
IF SHE HEARD (Book #7)

THE MAKING OF RILEY PAIGE SERIES
WATCHING (Book #1)
WAITING (Book #2)
LURING (Book #3)
TAKING (Book #4)
STALKING (Book #5)
KILLING (Book #6)

RILEY PAIGE MYSTERY SERIES
ONCE GONE (Book #1)
ONCE TAKEN (Book #2)
ONCE CRAVED (Book #3)
ONCE LURED (Book #4)
ONCE HUNTED (Book #5)
ONCE PINED (Book #6)
ONCE FORSAKEN (Book #7)
ONCE COLD (Book #8)
ONCE STALKED (Book #9)
ONCE LOST (Book #10)
ONCE BURIED (Book #11)
ONCE BOUND (Book #12)
ONCE TRAPPED (Book #13)
ONCE DORMANT (Book #14)

ONCE SHUNNED (Book #15)
ONCE MISSED (Book #16)
ONCE CHOSEN (Book #17)

MACKENZIE WHITE MYSTERY SERIES
BEFORE HE KILLS (Book #1)
BEFORE HE SEES (Book #2)
BEFORE HE COVETS (Book #3)
BEFORE HE TAKES (Book #4)
BEFORE HE NEEDS (Book #5)
BEFORE HE FEELS (Book #6)
BEFORE HE SINS (Book #7)
BEFORE HE HUNTS (Book #8)
BEFORE HE PREYS (Book #9)
BEFORE HE LONGS (Book #10)
BEFORE HE LAPSES (Book #11)
BEFORE HE ENVIES (Book #12)
BEFORE HE STALKS (Book #13)
BEFORE HE HARMS (Book #14)

AVERY BLACK MYSTERY SERIES
CAUSE TO KILL (Book #1)
CAUSE TO RUN (Book #2)
CAUSE TO HIDE (Book #3)
CAUSE TO FEAR (Book #4)
CAUSE TO SAVE (Book #5)
CAUSE TO DREAD (Book #6)

KERI LOCKE MYSTERY SERIES
A TRACE OF DEATH (Book #1)
A TRACE OF MURDER (Book #2)
A TRACE OF VICE (Book #3)
A TRACE OF CRIME (Book #4)
A TRACE OF HOPE (Book #5)

PROLOGUE

Trey Killian was feeling no pain.

He wasn't sure if it was the two rum and Cokes he'd had. Or the two vodka and cranberries. Or maybe it was the Jell-O shot he'd gulped down. Or the three beers. Or the weed.

Whatever it was, as Trey walked through the kitchen of Shasta Mallory's Manhattan Beach, California, beach house with a teriyaki tofu skewer in hand, he was borderline numb with good vibes. When he reached the entrance to Shasta's giant living room, he actually had to lean against the wall for support.

He looked out at the sea of people and allowed himself to take it all in. There were more gorgeous women here than his eyes could process. In addition, most of the guys looked like they had just come from auditioning for roles in action films. The music—a thumping dance track—was making Trey's bones rattle happily.

Who would have thought that a long-haired, scraggly-looking guy who was working as a Nashville session guitarist just six months ago would be in L.A. today, playing on the albums of some of the biggest artists in the world, and even getting an invitation to a huge Labor Day weekend beach blowout held by an uber-powerful music manager like Shasta Mallory?

Okay, maybe that was an overstatement. He didn't actually play on those mega-artists' albums. But he was there as a backup session performer if the regular guitarist ever got sick or didn't show. That hadn't happened yet. And while Shasta hadn't actually invited him to her party, her assistant had invited his buddy Dale, who ran the studio mixing board, and he'd mentioned it to Trey.

Since Trey lived in Hermosa Beach, just one beach town and half a mile south of here, he figured he'd crash the party. It turned out to be a good call. There was no security checking names at the door. In fact, there was no door to wait at. Everyone came and went as they chose through the open patio doors. The party spilled out onto the sand in front of the house.

Even though this was just the Thursday night before Labor Day, the place was rocking. To Trey's bleary eyes, there appeared to be at least a couple hundred people here already and it was only 10 p.m. He wondered what it would be like in an hour.

As he carefully made his way down the short set of stairs into the living room, he noticed something odd over on the parquet dance floor at the far end of the room. Some people were legitimately dancing, but one couple was acting oddly. The guy, heavyset with a long beard and wearing a white tuxedo and top hat, appeared to be choking out his dance partner, who didn't seem to be into it.

Everyone around the couple had stopped dancing and was staring but no one was doing anything, which made Trey think that maybe he was imagining things, that perhaps this wasn't anything disturbing after all, but just some weird West Coast party performance art that a guy who grew up in Louisiana wasn't clued into.

But then he realized he recognized the woman. It was Shasta Mallory, the big-time music manager who was also the owner of the house and hostess of the party. She definitely didn't seem to be on board with the tuxedo guy's act because she was swatting his hands away.

By the time Trey got to the dance floor, it was clear that some of the other onlookers were equally uneasy with what was going on. He exchanged looks with one big blond dude who looked like a long-lost Hemsworth brother, and they seemed to silently make the same assessment: they had to do something.

At the same time, they moved forward. Each of them grabbed one of the tuxedo guy's arms and yanked it off Shasta Mallory's neck. The guy tried to fight them off and grab at her again. That seemed to open the floodgates. A half dozen other people joined in, all helping pull the guy off Shasta.

The Hemsworth-looking dude even got in a couple of solid punches to the chest before the guy in the tuxedo scrambled away through the mass of bodies and darted out the door. Trey lost sight of him as he ran off into the darkness. When he turned around, he saw several people assisting Shasta to a nearby couch.

"Are you okay?" one young woman in a bikini asked. "Should we call the cops?"

Shasta waved her arms and shook her head vehemently. After swallowing a few times, she finally spoke.

"No, if the police come, they might end up closing down the party. I can't have that. I hired caterers. I have clients coming. I'm not shutting everything down because of some drunk psycho in a bad tuxedo. If someone could just get me some water, I'll be fine in a minute."

Trey was about to offer but someone else volunteered first. That was cool with him. He'd already done his part, and the idea of fighting through the crowd to go back to the kitchen for water and come all the way back here wasn't appealing. He was already on the verge of losing his buzz as it was. He had proven himself to be a Good Samaritan. He didn't need to go overboard.

Besides, this might be a good chance to earn some face time with Shasta, maybe see if he could actually play on one of her clients' albums for real. He kicked aside the top hat that the attacker had left behind and sat down on the couch beside her, nudging a petite young thing in glasses out of the way so that he could get closer and offer his best supportive smile.

***

The man walked casually back into the party a half hour later. Without the tuxedo, the beard, or the fat suit, no one had any reason to take extra notice of him, even with the small backpack he had slung over his shoulder. He maneuvered through the swath of people in the living room and found the top hat he'd left behind earlier still lying on the floor at the edge of Shasta Mallory's in-home dance floor.

He picked it up, took it to the kitchen, and stuffed it into one of the trash cans that he knew would be dumped out sooner rather than later. Now he wouldn't have to worry about residual DNA from the hat being used to identify him later. Then he unobtrusively made his way to the hallway and up the stairs.

He could see Shasta Mallory down below, chatting with some of her guests. But he knew that at some point during the night, she'd have cause to come upstairs. It might be soon. It might not be for several hours.

But whenever she came up, he'd be waiting for her.

CHAPTER ONE

Jessie Hunt took her time getting ready.

It was a rare day when she got to have a leisurely morning and she intended to make the most of it. She could already hear her police captain husband, Ryan Hernandez, and her younger sister, Hannah Dorsey, in the kitchen of their Mid-Wilshire Los Angeles home, prepping breakfast, but she refused to let that rush her.

Hannah wasn't leaving for another couple of hours. And since Jessie didn't have a pending case, she and Ryan were letting themselves arrive at LAPD's downtown Central police station at 9 a.m. instead of their typical 7:55.

Of course, the leisurely morning didn't mean Jessie wouldn't still dress for potential chaos. One never knew when investigative turmoil might strike for a criminal profiler like herself. That's why she was slipping into her black sneakers, which could almost pass for loafers to the casual eye but worked great when chasing a suspect.

It completed an ensemble that included loose-fitting athletic slacks, also great for physically tricky situations, and a lightweight gray top that looked professional but would hopefully afford her some reprieve from the sweltering late-summer days they'd been having lately. She tied her shoulder-length brown hair in a loose ponytail that wouldn't get in the way if she had to do anything more taxing than paperwork today.

She checked herself one last time in the mirror before heading out and let out a relieved sigh. None but those closest to her would guess that the put-together person looking back at her had been through such a rough stretch of late. They'd just see the attractive face, the beaming smile, the bright green eyes, the tall, athletic frame, and the confident posture and invariably assume all was well.

And technically it was. She reminded herself to be grateful. After all, there had been more than two months of relative calm since the madness of late June, when a series of coinciding nightmares had turned her life into a real-world horror show.

She hadn't had a near-concussion event since that night in June when a woman who had murdered her billionaire husband hit Jessie in the head with an ice bucket while trying to escape. Luckily, her doctor had determined that no additional damage had been done.

But considering that Jessie was still only five months removed from a major concussion that caused weeks of headaches, memory loss, confusion, and dizziness, she knew she wasn't out of the woods. Dr. Varma had warned her that she was still at risk of Second-impact syndrome, a condition where someone suffers a second concussion before completely recovering from the first one and gets brain swelling, seriously increasing the chance of death. It was a concern that was, quite literally, always on her mind.

But that worry paled in comparison to the other trauma that had upended her inner circle the same night she was getting hit with an ice bucket. At almost that exact moment, her little sister, Hannah, and Jessie's best friend, Kat Gentry, were almost murdered by a hitwoman named Ash Pierce, who was paid to kill them in order to punish Jessie.

Though they managed to ultimately outwit and defeat the assassin, it wasn't without consequence. Kat was only now nearing functional recovery from injuries that included a broken nose, a fractured left kneecap, and multiple stab wounds, the worst of which went deep into her right shoulder. She'd only gotten full range of motion back in the last week.

She'd been doing her rehab at the Lake Arrowhead mountain cabin of her sheriff's deputy boyfriend, Mitch, where she'd been staying this whole time. It was two hours northeast of L.A., so Jessie, Hannah, and Ryan hadn't gotten to see much of her this summer.

Because of that distance, Jessie hadn't been able to observe how Kat had been handling her emotional recovery either. But she'd been keeping a close eye on her sister's. To her relief, Hannah didn't show any outward signs of trauma from her run-in with Ash Pierce.

But Jessie knew better than to assume her sister wasn't hurting inside. Hannah had been through enough suffering in her eighteen years that she had become a master at hiding it from others. That didn't mean she wasn't absorbing every blow.

Jessie worried how both women would handle it when Pierce's case came to trial, which was only months away. They'd both have to testify and face in court the woman who had intended to torture and murder them on camera. Would they be ready when that scab was ripped off?

How could Jessie expect either of them—both civilians—to be up to such a monumental task when *she* wasn't sure that she was able to manage her own emotional burdens, both internal and, in one massive instance, external? And she was supposed to be a professional.

"Are you joining us?" Ryan called out from the kitchen.

Jessie snapped out of it, realizing that she'd been fiddling listlessly with her ponytail for the last minute, lost in thought.

"Coming!" she shouted as she left the bedroom and joined them.

Hannah's back was to her as she prepped something in a pan on the stove. Ryan was clumsily moving hot slices of toast from the toaster onto plates while trying to avoid burning his fingers. One of the pieces fell to the floor and he looked up sheepishly to see if anyone had seen it happen. Jessie shook her head in feigned disappointment.

"That one will be mine," he said.

"I should think so, Captain Hernandez," she replied officiously, trying to frown.

But she could only hold it for a second before his giant, warm brown eyes made her lips involuntarily reverse course and turn into a smile. He returned it and she felt herself melt. Even though their five months of marriage had been through more bumps than most couples would expect in a decade, she was still a sucker for his shy grin and adorable dimples.

She conceded that she wasn't immune to his other assets either. In addition to being a sharp investigator and tough cop who had graduated to leading both LAPD's Central Station and her specialized unit, he was sexy as hell. Six feet tall and 200 pounds, with short dark hair, a square jaw, and a well-muscled frame that strained at his dress shirts, he had the body of an MMA fighter and the brain of a sleuth.

She sat down at the breakfast table, where a mug of coffee was waiting for her. A moment later Hannah turned around and served her a big helping of cheesy scrambled eggs with avocado cubes, grilled mushrooms, and red onions. For Hannah, who until recently had been planning to go to culinary school, it was a relatively simple meal.

As Jessie watched her little sister scoop the food onto her plate, she marveled at how, less than two years ago, this young woman with the same green eyes, tall, lean figure, and intense focus as herself had been a complete stranger. Now it was hard to imagine a life without her, though soon she'd have to. College started for Hannah in less than three weeks. And even before then, she'd be losing valuable time with her.

"When are you going again?" she asked.

"The rideshare is picking me up at ten a.m.," Hannah said. "I should be at Patrice's beach house by eleven."

"And how long are you planning to be there?" Jessie checked, though she knew the answer and just wanted to make sure that her sister hadn't changed the plans.

"Don't worry," Hannah said. "I know Kat is planning to come back to town on Monday afternoon and you want me to cook a big welcome back Labor Day dinner for her. I promise I'll be back in time. I want to see her as much as you guys do, maybe even more. Does she still want to reopen Gentry Investigations on Tuesday morning?"

"Last I heard," Jessie said.

"Well, I don't start school until the nineteenth so I can probably help her out for a couple of weeks before I move into the dorm."

"I'm sure she'd really appreciate that," Ryan said, after swallowing a mouthful of cheesy eggs.

"Are you going to have any time to hang out with me?" Jessie asked, pretending to be hurt in order to hide the fact that she actually was mildly hurt. "You've got this beach house thing this weekend. You're moving in at school in two weekends. That only leaves one free weekend left for family."

She hung her head dramatically.

"Don't give me that," Hannah said, not falling for it. "If I had stuck to the original plan and gone to Cal State Fullerton, I'd already have been in school for two weeks by now. By switching to Cal-Irvine, you get an extra month with your charming sister."

"And I'm loving every second of it," Jessie noted, "but let's not forget how you got to switch schools at the last minute in the first place. I believe it was because I got my master's there and pulled strings with my thesis advisor, who just happens to be the head of the Criminology Department, which you suddenly decided to major in. So maybe a little genuflecting is in order."

"I think the complimentary cheesy eggs should suffice," Hannah replied with playful snark.

"Remind me who these beach house friends are again," Ryan said.

Jessie knew that he probably remembered who Hannah was meeting just fine. But he was intentionally playing the forgetful stepdad type to shake the sisters out of their teasing dynamic, which could occasionally turn acidic. She took the hint and eased up. So did Hannah, who answered the question sincerely.

"It's the gang from Wildpines," she said. "Remember when we had to hole up in that snowy cabin there last winter? These were the students from the Wildpines Arts Conservatory I met in town and ended up hanging out with. We all kept in touch. Anyway, one girl's family has a Santa Monica beach house and they're staying there this weekend. She's having her whole circle of friends over and they invited me to come too."

None of them mentioned the circumstances or final outcome of their stay in that mountain cabin last winter. They were holed up there because they were being stalked by a serial killer called the Night Hunter. Though they eventually managed to outmaneuver and capture him, Hannah had shot the elderly, unarmed, handcuffed man in a moment of delirious fury. The high she admitted to getting from killing the man was something that had scared all of them and that they'd been working through ever since.

"Must be nice to have a Santa Monica beach house they can visit on holiday," Ryan said, adopting a terrible faux British accent in the hope of moving quickly past the elephant in the room. "What kind of activities will you be partaking of?"

"I'm not sure," Hannah said. "Patrice mentioned that they had surfboards, jet skis, and kayaks. But I bet it will mostly be a lot of hanging out on the beach and walking along the pier."

"I'm actually kind of envious," Ryan said, giving up on the accent but not the silliness. "Maybe I should take a day off from this whole police captaining thing and join you crazy kids. I'm always game for water sports."

"We'd totally love to have you," Hannah said, managing to keep a straight face, "but I'm worried that the city would fall apart without you."

"Yeah, you're probably right," he said, before turning to Jessie. "I guess we should head out soon. I know we're being leisurely this morning but if we get in too late, I might lose my authority and not be able to keep Los Angeles on the straight and narrow."

Jessie offered a tight smile, hoping it would seem playful. She wanted to join in her husband and sister's shared jocularity, but her mind kept drifting to other, less lighthearted matters. Chief among them was the issue that had hovered over her marriage for the last two months, the one that neither she nor Ryan ever spoke of, which she morbidly called The Zoe Problem, though never out loud.

And then there was the other concern, the one they *did* talk about constantly, which would surely come up once they got to the station. But that could wait. For now, her little sister was going away for the weekend and that would be her focus.

"While Ryan is keeping our streets safe," she said to Hannah, "you do the same for yourself. Have fun. Relax, but please stay aware and keep in touch."

"I will," Hannah assured her, "but remember, we'll be less than an hour away."

"Still," Jessie reminded, "a lot can happen in an hour. You know that better than most. Just have an enjoyable, extremely alert weekend."

CHAPTER TWO

Jessie wasn't used to relief being her most anticipated emotion.

But somehow it had neared the top of the list of late, sometimes overtaking joy or pride. She'd felt it when she and Ryan got out of his car in the LAPD Central community police station parking garage without talking about The Zoe Problem, though she probably shouldn't have.

Her psychiatrist, Dr. Janice Lemmon, had told her on more than one occasion that the only way to solve this problem was to address it directly. But how was she supposed to tell her husband that she partly blamed him for her sister and best friend nearly being murdered by an assassin because he hadn't taken the threat seriously?

And what good would saying something do when he already blamed himself? Ryan was already fully aware that if he'd told his wife that Zoe Bradway—an incarcerated acolyte of a woman obsessed with Jessie—had made death threats against him, Hannah, and Kat, then she would have investigated them.

But he had assumed Zoe was just trying to get in Jessie's head and had no way to deliver on those threats. He was wrong and two people she loved had nearly paid the ultimate price. He beat himself up every day about that mistake. Jessie didn't need to make it worse. And yet she found forgiving him was beyond her, at least for now. So each conversation that concluded without the topic coming up was a reprieve.

She felt the wave of relief a second time as they walked into the detectives' bullpen at the station and noticed the relative quiet. That meant that there almost certainly hadn't been another recent murder by the killer who'd been haunting Jessie's dreams for months.

"Nothing new?" she asked Detective Karen Bray, who looked up as they walked in.

"Not so far," Karen said.

"But the morning is young," chimed in Detective Jim Nettles.

The other detectives in their unit, Homicide Special Section, weren't in the bullpen at the moment. Jessie wondered if Detectives

Susannah Valentine or Sam Goodwin might bring back news of a fresh murder with their coffee.

The four detectives, along with a two-person research department, and Jessie as criminal profiler, comprised HSS, an elite team which investigated cases with high profiles or intense media scrutiny—typically involving multiple victims or serial killers. Ryan led the group in addition to being captain of the station.

As Ryan headed to his office to check on what he'd missed overnight, Jessie stepped over to the corkboard where the team kept a list of all the victims of the killer that had been keeping her up at night, one who certainly met HSS's criteria. The media hadn't given him a name yet—and it *was* a him—because they weren't yet aware that the same killer was responsible for all the deaths in question. But HSS was and they were calling him the Clone Killer, at least for now.

So far, he'd killed four people, each about three weeks apart, although the timing wasn't exact. But that wasn't what had Jessie up at night. Each of those victims had almost been killed once before.

The HSS team didn't realize it initially, after the stabbing death of Woody Garnett, though perhaps they should have. Garnett had almost been murdered in March by a serial killer who stabbed people she thought had wronged their romantic partners. But Jessie and Ryan had saved him at the last second, capturing the unhinged young woman, Harper Grey, who had already plunged the knife into Garnett's abdomen in a hotel room. He recovered, only to be killed the same way a few months later on his boat docked in the marina. It was suspicious but there was no evidence, nor any credible suspects, as Grey was in prison.

Jessie started to put the pieces together immediately after learning of the murder of Janet Goodsen, who had acid sprayed on her a few weeks after Garnett's death. Goodsen had almost died by way of acid six months previously at her tenth wedding anniversary blowout party. A disturbed event photographer had been killing others the same way and Goodsen was next on her list, until Jessie stopped her in the nick of time.

But Jessie wasn't around when the woman was attacked again, this time in her own home, when her family was out. A small notebook, completely empty, was found lying on her chest, for reasons they had yet to determine.

The original culprit, Sloane Baker, wasn't responsible this time around. She had fallen to her death in a violent confrontation with

Jessie and Kat the night of the anniversary party. But it was clear that whoever was committing these crimes was painstakingly recreating the near-murders that a serial killer's next intended victims almost suffered. That was borne out several weeks later in mid-July.

"Looking for some sudden breakthrough?" Karen asked as she joined Jessie at the corkboard she was staring at.

"Yeah," Jessie admitted, "I figured that if I studied this thing five hundred and one times, something would come to me."

She was looking at the case of Sheena Lennox, a wealthy, married Santa Monica Realtor who had, like Janet Goodsen, been killed in her own home. While her physician husband was at the hospital, an intruder had broken in and made deep incisions in her arm and leg, slicing major arteries with one of her own kitchen knives, then locked her in a pantry, where she bled out. Her husband found her when he got home. In her case, a red apple was found on the floor just outside the pantry door.

The murder was eerily reminiscent of a series of killings committed by an in-home chef named Kurt Sumner last January who used precise cuts to major arteries using household knives to kill his victims. He considered it a form of art and had intended for Sheena to be his next canvas before Jessie captured him. He was currently serving multiple life sentences. Unfortunately, Sheena wasn't so lucky this time around.

After the third murder, HSS had snapped into action, reaching out to every near-victim in cases Jessie had investigated that involved serial or spree killers. They especially focused on the last potential victim who would have been killed if Jessie hadn't solved the case in time.

For all of those people, who numbered in the low double digits, they helped set up or improve home security systems, provided complimentary pepper spray and Tasers, taught basic self-defense techniques, and, in some cases where folks were particularly vulnerable, even put units outside their homes at night. But all of those efforts were blown up after the fourth murder.

"Has anything come to you?" Karen asked.

Jessie was so deep in thought that she'd forgotten that the other detective was still standing beside her. She looked over at the woman, who at thirty-eight was seven years her senior. Karen Bray, petite and self-effacing, was the only team member with a young child, and her maternal instinct was coming out now in the concerned tone she used as she checked in on how Jessie was doing.

"It's just that I don't think I've ever been more frustrated by a case," she admitted. "I come in here every day and yet I don't have a single lead to pursue. If Ryan were to get a new case today and assign it to me, I'd have to take it because I don't have anything fresh to work with on this, even after Melissa Ferro's murder, and that's with the video."

Karen nodded in shared disappointment. The one positive that was supposed to come when a serial killer took another life was the possibility of new evidence, especially when there was video footage of the killer. But other than brief snippets that showed the masked assailant entering and leaving Ferro's home the night she died, there was nothing. Actually there *was* one more thing: he waved. Both when he accessed the house and when he left, he made sure to wave dramatically for the camera.

Melissa Ferro, the most recent victim of the Clone Killer, as they dubbed him when his methods became clear, was killed almost three weeks ago, on August 12. She was found the next day, sprawled on the floor of her living room, dead of a massive dose of the sedative trazodone, which had been added to the oat milk creamer she put in her coffee each morning.

She was discovered by a friend who became concerned when she didn't meet for lunch that day. When they investigated, they found a brand new, unsharpened pencil in her mailbox. It had been rubbed in the same poisoned oat milk that killed her.

The team had spent hours trying to discern the meaning of the items left near the bodies. Did the apple found near Sheena Lennox's have to do with the original intended killer being a chef? Did the notepad found on Janet Goodsen's chest have any connection to how obnoxiously obsessive she was about list-making for her tenth anniversary party? No one could glean any particular correlation between Melissa Ferro and the pencil.

Someone had posited that the items might all be connected to a shopping list: the pencil for writing items down, the notebook keeping the list, and the apple as the first purchase. Jessie even threw out the idea that there might be some kind of school association with the notebook and pencil being supplies and the apple being for a teacher. The truth was that they were all grasping at straws.

There were only two things they knew for sure: the killer was male and over six feet tall. That limited information came from the surveillance camera outside Melissa Ferro's house. But because the camera that caught the glimpse of him was perched high above her front door at an odd angle, was black and white, and was partially blown out by an overly bright porch light, they couldn't tell anything else.

He was masked. He wore all black. And he had on a thick coat so they couldn't determine his weight or body frame. Only his stride style, in combination with his height, had convinced their research genius in residence, Jamil Winslow, that they were dealing with a man. But that one bit of positive news was overwhelmed by a much bigger negative.

Melissa Ferro, victim of the poisoned oat milk, had almost died once before, last January, when her husband, Richard, drugged her in their Bel-Air home, also using a massive dose of trazodone. It was a panicky decision, borne out of fear that she would discover that he'd murdered his mistress, who was pregnant with his child.

Jessie eventually determined that Richard Ferro was the killer and saved his drugged wife. Ferro, convicted for both killing his mistress and the attempted murder of both his wife and Jessie, was serving a life sentence.

But because Ferro wasn't a serial killer, no one had thought to warn Melissa that she might be the future victim of a copycat killer. Ferro's case had seemed straightforward: he had killed his mistress, who was going to reveal their affair and her pregnancy. Then he decided to kill his wife when he thought she might discover the truth. And finally, he tried to choke Jessie to death when he realized she'd figured out his crime.

This wasn't a man who had conceived an elaborate plan to kill multiple people. He was just an amoral scumbag whose world spiraled out of control and whose every attempt to solve his problems ended in violence. That didn't fit the pattern of the Clone Killer.

But if the original murderer in this fourth case—Richard Ferro—wasn't a serial killer and his final near-victim wasn't a planned selection on some list, then how were they supposed to protect other potential future victims? It was one thing to put squad cars outside the homes of people who had almost died at the hands of serial killers caught by Jessie Hunt. But to put cops at the homes of every near-victim of every killer Jessie brought to justice?

That wasn't just eleven people. Depending on how one counted, that number could range from about fifty people to well into the hundreds. LAPD didn't have anywhere near the resources for that level of personal protection. And yet, they couldn't just leave all those folks in the dark.

"I'm going to check in with Jamil and Beth," Jessie said to Karen as she headed toward the research department, silently making a decision that she realized she should have come to some time ago.

"Go easy on them," Karen called after her. "You've got that uber-purposeful look to you. Just remember—whatever you've got in mind, they'll be hearing it for the first time."

"I'll be like a gentle, soothing rain," Jessie promised, marching down the hall as quickly as she could without breaking into a jog.

***

"We have to call *all* of them?" Beth Ryerson, HSS's junior researcher repeated incredulously.

"It's something I should have had you guys do the day after Melissa Ferro was killed," Jessie said. "I guess I just hoped that the new evidence from the crime scene—the video footage, the autopsy, something—would have cracked the case open. But there's no excuse now."

"So just to be clear," Jamil Winslow, the head of HSS research said, "you want us to reach out to every person who was in potentially mortal danger when you caught the killer involved in their case?"

"Correct," Jessie told him.

"So in the case where a woman tried to poison her husband on a private jet and inadvertently poisoned someone else and went to prison for it, we need to warn the husband she didn't successfully kill?" he checked.

"You're getting it."

"Ms. Hunt," Jamil said, polite as ever, "you do realize that in many of these cases, the person these killers were hoping to eliminate next was *you*, right?"

"It's an irony that I'm well aware of, Jamil," Jessie said. "But it's also clear to me that if our copycat wanted to make me his next victim, that would kind of defeat the point of this whole endeavor for him. These murders are his way of sending a message to me. He'll only come after me when he's done sending messages. Also, I've told you a million times to call me Jessie, Jamil. Now can you guys do this?"

Jamil looked over at Beth, who shrugged in return. It was her way of acknowledging that he was the one who knew the answer to that question better than she did. Jamil Winslow didn't look imposing but everyone in HSS agreed that he was the unit's resident genius.

Short and skinny with thick glasses and a perpetually serious expression, he made up for his lack of physical prowess with his mental ability. At just twenty-five, he was already an expert at filtering through massive databases, sorting surveillance video into manageable buckets, and making complex financial records understandable, all seemingly in the blink of an eye.

"In theory, yes, we can reach out to all these people," he said. "Partly because it's not crazy busy with other cases right now. And sadly, because we have no leads on this one. But it will be a daunting undertaking. We're talking a *lot* of people. It could take a while."

"Do it anyway," Jessie said. "The idea that there are vulnerable citizens out there who could be safer if only they knew they were in danger—we have to do whatever we can for them."

Beth sighed heavily and Jessie turned to face her. The junior researcher had only been with the unit for a few months but she'd already more than proven her mettle. When she showed signs of apprehension, Jessie knew to take it seriously.

Like Jamil, Beth Ryerson was twenty-five. Unlike him, she was a daunting physical specimen. Over six feet tall with brown hair that she liked to keep in a ponytail, Beth was a former college volleyball star at UC-Santa Barbara. Unfussily attractive, she never wore makeup, and her razor-sharp mind was often hidden under a relaxed demeanor. Her perpetual chill was a total contrast to Jamil's constant, jittery intensity. She almost always had a sunny disposition. But she wasn't smiling now.

"What is it, Beth?" Jessie asked.

"There's another concern with reaching out to so many people," she said reluctantly. "The more folks we contact, the more risk there is that some of them might speak to the press. We've been lucky so far that the media hasn't made any connection among the cases, probably because the general public wasn't aware that these victims were on past serial killers' hit lists in the first place. But that could change if reporters start getting calls from people who've been warned by HSS."

"Frankly," Jamil added, "I'm surprised that the Clone Killer hasn't already reached out to the media himself."

"He will when it serves his purposes," Jessie assured him. "He's striking fear in victims right now. His next step is to strike fear in the whole city. He doesn't want to play that card until he's ready. As to your concern, Beth, it's legitimate, but it's a risk we'll have to take. If making these calls saves even one life, it's worth it."

Just then, Ryan bolted through the research office door. The second Jessie saw his face, she knew her relaxed day was over.

CHAPTER THREE

"Another victim?" she asked, her heart sinking even as she knew it might be the best chance to catch the bastard.

Ryan shook his head.

"Not in the Clone Killer case," he said. "But a new one came in. We just got a call from the Manhattan Beach Police Department. A woman named Shasta Mallory was found dead there this morning at her beachfront mansion."

"Manhattan Beach?" Jessie repeated. "That's not in LAPD jurisdiction."

"No, but they've specifically requested the assistance of HSS," Ryan told her. "Apparently the victim is a big-time music manager who was throwing some blowout Labor Day weekend party at her place last night. Some of her clients are major stars and they've put pressure on the local police to bring in HSS—specifically you—to help. They basically begged me to make you available. Since you didn't have anything else on your plate, I couldn't in good conscience say no."

Jessie couldn't blame him for agreeing to the request but shared his reservations nonetheless.

"Okay, but what happens if something breaks on the Clone Killer front while I'm working this case?" she asked.

"We'll cross that bridge when we come to it," he replied. "In the meantime, we can't just stay in a holding pattern, not having you take other cases on the chance that something might happen with this one. We've been dealing with this situation for months now. We'll address any new developments as they arise."

Jessie knew he didn't intend to sound like he was chastising her, so she let the intensity of his tone slide. Before she could respond, Jamil piped in.

"Don't forget, I got my start with MBPD. So anything you need, don't hesitate to ask. I might be able to offer some local insight that an outsider like yourself wouldn't be privy to."

Jamil was making a rare attempt at levity with his "outsider" crack, but what he said was true. Jessie and Ryan had actually met him in a similar situation, while working a prior case in the beach town just southwest of L.A. He was the researcher for the local department and his assistance had been invaluable. After working together, he had applied to join LAPD and requested to join HHS specifically so he could work with the two of them again. Upon discovering his qualifications, he was hired immediately.

"Noted," Jessie said. "If you were Academy-trained, I might even ask you to tag along. But since you're not, I guess I better find out which detective I'm being paired with."

She noticed Jamil try to hide a shy smile, well aware that he'd been toying with the idea of applying to the police academy in the hopes of joining the force. Only his concerns about his small stature and physical fragility had prevented him so far.

"I'm assigning Valentine to work with you on this one," Ryan told her. "You cool with that?"

Susannah Valentine had joined the unit seven months ago, when Jessie was on sabbatical from the department and teaching a course at UCLA. Their working relationship started out extremely rocky, in large part due to Susannah's "take no prisoners" investigative techniques. It didn't help that she had also flirted relentlessly with Ryan, unaware that he was engaged to Jessie, back when the couple was keeping their relationship secret.

After a brutally honest airing out session, the two women eventually made peace. Since then, they'd developed a friendly, teasing rapport that played off their former combativeness. That's why Jessie was a little surprised by the question.

"Why wouldn't I be cool with it?" she asked suspiciously.

Right at that moment, Susannah walked in. As usual, she was dressed in the standard attire that used to make Jessie equal parts self-conscious and distant. She wore a tight-fitting turquoise top and hip-hugging slacks, an ensemble that might typically work better for a night out than for investigating a murder.

The outfit was only half of what made Susannah Valentine such an unconventional-looking LAPD detective. She was also, by all accounts, a bombshell. Almost impossibly gorgeous, she had hazel eyes, deeply tanned skin, and long, black hair to go along with a curvy figure that suggested swimsuit model more than cop. Of course, the woman knew how she was perceived and rather than hide from it, she preferred to lean into the persona, to use it like a weapon.

Ryan still hadn't answered Jessie's question about why she might not be okay working with Susannah Valentine on this particular case, so she posed it again, this time with more bite.

"Captain Hernandez," she said sharply, "why wouldn't I be cool with it?"

Ryan looked at her with trepidation before offering a reluctant reply.

"I'll let her explain," he said.

***

They were in the car before Valentine explained why she'd been assigned. Once she did, Jessie understood why she'd held off.

"I didn't want to say anything in front of the research crew," the detective said as she pulled out of the parking garage and merged into traffic. "I know this may come as a shock, but I *am* capable of being embarrassed."

"It does come as a shock, actually," Jessie teased from the passenger seat. "Now you've really got me intrigued."

Susannah gave her a smirk. It was clear to Jessie that she was pretending to be offended. By now, she had to know that Jessie wasn't going to judge her based on what she might reveal. She'd already shared the truth about the sexual assault that had defined her younger years and how she subsequently decided that she wouldn't allow herself to be ashamed of her body or her brash personality.

It was why she dressed so brazenly, almost like a dare to anyone who might challenge her right to be who she wanted. It was why she joined the force, so she could protect herself and the rights of other people to live their lives safely, without having to worry about constant harassment. She knew Jessie had her back and she was right.

"When Captain Hernandez told us this case had come in, I volunteered," she said. "Turns out I have some personal experience that might prove useful to our investigation."

"What do you mean?" Jessie wanted to know.

"I used to go to some of these annual parties."

"Wait, there's more than one?" Jessie asked, surprised.

"Sure," Susannah said, pulling the car onto the 110 freeway and heading south toward the Beach Cities. "It's a whole thing. Over the big summer holiday weekends, the beachfront communities in the South Bay have these massive, unofficial parties that travel from mansion to mansion. They have them for Memorial Day, the Fourth of July, and finish up with a giant end of summer extravaganza for Labor Day. That's why the party was last night—on a Thursday. They'll run all the way through Monday night."

"And you used to go to these?" Jessie asked. "That doesn't seem like your scene."

"It's not anymore," Susannah conceded. "But back in my late teens, when I was in high school, after…what happened to me, I was kind of lost. I was drinking too much, partying too much, trying to numb the pain. So some girlfriends and I would take the metro green line down from our crappy neighborhood to Redondo Beach, catch a bus to the Manhattan Beach Strand, hop out, and act like we owned the place. And because I look like this and could fill out a bikini, we could get in pretty much anywhere we wanted. I can go into more detail later, but that's why I'm on this case—because I know the milieu."

"And maybe because you can still fit in at these parties today?" Jessie added, now understanding why Ryan was reluctant to explain his reasoning. He was trading on Detective Valentine's sex appeal as an asset in their investigation and he felt guilty about it. He might also have worried that Jessie would be jealous, wondering if he didn't think she had enough sex appeal of her own to get the job done.

While she was more than secure in that department, she didn't kid herself. She wasn't the voluptuous pinup type that her partner was, and having Susannah available and willing to make use of her special appeal would be a great advantage. Still, she made a mental note to tease her husband about his discomfort later.

"It's worth a shot," Susannah said with a shrug. "If me fitting in down there helps get us an edge, I think we should use it."

"I agree," Jessie said. "I just have one question for you."

"What?" Susannah asked hesitantly.

"Did you remember to bring your bikini?"

She just barely managed to avoid the detective's attempt to punch her shoulder.

CHAPTER FOUR

By the time they arrived at the Manhattan Beach Strand forty-five minutes later, Jessie was half-wishing she'd brought a bikini of her own.

It was barely 11 a.m. and the temperature was already approaching ninety degrees. Jessie had to remind herself that they were the lucky ones. If it was this hot here, that likely meant it was closer to 105 downtown, where Ryan and the rest of the HHS team were stuck. They parked in the alley behind the address they'd been given.

"Should we just go in the back way?" Susannah asked.

"I think we should enter through the front door," Jessie suggested. "That's more than likely how the killer got in, right? Mixing in among the partygoers. I'd like to try to get into the murderer's head from the very beginning."

"Fine by me," Susannah said, "let's go around."

They walked the half block down the alley until they got to the small residential street leading to the beach. Once they rounded the corner they were greeted by the unobstructed warm breeze and salty scent that accompanied it.

Just in front of them was the Strand. Beyond that was the beach, which was an endless sea of humanity, along with countless umbrellas, towels, and beach coolers, with multiple crowded volleyball courts mixed in. Past that was the Pacific Ocean, already packed with people. Jessie could see the waves, oblivious to it all, collapsing in on each other, creating a frothy surf that bubbled tantalizingly white.

She and Susannah stepped onto the Stand and walked in the direction of the mansion where the murder occurred. The Strand was the name of the pedestrian-friendly, north-south cement path that often came within a casual newspaper toss of many homes in the towns of Manhattan Beach and Hermosa Beach. It was popular with tourists, runners, moms pushing strollers, or simply locals taking a walk with their morning coffee.

Looking at the long line of impressive homes along the Strand, Jessie silently noted again what always struck her when she came to this neighborhood: the place oozed rich. It didn't have the same ostentatious, perfectly manicured persona of a place like Beverly Hills. But the casual, beachy vibe couldn't mask the wealth of the people who lived here or the reality that many of the houses she and Susannah walked by cost close to eight figures, with some going for multiple times that.

It wasn't hard to find the residence they were looking for as it was surrounded by police tape and had an officer standing guard out front. The home was narrow but tall—three stories high with front-facing windows and large terraces on each level that took up the entire front of the home.

Jessie couldn't help but notice the giant sliding door that led from the courtyard patio into the house. If that had been wide open last night, any number of people could have shuffled in and out without being noticed.

They approached the officer and Susannah flashed her badge. The cop, a young blond guy who looked like he'd rather be in the water than sweating through a dark, navy uniform in an unshaded courtyard, sullenly waved them through.

"Who's in charge?" Susannah asked him sharply, annoyed at the officer's lack of civility.

"Sergeant Breem," he answered. "He's in the living room."

"I know him," Jessie said as they walked up the steps toward the front door. "He was involved the last time I worked a case down here."

"Oh yeah? What's he like?"

Jessie struggled with how to answer. Her feelings about everyone related to that time were colored by the fact that she'd been down here investigating the murder of her friend and mentor, the celebrated criminal profiler Garland Moses. It turned out that he'd been killed by her own ex-husband, Kyle Voss, as a form of vicious payback.

"He's a good guy," Jessie finally said. "Very experienced. Chill. He's a surfer. He'll be an asset."

They opened the front door and stepped inside. At first glance, it seemed like a tornado had passed through the interior of the home. Sofas were turned over. A coffee table was on its side, with two broken legs lying nearby. Plates and cups were everywhere. Beer bottles—some broken—were strewn all over the floor. Pieces of food rested on every surface, from countertops to tables, to the parquet dance floor, to the carpet, where it had been ground in. There were several puddles of liquid, some of which Jessie didn't want to guess the contents of.

In the far corner, near the kitchen, another officer was talking to someone with his back to them. The officer stopped speaking and nodded in their direction. The other person turned around. It was Breem.

Sergeant Drake Breem looked just as Jessie remembered him: a deeply tanned, weathered but wiry guy in his forties with shaggy gray hair that was just this side of acceptable for a law enforcement officer.

"Jessie Hunt," he said, breaking into a wide smile as he walked toward them. "It's been too long. How the hell are you?"

"I'm good," she said, accepting the unexpected hug she got instead of a handshake. "Sergeant, this is Detective Susannah Valentine. She's on our team at HSS. Detective, this is Sergeant Drake Breem of MBPD."

"Nice to meet you, Detective," Breem said, extending his hand to Susannah for a more traditional handshake. Jessie noted that he looked her straight in the eyes and never made any attempt to glance below her collarbone. That was a rarity for her partner, especially when it came to male cops.

"You too, Sergeant," she replied. "Jessie speaks highly of you."

"Nice of her to lie on my behalf," Breem said. "In order to keep the façade going, I suppose my best move would be to fill you in on what we know so far and show you the crime scene. Sound good?"

"Lead the way," Jessie said.

"We actually don't know a ton," he admitted as he started toward the stairs. "Here's what I can tell you for sure. There was a ruckus during the party earlier in the evening, an altercation of some kind. Multiple folks have mentioned it, but we can't find any witnesses who actually saw it take place, so we don't know the nature of what happened, who was involved, or if it was in any way connected to what happened to Shasta Mallory later on. We're still hoping that when someone wakes up later this morning, they'll come forward with something useful. But as of now, that's all we've got: something definitely seems to have happened. But we don't know what, when, or with who."

He paused briefly to catch his breath as they reached the landing between the first and second floors. After a few seconds, he resumed trudging up the stairs and talking.

"What we do know is that Mallory's body was found this morning by her personal assistant, who is currently in a guest room on the third floor, still in a very emotional state. She wanted to take something for anxiety, but I told her she had to wait until you had a chance to interview her."

"We appreciate that," Jessie said. "We'll try to get to her quick."

"Thanks," Breem replied. "She's been a handful. Lastly, the coroner hasn't transported the body yet, so you can get a look at the scene as it was, but his preliminary analysis is pretty straightforward. It looks like she was choked to death. He doesn't seem too uncertain on the matter."

They reached the top of the stairs, and all stopped to gather themselves. Jessie used the opportunity to take in the view through the wall-sized, beach-facing window in front of them. From this height, she could see the entirety of the Santa Monica Bay, from the Palos Verdes Peninsula all the way north to Malibu. Just south of that was Santa Monica, where Hannah was already likely settling in at her friend's beach house right about now.

"You know," Breem said, pulling her out of her thoughts, "if it was anyone but you handling this, there'd be some hard feelings. When Shasta Mallory's clients started demanding we bring in HHS, the chief got his back up a little. I think he was mildly insulted. But after we reminded him how effective you were the last time around, he relented pretty quickly."

"Are you sure he wasn't just a little happy to pass the buck too?" Susannah asked, with her trademark bluntness. "If this investigation gets screwed up, it's on us and those pop stars will blame HSS, not his department."

"That may have played a role too," Breem acknowledged wryly, leading them to a door at the end of the hall. "This is Shasta Mallory's bedroom."

Jessie noted that the door didn't seem to have any damage indicating that it had been forced open. They stepped inside. Out of the corner of her eye, Jessie could see a body lying on the bed but chose to ignore it for now so she could take in the rest of the room. It had a door leading out to a terrace the size of a bedroom.

In one corner of the bedroom was a Peloton bike. In another was a fireplace surrounded by an easy chair, a love seat, and a small coffee table. None of it looked disturbed. She looked in the bathroom, which was messy, but not unusually so. There was no indication that a struggle had occurred there.

"Nothing out of the ordinary, right?" Susannah said, voicing Jessie's thoughts.

"Not as far as I can tell."

"You ready to look at the body?" Susannah asked, well aware of Jessie's preference to save that for last.

"Yeah."

They walked over to the bed, where Shasta Mallory was lying on her back. Standing next to the bed was Carl Pugh, the Manhattan Beach deputy coroner, whom Jessie remembered from her previous case. A short, balding man in his late thirties with an unassuming demeanor, he said nothing as she and Susannah looked over the body.

Shasta Mallory's brown eyes were open wide with red dots where capillaries had burst. There was obvious bruising around her neck, which was exposed. She was wearing a blousy, emerald-green top. The top button had popped off, revealing part of her bra. She had on a pair of loose-fitting, striped, wide-legged trousers. Her brown hair was short and unfussy. Jessie guessed that she was in her mid-forties. Her fingernails were relatively short and didn't look broken or bloody. It didn't appear that she'd had the chance to fight back.

Jessie felt a small ache for this woman she didn't know. How terrified she must have been as she gasped for breaths that wouldn't come, unable to save herself, perhaps unaware of who was doing this to her or why.

"What can you tell us, Pugh?" she asked quietly, sensing the coroner's anxiousness.

"Initial evidence suggests strangulation," he replied without hesitation, "though you don't need me to draw that conclusion. We'll confirm officially once we get her back to the office. The grip markings indicate an attack from behind and that gloves were used, probably latex. We'll do testing but I don't think we're going to get lucky with any fingerprints or DNA. I'm estimating time of death between eight and twelve hours ago. We should be able to eventually narrow that down a little, maybe an hour on either side if we're lucky."

"So," Susannah said, looking at her phone, "you're thinking she was killed sometime between eleven p.m. last night and three a.m. this morning. The party was going that whole time, right?"

"That's my understanding," Sergeant Breem said. "It quieted down a fair bit after about one a.m., but patrols told me there were still people drifting in and out as late as four this morning."

Jessie couldn't help but wonder what the woman's life was like that she'd lain here for potentially hours while her own party raged on without anyone noticing her absence or checking on her. Perhaps they could get insights on that front from her assistant.

“Unless you have other questions, I’m okay with them taking her,” she said to Susannah.

“I’m good too,” the detective agreed. “The quicker we get those results, the better data we have to work with. Besides, we should probably talk to that antsy assistant, no?”

“She’s just across the hall,” Breem said.

They left Pugh to wrap up and crossed the hall. Breem knocked on the door softly. When it opened, Jessie had to stifle a gasp.

CHAPTER FIVE

Though the face was familiar, and friendly, the sight of it still brought her pain.

Jessie vividly remembered Officer Will Timms. Though it had been over a year since she'd last seen him, the fresh-scrubbed young cop still looked like he'd just joined the force, which was true. He'd only been on the job for eighteen months.

She offered him a smile, though it was hard. Timms was the officer who had found Garland Moses's body, though Jessie hadn't known that at the time she first met him. But she still remembered how shaken the kid had been at the sight of the body she would later learn was her mentor. It was hard to separate that memory from the young man in front of her now.

"Hi, Officer Timms," she said as warmly as she could.

"Hello, Ms. Hunt," he said, his cheeks turning pink as he nervously wiped his sandy-colored hair out of his eyes. "It's good to have you back again, even if it is once again under unpleasant circumstances."

"Thanks," she said. "This is Detective Susannah Valentine. She's working the case with me. Are you supervising the witness?"

"Yes, ma'am," he answered quietly, stepping out into the hall and pulling the door closed. "Her name is Paisley Sorrento. I've mostly been trying to keep her calm, but you should know that she's really on edge. I just wanted to make you aware of that before you go in."

"Thanks for the heads-up," Jessie said. "Why don't you stick around? Maybe having someone she already knows nearby will help keep her from spinning out when we question her."

"Sure," Timms said with a look of surprised excitement. Sometimes Jessie forgot how big a deal it was for other law enforcement officers to participate in an HSS investigation.

He opened the door and they, along with Sergeant Breem, entered the room, where Paisley Sorrento was curled up in a tight ball on a lounge chair in the corner. She looked to be in her mid-twenties. Skinny and pale, with a bright bob of red hair and heavy, black eye makeup, she looked more like a member of a goth rock band than an assistant to a music manager.

Only her outfit, comprised of a sensible, sleeveless white top and billowy black slacks, suggested that she was more interested in receipts than rocking out. The way she was hugging herself tightly, Jessie could almost feel her vibrating with anxiety.

"Hi, Paisley," she said softly, as she entered the room and sat down on the bed across from her, "my name's Jessie and this is Detective Valentine. We appreciate your patience. We have a few questions for you and then we hope to let you get clear of all this. How does that sound?"

Paisley looked up to reveal dark shadows under her eyes. Jessie wondered if they were due to the stress of the moment or a general lack of sleep because of her job.

"I gotta say," the young woman grumbled, "I'm not sure I'm ever going to get clear of this, especially with Shasta's superstar clients bombarding me every two minutes with texts demanding to know how the investigation is going. How the hell am I supposed to know that?"

"From now on, you can just tell them to pose all their questions directly to HSS," Susannah told her, using a surprisingly gentle tone for her. "No matter how much they press you, just tell them you've been instructed to direct all questions to us. That should get you off the hook."

"Thanks," Paisley said, seeming to relax ever so slightly.

"You're welcome," Susannah said, sitting down next to Jessie. "That said, we do need you to answer *our* questions, so let's get started with an easy one. When did you find Shasta and why did you come to her house?"

"I found her around eight-fifteen this morning," she said, once again wrapping her arms around her knees. "She had a nine a.m. meeting with some promoters for Chantilly Mace's upcoming fall tour and I couldn't get in contact with her."

"Wait," Susannah said, "the meeting was at nine, but you were so freaked out that you couldn't get ahold of her that you showed up at her home at eight-fifteen? Isn't that a little excessive?"

"Not if you know Shasta," Paisley said irritably. "She's amazing at what she does, one of the best music managers in the business. Clients adore her. That's why so many big names sign with her. But she's also incredibly demanding. The word 'taskmaster' isn't unreasonable. She specifically told me that she was worried about being ready for the meeting after having the party the night before. So even though she planned to do it over Zoom from her home office, she insisted that I be at her place at eight a.m. to make sure she was awake in case she slept through her alarm. She wanted me to help prep her for the meeting, to review notes and help with hair and makeup touchups."

"So you were actually here at eight?" Jessie confirmed.

"A little after, with traffic," Paisley said. "I live in Mar Vista so it takes a while to get here. By the time I walked through the front door—which wasn't locked, by the way—it was more like eight-ten. I was actually surprised that I hadn't gotten any angry texts from her. As I'm sure you saw, this place was a pigsty. I was coming up here to her room when I got cornered by Jelly, who wouldn't leave me alone."

"Who's Jelly?" Susannah asked.

"She's part of Chantilly's entourage," Paisley explained. "Apparently she crashed here last night. She was talking about what a rager the party was. I wanted to blow her off but I couldn't just do that because she's tight with Chantilly and if she badmouths me to the star and the star says something to Shasta, then I'm screwed. So I had to listen to her blather on for a few minutes. That's why I didn't get up here until eight-fifteen, which is when I found Shasta on the bed. I started screaming. That's how everyone found out about her death so quickly. Jelly came in the room, saw her body, and called Chantilly right away."

She looked straight at Jessie when she continued.

"I couldn't believe how blank her eyes were."

The pale young woman shuddered at the memory of it. Jessie noted that she didn't seem emotionally overwrought at the loss of her boss so much as grossed out. While her lack of empathy wasn't ideal, the fact that thinking about a dead body seemed to repulse her suggested that murder might not be in her skill set. If her alibi held up, she probably wouldn't ultimately be at the top of the suspect list.

"Paisley," she said, "were you at the party last night?"

"Are you kidding?" the assistant snorted. "I don't get invited to stuff like that unless I'm going to be on call. And I had another assignment. I spent last night prepping for the promoter meeting, then crashed by eleven."

"But you know who she invited, right?" Jessie pressed.

"Sure, I was the one tasked with sending out the invites."

"Was there anyone on that list she had major beefs with?" Jessie asked. "Anyone you could see her getting into a dispute with, especially if alcohol or drugs were involved? Maybe an ex there was tension with? She was divorced, right?"

"She was," Paisley said, "but I don't think her ex-husband would make a great suspect. They despise each other but he's the band manager for Calico Kitten Co-op and they're currently on a European tour. I think they're in Prague right now."

"What about other exes?" Susannah asked. "Or business relationships that soured? How many of those folks were on the guest list you organized?"

Paisley laughed bitterly.

"The formal guest list for the party was around a hundred people, about a third of whom she's pissed off or vice versa. But based on what she told me about parties in previous years, I'm guessing that she expected close to five hundred people to show up here last night, invited or not. So good luck with your suspect list."

For the first time since they'd entered the room, Jessie saw Susannah start to lose patience with Paisley. The detective's back stiffened and her nostrils flared ever so slightly. In order to nip any unneeded conflict in the bud, she popped up and spoke before her partner could.

"Thanks, Paisley. We'll be in touch."

She nodded to Susannah, who reluctantly followed her out of the room, along with Sergeant Breem, who hadn't spoken the entire time. Officer Timms remained behind. Once they closed the door, Breem spoke before Susannah could express her irritation.

"I'm afraid Paisley's guess about attendance at the party last night may be low," he whispered. "I'm hearing well over five hundred people passed through this place."

"Wonderful," Jessie muttered, wondering how they would even begin to put together a cohesive suspect list.

"That's the bad news," Breem said. "The good news is that you should be able to talk to some more of them now."

"What do you mean, *now*?" Susannah demanded, still surly about the backtalk they'd gotten from Paisley at the end of their interview.

"Well, you remember how I said earlier that when people started to wake up, we hoped some of them might come forward with information?"

Both women nodded.

"Well, a lot of them weren't just sleeping," he said. "Until recently, most of them were too drunk or high—or both—to be of much use to you. But now a few of them are conscious and coherent. Would you like to chat with them?"

Jessie looked over at Susannah Valentine, who appeared to have a profanity on the tip of her tongue, and shook her head in resigned dismay.

"This just keeps getting better and better."

CHAPTER SIX

Hannah tried to hide her nerves.

As her rideshare pulled off the Pacific Coast Highway into the driveway of Patrice's family's beach house at the northern end of Santa Monica, she felt a flutter of butterflies in her belly and did her best not to squirm in her seat.

There was a time, not so long ago, when she almost never got nervous at all. Of course, that was back when she was numb most of the time, so closed off after the horrors she'd experienced that it took extreme experiences—either positive or (mostly) negative—for her to feel much of anything, and even then typically only passionate hate or giddy elation.

It was only recently, when she'd allowed herself to actually care about the well-being of other people besides her sister, that more subtle gradations of feeling had worked their way back into her emotional palette. Among them were pride, regret, concern, enthusiasm, and, apparently at the moment, nervousness. She had a sneaking suspicion that she knew why.

The car came to a stop. She got out with her small travel backpack and walked toward the front door of what was less a house and more of a chateau plopped down in front of the beach. It had steep, hipped roofs and twin chimneys, along with an actual tower and battlement-style walls that had to be at least fifteen feet high. It was a definite, bold statement of style.

Before she got too far, the door flew open, and someone charged out toward her. For half a second, Hannah had the urge to turn and run. She only relaxed when she saw who it was: Patrice.

The last—and only—time Hannah had seen Patrice Buono had been in the small mountain town of Wildpines over eight months ago when she, Jessie, and Ryan had been hiding out from an elderly serial killer. Somehow, during that high-tension period, she'd managed to make friends with a group of students from a nearby arts-centric high school who liked to hang out at the coffeehouse where Hannah had been spending time.

After the threat was eliminated and the real reason Hannah was in town was revealed, they'd all exchanged numbers and stayed in touch. But this was the first time she was seeing any of them in person since that wintry mountain getaway. And apparently whatever nerves she felt were not reciprocated by Patrice.

The petite blonde with blue and purple streaks in her long, wild hair flung herself into Hannah's arms, with complete confidence that she wouldn't be dropped. Hannah squeezed her tight as she tried to keep her balance. Patrice gave her a big kiss right on the lips, then on both cheeks, before sliding down her front like she was an amusement park ride.

"I forgot how tall you were, girl," she said happily.

"And I forgot how crazy you were," Hannah shot back, trying not to chuckle. "What are you wearing?"

Patrice was known for her bold fashion choices but this one was especially outré. She had on a barely-there vintage red floral crop top and yellow-and-white-striped short shorts that might as well have been bikini bottoms.

"I'm going for a 'sixties flower child at the beach' vibe," Patrice replied. "Did I nail it?"

"I think you did," Hannah assured her, noting the rest of the Wildpines crew start to pour out of the house as well.

"Please don't comment on the house," Patrice whispered in her ear as the others approached. "I know it's awful but if you say anything, it'll just set Doug off on another ten-minute style rant that I'll have to make sure my mom isn't around to hear. I can't deal with that."

"My lips are sealed," Hannah promised before they were surrounded.

There were Melina, Carlos, Annie, Doug, and, leisurely pulling up the rear of the group, Chris. At the sight of him, and completely without warning, the flutter of butterflies in Hannah's belly took flight again. She noted that his thick blond hair was almost as long as her own. As he held up a hand to shield his sky-blue eyes from the late morning sun, he smiled amiably, and his white teeth sparkled.

He wasn't especially tall or ripped and his nose bent awkwardly to the right—she liked to think that it had been broken in a pre-teen soccer mishap or an ill-advised middle school fight. But he had a quirky charm that had appealed to Hannah from the first time she'd seen him. And standing reservedly behind everyone else in his swim trunks and a gray

T-shirt that read *Poly-State University Mascot Go Team!* only added to his allure.

He waited until the others had all given her hugs before coming over and asking with a wink, "How's it going, Heidi?"

Despite her best efforts, she felt a surge of pink heat paint her cheeks. Heidi was the fake name she'd used in Wildpines when she, Jessie, and Ryan were trying to keep their identities hidden. Once the Night Hunter was dead, under complicated circumstances that the gang didn't need to know the specifics of at the time, she was able to reveal her real name to them.

They had all thought it was pretty damn cool that she'd had a pseudonym—that she'd had cause to need one. So there was no reason to be embarrassed about having used it. And yet hearing the name said by Chris Balfour, especially so softly and in such close proximity, was doing a number on her.

"It's going well," she said, managing to regain some of her equilibrium and nodding at his T-shirt. "By the way, is that where you're going to school in the fall?"

Chris smiled at the crack and Hannah fought hard to keep her knees from turning to pudding.

"Hey, Chris," Patrice instructed, "be a gentleman and grab the lady's bag. Let's get her settled into her room so we can hit the beach. Daylight's wasting!"

Chris turned to Hannah.

"My lady," he said, extending his hand to take the backpack.

"Good sir," Hannah said, handing it over and walking ahead of him toward the beach house. It took all of her will power not to look back over her shoulder.

***

A half hour later they were on the sand.

Patrice's parents and younger brother, who were staying in a separate wing of the house, had come to the beach earlier and staked out a good spot so they didn't have to battle the growing pre-holiday crowd for space.

Once they were all settled in, with giant umbrellas set up, beach towels down, sunblock applied, and lemonades in hand, the interrogation began. Apparently the whole Wildpines crew had been holding off on pummeling Hannah with their myriad questions until she at least had a chance to lie down.

They lulled her into a sense of complacency with a question about her summer. Everyone listened politely as she talked about how, after her internship with Kat had to be put on hold, she decided to go to summer school at UCLA, where she took classes in both Abnormal Psychology and Anthropology of Food, finishing up just yesterday. After offering congratulations, they apparently decided the gloves were off, and pounced.

"So did you really stop an assassin who was trying to kill you and your boss?" asked Doug Mercy, the fair-skinned, red-headed young man in the pink sundress and wide-brimmed floral hat. He'd been a violin prodigy at the Wildpines Arts Conservatory and was headed to Juilliard in the fall.

In fact, all of the people surrounding her were incredibly talented in one way or another. Though the conservatory was nestled in an isolated, artsy mountain town, it was considered one of the top arts-based high schools in the country and drew students from around the country, as well as internationally.

It was also extremely expensive, which apparently wasn't an issue for Patrice's family. But no one seated on the beach towels around her was interested in discussing their curriculum. All of them, save for Chris, were staring at her intently, waiting for an answer to Doug's question.

Normally, Hannah would have been reticent to satisfy the curiosity of folks who were interested in the titillating details of her trauma. She didn't love reliving it and *definitely* didn't like when people pried. But these guys were different. Because they met her under a fake name and already knew that she'd been in Wildpines to hide from a serial killer, the interest felt somehow less intrusive.

"It's a little more complicated than that," she replied, "but the short version is yes, a hitwoman named Ash Pierce was hired to kill me and my friend Kat Gentry, the private detective I was interning with. Together we were able to stop her."

"I read that you kicked her ass," Melina Katsaros volunteered with a wicked grin, throwing back her endless, curly black hair. Melina, olive-skinned and gorgeous, was wearing a white, one-piece bathing suit that accentuated her long dancer's legs.

Hannah and Melina had gotten off on the wrong foot up in Wildpines. Both of them had sharp-edged personalities and they kept bumping up against each other. Hannah also suspected that Melina had a little thing for Chris. But after Hannah confronted a leering jerk who'd been harassing them at a local restaurant one night, embarrassing him in front of dozens of customers, Melina was won over. They'd had no major issues since.

"We needed to make sure she was really incapacitated," Hannah said diplomatically. She had no intention of sharing the fact that she'd come dangerously close to bashing in Ash Pierce's head with a police baton.

Luckily, her response was enough, making everyone laugh. Several people nearby turned around to see what all the commotion was about before returning to their fun in the sun. She did notice one tall, gangly guy with glasses over by an ice cream stand who continued to look their way, like he wanted in on the joke and was annoyed that he was too far away to hear it.

"And she's going on trial soon, right?" Melina said, recapturing Hannah's attention. "Are you going to have to testify?"

The question made Hannah squirm uncomfortably on her towel. Suddenly, she felt extremely vulnerable, even in her fairly modest twist bralette and spliced high-waist green bikini set, which was intended to highlight her green eyes. The thought of having to face Ash in court, potentially in as little as a few months, made her vaguely queasy.

"It's possible," she admitted.

"And all of that happened because of the thing where your sister was kidnapped on her wedding night by the crazy woman and you and that Gentry lady helped save her from the collapsing mine?" pressed Annie Prentiss, the aspiring theater actress with short brown hair who matched Hannah's five foot nine height and was about to start at Carnegie Mellon University School of Drama.

"Not just us," Hannah made sure to clarify. "Jessie was also rescued by a retired detective named Callum Reid. Unfortunately, he died in the mine collapse. He sacrificed himself to get information that saved us and hundreds of other people. But in doing that, he left behind a wife and two young kids. I think about them a lot, and how they won't have a father to help them grow up."

It was true. Callum's death was the reason she regularly attended weekly survivors' guilt group meetings with Jessie and Jamil, who were each working through issues of their own. They had helped her tremendously, but sometimes when she closed her eyes, she still saw his sad, knowing half-smile as he disappeared into a hole in the earth not thirty feet away from her.

Carlos Margolis, a talented saxophonist with a bird's nest of flyaway black hair, looked like he'd been on the verge of asking a question of his own, but Hannah's response to Annie stopped him short. In fact, the whole gang went silent.

Hannah looked away uncomfortably and noted that the tall, gangly guy with glasses was still looking their way. Oddly, he didn't seem to have made any attempt to buy ice cream but appeared much more focused on their little group. His interest had her mildly unsettled.

"Okay, guys," Chris said wearily, pulling her attention back, "do you think we've put her through the third degree enough for now? Enough questions about Hannah's past. Let's get answers about her future!"

Hannah went from relief to anxiety in a fraction of a second.

"I'm just kidding," he said quickly, standing up. "There's lots of time for that later. How about a dip in the water? It's really scorching out here."

"Sounds good to me," Hannah agreed, popping up, happy to end the interrogation for now.

"Anyone else?" Chris asked.

"I'm just getting settled in," Patrice said.

"Yeah," Melina added. "Maybe in a few minutes."

"I burn like an unprotected baby's bottom," Doug announced, "so I'll stay in the shade."

"Thanks for that mental visual," Chris replied, turning to Hannah. "I guess it's just you and me for now."

"Cowards," Hannah said to the rest of them as she grabbed a hair tie and headed for the water. She gave a half glance back to the ice cream stand, but the gangly guy was gone and so was her unsettled feeling.

"Race you," Chris said, breaking into a run as he said the words.

"Cheater!" she called out as she charged after him, half trying to catch him, and half just trying to get to the water before the sand burned the undersides of her feet.

It was turning into a pretty good day.

CHAPTER SEVEN

"How many did you say?"

Jessie listened to Susannah pose the question as if she expected a different answer this time around and did her best not to roll her eyes. This was when Detective Susannah Valentine could be a bit much.

"Fourteen, Detective," Sergeant Breem repeated patiently as they stood on the balcony overlooking the living room in Shasta Mallory's beach house.

"So you're telling us that out of the over five hundred people who attended the party at this house last night, you have a grand total of fourteen people assembled here for us to question?"

"That's right," Breem said, with what Jessie considered admirable restraint. His chill surfer vibe was serving him well right now. "And of that group, I can't promise that all of them will be of much use. We're still trying to rouse a few of them enough to engage in coherent conversation."

"It's almost noon!" Susannah seethed.

"Yes, Detective," Breem replied. "We've sent an officer on a coffee run."

"Thank you, Sergeant," Jessie said, finally intervening. "We know you're doing the best you can, and we'll make do. Do you have officers keeping the witnesses separated?"

"Yes," he confirmed. "They're being held in rooms throughout the house in groups of two and three. We've cordoned off a small office and Mallory's meditation room for interrogations just in case you wanted to split them up to get to more people faster."

"What do you think?" Jessie asked Susannah, knowing that she'd like the idea of expediting the process *and* wanting her to acknowledge that it came from the sergeant she'd just been needling.

"I think that's a good plan," she conceded reluctantly, and after Jessie glared at her, added, "Thanks for coming up with that, Sergeant Breem."

"Not a problem," he replied genially. "Why don't you two pick your preferred spaces and get set up? We'll bring folks in based on who is most awake and hope that by the time you're done with them, the laggards will have come around."

Jessie offered Susannah the office, mostly because she thought it would be good for witnesses being questioned by the detective to have a desk as a physical barrier between themselves and her when things got intense, as they inevitably would. The library was really just a converted walk-in closet that had book-covered shelves, with just enough room for two smallish, plush chairs and a side table with a lamp.

She was assigned a young officer named Jaquez, whose job was to stand by the door just in case any witnesses got difficult. The first of them was a young woman named Marta who lived down the Strand about a mile south in Hermosa Beach. She was in her early twenties, super-tan, with dyed blonde hair. Dangerously skinny, she was still wearing the tiny bikini that highlighted her skeletal figure.

"So you didn't know the woman who owned the house and threw the party—Shasta Mallory?" Jessie asked, after getting her basic information.

"I didn't even know it *was* a woman," Marta said, in a voice that was either naturally raspy or blown out from partying. "I just heard that it was kicking from some friends and showed up."

"Do you remember when?"

"I think it was around midnight," she said without much conviction. "We were raging pretty hard here for a few hours, then it got kind of hazy. I didn't feel like walking all the way back to my place and needed to crash. I wanted to ask for permission but didn't even know who to go to, so me and my friend Trista found this ratty couch in the garage and just zonked out. We got woken up by the cops this morning and told not to go anywhere. I've been waiting ever since."

***

The rest of the interviews weren't much more informative.

Over the next hour and a half, Jessie interviewed five more people. None of them had been formally invited to the party. Three of them had heard of Shasta but only one guy actually knew what she looked like. He said that he never actually saw her at the party but that he didn't get there until close to 1 a.m. when he was already wasted and wasn't in the headspace to be looking for the hostess to thank her for her hospitality.

When Breem brought in the seventh person, a middle-aged woman with unkempt gray hair, crinkly skin, and some serious body odor, he leaned over and whispered, "This is Mary Mary. She's one of our neighborhood alcoholics. She's been awake for about fifteen minutes now."

"Mary," Jessie said, her eyes watering, "why don't we have this conversation on the patio?"

"It's Mary Mary!" the woman slurred.

"Okay," Jessie said.

As Jaquez guided the woman outside, Jessie leaned over to Breem.

"How's Susannah doing?"

"She's talking to her last witness right now," he said. "I get the impression that none of them have been the holy grail of information. Have you fared any better?"

"No," Jessie said. "But maybe Mary Mary here will change all that. Anything special I need to know about her?"

He shrugged.

"Real name is Mary Morrison but she insists on being called Mary Mary. Divorced. Hugely wealthy. Took to drinking heavily after the breakup about fifteen years ago. Has slowly deteriorated ever since. Has never committed any crimes other than public intoxication. But she doesn't *do* anything objectionable when she's drunk, so we don't arrest her. She just gets loaded at local bars and walks home to her incredibly nice house, where she lives alone. In this case, I guess she got loaded here and passed out last night."

Jessie nodded and joined Mary Mary on the front patio. The woman, who was wearing cargo shorts, an untucked button-down shirt, and flip-flops, was splayed out on a patio chair with her eyes closed, soaking up the sun. Jessie sat down across from her.

"Do you know why I wanted to talk to you, Mary Mary?"

"You're trying to find out who killed that surly shrew, Shasta Mallory."

"Basically," Jessie conceded. "Do you have any thoughts on the matter?"

Mary Mary opened her eyes and squinted sharply at Jessie.

"I'd hazard a guess that it was that guy who was choking her on the dance floor last night," she replied casually, as if she was mentioning that it might get cloudy later this afternoon.

"Excuse me," Jessie said, leaning forward in her chair, "you saw a man choking her?"

She wondered if this was the vaguely referenced "ruckus" that Sergeant Breem had gotten wind of. But general talk of a ruckus was a far cry from someone getting choked in the middle of a party. No one else had claimed to witness that until now.

"I can't be the first person to mention this to you," Mary Mary replied with a mix of amusement and disbelief. "A bunch of people had to pull him off her. They started beating him up before he ran out of the house."

"This is the first I'm hearing of it," Jessie conceded with a modicum of doubt. "Why do you think no one else has brought it up? Wouldn't someone have taken photos or video of that on their phone?"

"I don't know," Mary Mary said. "It was a big party. There was a lot going on. And it all happened really fast."

"And no one called the police?"

"I don't know about that either," Mary Mary admitted. "I was across the room, sitting on the stairs. That's how I had such a good view. I could see over everyone. But I couldn't hear what anyone said."

"Can you describe the guy?" Jessie asked.

"He was white."

"That's it?" Jessie pressed skeptically. "Was he tall or short? Skinny or heavy? What was he wearing?"

Mary Mary cackled at the question, revealing a set of teeth that were in dire shape.

"I was drunk, lady," she said. "I wasn't exactly focused on those kinds of details. Here's what I know: he was white, he was choking Shasta until a bunch of people yanked him off her and started beating the hell out of him. Then he bailed. I can tell that you don't buy what I'm selling because of my…compromised faculties. But that's my testimony for the court, so help me god."

"This isn't a courtroom, Mar—," Jessie started to tell her.

"Did you say she was choked?" someone asked from behind them.

Jessie turned around to see Susannah escorting out another witness who looked the worse for wear. In her thirties and wearing a cover-up over a bathing suit, the woman had on sunglasses but was still shielding her eyes from the invading sun. Her dark hair looked like it had been electrified and her skin was dry and burned.

"This is Linda Blane," Susannah said. "She was at the party last night, and she apparently knows Shasta. Unfortunately she doesn't remember much of anything, including whether she saw her at any point during the evening."

"No," Linda conceded. "But if Shasta was choked, I know of a guy you might want to talk to."

"Who?" Susannah demanded more intensely than she probably intended.

Linda looked at Sergeant Breem nervously.

"Is he going to arrest me if I mention stuff that might not be strictly legal?" she asked.

"You know that I'm an LAPD detective, right?" Susannah asked incredulously. "I can arrest you too."

"Yeah, but he's wearing a uniform," Linda pointed out. "You're super-hot so I kind of forgot that you're a cop."

Jessie cringed in anticipation of what she sensed was about to come. Dismissing Susannah Valentine's investigative chops while focusing on her physical attributes was a ticket to getting scolded at best and aggressively arrested at worst. Before she could jump in to save the unsuspecting woman, Sergeant Breem took a step forward.

"Detective Valentine," he said, with a tone of deference that Jessie hadn't encountered from him all day, "if you find that Ms. Blane's information is useful and she hasn't personally committed any crime, we would of course defer to your authority in regard to any potential arrest."

It was a mishmash of words. Of course he wasn't going to arrest Linda Blane if she didn't admit to any wrongdoing, and they couldn't prove that she'd done anything wrong. But that wasn't the point. Breem was attempting to thread a tricky needle: he was clearly trying to short-circuit the confrontation he too could feel coming on. But he was also making it clear to everyone here—Linda *and* Susannah—that he understood who was in charge.

Susannah got it too. And to Jessie's amazement, she did something unexpected in response: she smiled.

"Thank you, Sergeant Breem," she replied, playing along. "LAPD appreciates MBPD's cooperation in this matter. We're willing to be lenient, depending on the value of what Ms. Blane has to say. Linda—spill."

Linda Blane, oblivious to the fact that she'd just managed to avoid being reamed out by an angry detective on a crowded Southern California beachfront, proceeded as if everything was copacetic.

"Okay, there's this dude, kind of a boy-toy type who I know gets passed around by some of the older ladies in the community. He does what they want, and they pay his bills. But here's the thing: he's got a reputation for being into the rough stuff. I also heard he's got a bit of a temper. I didn't know Shasta well enough to say if they had anything going on, and I wouldn't have thought to mention it except that I saw him here last night."

"What's his name, Linda?" Jessie asked as casually as she could, trying not to sound as if this was the only decent lead they'd gotten all afternoon.

"Richard Vance," she said. "But everybody calls him Richie Boy."

Jessie turned to Breem, who had a knowing look on his face.

"Thanks, Linda. Why don't you hang here for a minute?" she said, before motioning for Susannah and the police sergeant to join her in a secluded corner of the courtyard.

"Have you heard of this guy?" she asked him.

"I have," he said. "We brought him in a few times for being drunk and disorderly. He was even charged with assault for going after a guy in a bar down in Redondo Beach last year, but he beat the rap. I knew he was a lothario but I didn't realize it was a vocational type of thing."

"I guess we need to find out if his work involved Shasta Mallory and if he can account for his whereabouts last night," Susannah said.

"The best person to ask the first question is probably her assistant, Paisley," Jessie said. "Any chance she's still here?"

"Funny thing," Breem said, "after being so anxious to get out of here, she ended up crashing hard on that bed in the guest room."

"I guess it was all the stress," Jessie said.

"Let me check on her status," Breem said, pulling out his radio. "Timms, is Paisley Sorrento still asleep in the upstairs guest room?"

"Yes, Sergeant," Timms answered, "for over an hour now."

Breem looked at Jessie and Susannah questioningly, waiting for instructions.

They gave them in unison.

"Wake her up."

CHAPTER EIGHT

"She's dead, Paisley," Susannah said with her typically direct bedside manner, "it's not like she can fire you for violating her confidentiality."

Jessie stood next to the detective who was hovering over the bed where Paisley Sorrento was still lying down, shaking off the cobwebs from her mid-afternoon nap. The young woman had protested that revealing anything about her boss's personal life would be a violation of the nondisclosure agreement she signed when she was hired.

"Listen," Jessie said gently, sitting down on the bed in the hopes of changing the combative dynamic her partner was in the process of creating, "we get it. Shasta might not have been the nicest person in the world, but she gave you a job and a shot and you don't want to reveal her secrets just hours after she died, right?"

Paisley nodded as she sat up in the bed, taking a sip of water from the bottle on the bedside table. Jessie could feel Susannah's irritation at the delay without even looking at her but proceeded as if she was unaware of it.

"That's a completely understandable reaction," she confided, "and a very human one. But in this situation, it's the wrong instinct. That agreement isn't legally relevant anymore. Think about it, Paisley. It was designed to protect Shasta's reputation, but she's not here anymore. There's no reputation to protect. Like Detective Valentine said, she can't fire you. She's not going to sue you. On the contrary, holding back could actually do her harm. We're trying to find her killer. Don't you think that if you had information that could help us find out who choked the life out of her, she'd want you to give it to us, even if it cast her in an unflattering light? It's not like people in the music industry thought she was pure as the driven snow, am I right?"

She had watched Paisley's reservations fade as she spoke to the point that by the time she finished, she knew the woman would help. She was glad because, while they could have compelled her assistance, it just would have taken longer and been more unpleasant. This way they could get the answers they needed fast and from someone who wasn't holding vital details back.

"What do you need to know?" she asked.

Jessie looked up at Susannah, who looked like a racehorse at the starting gate, raring to go.

"What was the nature of Shasta's relationship with Richard Vance?" the detective asked.

Paisley sighed and blew a strand of red hair out of her eyes, before leaning back against the headboard of the bed.

"He went by Richie," she said. "Shasta told me she met him at some beach festival concert thing earlier this summer, like sometime after Memorial Day. There was some Fleetwood Mac cover band playing and they bonded over that. They ended up hooking up back here that night. And again the next night."

"She told you all of this?" Jessie asked, surprised.

"She told me pretty much everything," Paisley said. "Because of the nondisclosure agreement, she knew I wouldn't repeat it, and because she was such a workaholic, she didn't really have any close friends to speak of, so who else was she going to confide in?"

"Okay," Jessie told her, "go on."

"Anyway, next thing I know, he's shacking up with her and I'm supposed to pick up his dry cleaning and make tanning appointments for him," Paisley said, shaking her head at the memory. "Shasta started taking him to events, like album release parties and private artist performances and stuff. She was really smitten."

"I assume it didn't stay that way," Susannah pressed, as usual intent on cutting to the chase.

"No," Paisley said. "I guess he was into some hardcore stuff in the bedroom, which she said was pretty exciting at first, because she hadn't had anyone really show a ton of interest in her like that since her divorce. But then it kind of tipped over into a place that she wasn't comfortable with."

"What do you mean?" Jessie asked, noticing Officer Timms shift uncomfortably from one foot to the other in the corner of the room. He clearly hadn't expected babysitting duty to take this turn. Paisley looked uneasy too but answered anyway.

"She said that sometimes she had to use the safe word they agreed on a couple of times before he would stop what he was doing, and afterward he would get pissed that she made him stop at all. She didn't say so but based on her description, I'd say that he was verbally abusive."

"And she put up with that?" Susannah asked, her voice reflecting her indignation at the thought.

"Actually," Paisley told her, "while she was describing the situation to me, she had this moment of clarity, like hearing herself say out loud what had been going on made it obvious just how not okay it was. So that very afternoon, she had me call the security company we used for some events to provide protection for clients."

"She didn't call the police?" Jessie asked.

"She was worried that if she did anything official like that, word would spread in the community around here, and she didn't want to deal with that hassle."

Jessie looked over at Breem, who nodded.

"Probably a smart move," he conceded. "I wish I could say otherwise, but it almost certainly would have gotten out."

"So you called the security company," Susannah prompted.

"Right," Paisley resumed. "They assigned a team—four guys—who met her down here. The team 'escorted' Richie out of the house, by which I mean they tossed him and his belongings out onto the sand. They warned him that he was no longer welcome and that if he ever stepped foot on the property again, it would be considered trespassing, and he would be dealt with accordingly. Did I mention that all these men were armed?"

"You did not," Jessie noted. "So was that the end of it?"

"I thought so," Paisley answered. "We kept security on for another week after that, one guy as a body man with her during the day and another at the house at night. To my knowledge, Richie never showed his face again."

"Until last night," Susannah pointed out, "which wouldn't have been a violation of any restraining order because Shasta never requested one, right?"

"Not that she ever told me about," Paisley said. "I don't think she thought she ever needed one. To be honest, neither did I. Their 'relationship' was over by the end of June and Richie dropped out of sight after being warned away. Maybe he thought that after so much time had passed and with so many people around last night, he could sneak in without anyone noticing."

"But certainly people would have noticed him choking her," Sergeant Breem objected. "That's a crazy risk to take."

"Thanks for your help, Paisley," Jessie said quickly, not wanting to discuss the other details of the case in front of the already frazzled assistant. "You should continue to rest here until you feel up to moving. We're going to step outside."

Once she moved into the hall with Susannah and Breem and closed the bedroom door behind them, she countered the sergeant's assessment.

"Maybe it wasn't such a crazy risk to take," she suggested. "This place was a madhouse last night. We didn't even know she *had* been choked until someone mentioned it in passing a few minutes ago. I'm still not a hundred percent sure I believe it happened, considering that so far, our only witness to this supposed choking is the neighborhood drunk, Mary Mary, who says it was a white guy. And even if that's true, our only potential lead is a dude who likes the rough stuff named 'Richie Boy.' And that lead is based on a sighting by a woman who was worried that she could be arrested by a cop in uniform but not by a female detective because she was too 'hot.'"

"When you put it that way, it doesn't sound super promising," Susannah said, borderline pouting.

"I just wanted to be clear about what we're up against," Jessie replied.

"Well," Sergeant Breem said, looking at his buzzing phone, "I don't want to mess with your Debbie Downer thing, but I might have some moderately good news for you."

"What?" Jessie asked, choosing not to take the bait on the crack at her expense.

"I asked our people to put out a BOLO on Richard Vance when his name came up and we just got a hit on his location."

"Where is he?" Susannah demanded, as if the sergeant wasn't about to reveal that information in his next breath.

"About three blocks north of here," he said. "Apparently he's visiting with another lady of the more mature variety who also owns a home on the Strand. Obviously he has a type. Would you like me to accompany you over there?"

"That's okay," Susannah said, already bolting out the door, "just text us the address. We'll let you know if we need any help."

Jessie could already hear her footsteps pounding down the stairs. She offered Breem a shrug.

"Thanks for the info," she said, starting for the door herself. "Good to know you're not too far away if we need backup."

“No problem,” Breem said. “Your partner is definitely enthusiastic. Just make sure that her enthusiasm is tempered with some caution. Richie Boy can be a handful.”

“Sergeant,” Jessie called back to him as she headed down the stairs, “between Richie Boy and Susannah Valentine, I feel like I’m sitting on a pile of fireworks. I just hope I get there before one of them lights a match.”

CHAPTER NINE

Susannah was itching to go in.

She was tempted to knock on the door of the address belonging to Ilana Owens but knew that Jessie would never let her hear the end of it if she did. So instead, she stood on the Strand by the gate leading to the house and waited as her partner jogged over.

Susannah sensed that she was testing Jessie's patience. After the rough start to their working relationship several months ago, and their eventual mending of fences, the last thing she wanted was to reopen that fissure by alienating the woman who had inspired her to join HSS in the first place. Jessie Hunt's fearless takedown of serial killers had convinced Susannah to return to her hometown and pursue a position with the most elite investigative unit in the department. She wanted to work with Jessie, not piss her off.

Yet all morning, despite her best efforts to rein herself in, she'd been giving in to what Jessie diplomatically called her "bull in a china shop" instinct. She's been exasperated and short with witnesses and law enforcement officials alike. And she thought she knew why.

"Thanks for waiting for me," Jessie said wryly when she caught up. "I wasn't sure you would."

"Honestly," Susannah admitted, "I was on the verge of marching up the walk and banging on the door. I had to force myself not to."

Jessie looked down at her with an apparent mix of amusement and confusion. For a second, it seemed she might let the comment slide, but then, of course, she didn't.

"You want to tell me what's going on?" the profiler asked. "You're always a…go-getter, but you're bringing an extra level of intensity to the job today, more so than in a while. I feel like something's building up in you and I'm a little worried it's going to explode if you don't pull the release valve."

Susannah sighed. Normally she'd tell her assigned partner to screw off. But Jessie Hunt wasn't just any partner. She's been to hell and back multiple times and deserved better than to spend the day working with a half-cocked detective that she wasn't sure she could count on.

Besides, the criminal profiler could read people like books, and she wasn't going to let this go.

"Fine," Susannah relented. "Remember how I said I used to come to these blowout parties when I was younger, and that it might prove useful as we investigated the case?"

"Vividly," Jessie replied.

"Well, that's the advantage of me having partied here: my experience with this world and the people in it," she said. "But there's a disadvantage too."

"What's that?" Jessie asked.

"I didn't really like who I was back then," Susannah said, looking away from Jessie and focusing on a wave crashing on the beach. "I mentioned that I drank a lot at the time. I also got around a lot, and not in an 'empowered sexuality' kind of way. I told you that I was raped a couple of years prior to that. But at that point, I hadn't really processed it. I was just trying to numb myself to the pain of that memory with booze and sex with guys that I could easily control. It's not a time in my life that I'm very proud of. And I guess being back here reminds me of being that person and I've been trying to avoid her at all costs. Maybe I'm overcompensating a little."

To her surprise, Jessie smiled and pulled her in for a hug.

"Maybe you are," the profiler whispered in her ear, "that's understandable. Personally, I don't think you need to do any compensating. You should be proud of yourself. I know she is."

"Who?" Susannah asked.

Jessie broke off the hug and grabbed her by the shoulders.

"Nineteen-year-old Susannah," she said.

"I went by Susie back then."

"Okay, Susie then," Jessie said. "Imagine her a decade ago at one of these parties—terrified, full of self-doubt, self-medicating, wounded inside and out, not sure if she would make it. If you told that young woman that ten years later, she would be a badass detective, able to kick the butt of anyone who gave her crap, who walked proudly in her bodacious body, and who regularly brought the worst scum in this city to justice on behalf of the vulnerable, what do you think Susie would have thought of her future self? Do you think she'd have endorsed future Susannah, the one who is standing in front of me right now?"

Susannah felt the beginning of a tear fighting its way to the edge of her eye and fought it back with some aggressive blinking and a shrug.

"Maybe?"

"Now you're just fishing for compliments," Jessie said, "and I'm fresh out of them for the afternoon. So what do you say we put your manic, hyper-probing energy to productive use with the first half-decent lead we've had today and see if Richie Boy ends up being worth our time?"

"Let's do it," Susannah said, opening the gate and letting Jessie go in first.

"From what Breem sent us," the profiler said, looking at her phone, "it appears that Ilana Owens is divorced too. She got the house. Her ex is a lawyer who moved to Palos Verdes with his new wife about six months ago."

As they approached the front door, Susannah noted that while the place was nice, it wasn't anywhere near as extravagant as Shasta Mallory's. The home was two stories instead of Mallory's three and even narrower. It looked to be about thirty years old whereas Shasta's place couldn't have been more than ten. Instead of a giant courtyard, it had a modest patio.

Still, it was well-maintained, had a second-floor balcony, and was situated on the Strand, five paces from the beach and about 150 unobstructed yards from the Pacific Ocean. She was doing just fine. They reached the front door, and Susannah looked over to see if Jessie wanted to take the lead.

"Go for it," the profiler said.

"How do we want to play it?" Susannah asked. "Direct or sneaky-like?"

"I didn't know you knew any way other than direct," Jessie teased before adding, "I say we play it by ear, but based on the description we have of Richie Boy so far, I'm leaning toward charm the lady and poke the bear."

"You know how I love to poke the bear," Susannah said.

The door opened before Jessie could reply. Standing in front of them was the same man they'd seen in the mug shot that Breem had sent them from his assault arrest last year. Based on the basic information that had accompanied the photo, they knew that Richard "Richie Boy" Vance was twenty-eight, lived in Lawndale, and worked as a part-time personal trainer.

"Yeah?" Richie Boy demanded brusquely. He wasn't even looking at them as his attention was focused on something in the house behind him. His disinterest gave Susannah a chance to take stock of him.

Richie was shirtless. In fact, other than a snug pair of bright orange boxer briefs, he was basically naked. As a result, his completely tanned body was on full display, as was his hairy but clearly professionally groomed chest hair. He was Jessie's height and in good shape with a swimmer's body. His dark hair was just shy of needing a cut and he had a closely trimmed mustache and perfect two-day stubble. He reminded Susannah of a leaner version of Burt Reynolds, the actor that her mom used to have a crush on. She could see why middle-aged women would be drawn to him, though he screamed cheesy to her.

When he actually fixed his brown eyes on what stood in front of him, his brusque demeanor was immediately replaced by what he likely thought was roguish charm. Instead, it just came off as lecherous, with a hint of menace.

"Excuse me," he said, suddenly much warmer now, "I thought I was dealing with another annoying solicitor. What can I do for you lovely ladies?"

"Good afternoon," Jessie said. "This is Detective Valentine. I'm Hunt. We're looking into an incident that happened down the block and we think that Ms. Owens might have some information that could be useful to our investigation. Is she in?"

His face fell but he managed to recover quickly.

"And here I thought you were here to see me," he said with a tight smile. "Come on in. She's in the living room."

Susannah wondered if the brief break in his façade was really because he was disappointed or because he feared they were on to him and a potential crime he committed last night. She bet that Jessie had an opinion on the matter.

"Thanks," she said, stepping inside after the profiler and pretending not to notice Richie staring unsubtly at her chest as he closed the door behind them. Normally she would have made a cutting comment that set him back on his heels, but for now she held off, happy to let him horndog it up if it kept him unaware of their real reason for being here.

She allowed herself a moment to luxuriate in the change in temperature as they left the mid-afternoon heat and entered the air-conditioned house. Within seconds, the beads of sweat on her forehead had evaporated.

They rounded a short corner into the living room, which looked out onto the patio they'd just come from and the ocean beyond. Lounging on a cream-colored sofa, reading what looked like a magazine about yachts, was Ilana Owens.

She was wearing a bathrobe and her brown hair was tied up in a messy bun. Pleasantly attractive, Susannah guessed that she was just a little past forty, which seemed a little young for Richie Boy. As they got closer, she also noticed dull bruise marks on the woman's wrists and around her neck. When Owens looked up, she almost jumped off the couch.

"Richie, you didn't tell me we had guests," she said, startled. "I would have put something more appropriate on."

"Sorry, Loni," he said, "these didn't seem like the kind of guests I could keep waiting."

"Please," Susannah said, "don't worry about changing. This isn't a social call. We're with the LAPD on a case. I'm Detective Valentine and this is Ms. Hunt. May we sit?"

Ilana Owens sat upright and checked that her robe was properly covering her before responding.

"I'm a little thrown, but of course," she said. "Would it be all right if Richie changes at least? Whatever this is about, I don't think that I'll be able to concentrate on it if he's standing there in his underwear."

"By all means," Jessie said, sitting down on the sofa opposite Ilana, "please, Richie, go right ahead."

While he went off to change, Susannah took a seat next to Jessie. Since the real reason they were here had just stepped out of the room, she viewed this as potentially the only opportunity to speak to Owens without Richie influencing her answers.

"Before we get into the nitty-gritty of why we're here," she whispered, leaning in conspiratorially, "I have to ask you, how did you and the underwear model get together?"

Ilana Owens blushed and began fiddling with her hair as a goofy smile came over her face.

"I know he seems more like the kind of guy who'd be with a woman who looks like you, right?" she whispered back. "I was at this fundraiser for injured sea mammals and Richie was there and we started talking. We just kind of clicked. He has a passion for animal rescue, as I do, and that passion just sort of transferred elsewhere, if you know what I mean."

"I certainly do," Susannah said. "Well, good for you. And it's especially great that you have someone around in light of the reason we're here."

"Yes, why are you here?"

"Do you want to explain, Jessie?" Susannah asked.

"Wait, you're Jessie Hunt?" Owens suddenly exclaimed. "I knew you looked familiar. You're the profiler I always see on the news."

"Yes, ma'am," Jessie said, clearly uncomfortable with the notoriety.

"To be honest," Owens said, "with everything you've been through, I'm amazed you're here in our little beach town handling a case. If I was in your shoes, I'd have retired and moved to a tropical island by now."

Jessie forced a smile.

"But if I did that," she said, "who'd be here to help Detective Valentine assist you and the fine folks of Manhattan Beach get to the bottom of the crime we're investigating?"

"What crime?" Richie asked from behind them, now dressed in gray silk slacks and a sleeveless, torso-hugging white shirt.

"That's what we were about to get to," Jessie said. "Feel free to have a seat if you like. Richie, is it?"

"That's right," he said warily, joining Ilana.

"Well," Jessie continued, "sometime last night, your neighbor down the way, Shasta Mallory, was murdered. Had you heard about that?"

"Oh my god, no!" Ilana exclaimed, bolting upright on the sofa. "That can't be!"

"I'm afraid it's true," Jessie said.

"Oh dear," Ilana said, putting her hands to her cheeks. "I went to bed early last night and haven't left the house yet today. I heard some sirens earlier this morning, but I had no idea what it was about."

Susannah took note of Richie's silence, his squinty eyes, and his cloudy expression.

"Did you know her?" she asked Ilana, though she kept her eyes on the man beside her.

"A little bit, just from the neighborhood," she said, "but you used to date her for a little while, didn't you, Richie?"

Susannah turned to him as if this was completely new news.

"Is that right?" she asked mildly.

"Briefly, yeah," he said, the relaxed charm from before nowhere in sight. His brow was furrowed, and his eyes were steely. "For like a month, maybe. That's really terrible to hear. Have you caught the person who did it?"

"No, actually," Jessie told him. "That's why we're canvassing the neighborhood. We're hoping to get as much information as we can. You might actually be able to help us out, Richie. Since you dated her, you'd probably know her routine better than most, maybe even be able to share the names of folks that she had conflicts with, that sort of thing. Maybe we could talk to you separately for a few minutes."

"I don't know," he replied hesitantly. "I haven't seen her since June, and we only went out for a month or so. I don't think I'd be of much help."

"You'd be surprised, Richie," Jessie pressed. "Sometimes people don't even realize how much they really know until they're asked the right questions. Your help could be the reason we catch this bastard or not. What do you say?"

"Richie, you should do it," Ilana implored, tapping him on the knee. "It can't hurt, and you could end up being the hero of this thing if what you say helps. Remember, this is Jessie Hunt. She catches serial killers for a living. They call her the Angel of the City of Angels. Don't you want to be able to say you made a difference in her nailing a killer around here?"

"Yeah, Richie," Susannah added, unable to stop herself, "don't you want to make a difference? Let's just have a chat out on the patio and see if you have any nuggets in that brain that could break this case open."

Richie stared daggers at her. Then without any warning at all, he stood up. Susannah felt the urge to reach for her gun and let her fingers inch in that direction. Unexpectedly, she felt a hand on her own, preventing her from grabbing her weapon.

CHAPTER TEN

Despite her best efforts, Susannah flinched.

Glancing to her right out of the corner of her eye, she saw Jessie imperceptibly shake her head, warning her not to take any action. She didn't trust Richie, but she did trust Jessie Hunt, so she returned her hand to her lap.

Richie, still hovering over them with a hostile glower on his face, raised his arms with his palms up and muttered, "I give up already. Are we doing this or what?"

"We are," Jessie said sweetly, standing up and heading for the sliding door that led to the patio. Richie reluctantly followed her. Susannah walked behind him, just in case he made an unexpected move.

Even though she knew it was coming, the blast of heat that walloped them as they exited the cool house was brutal. Once they were all outside and seated on wicker chairs, with the sliding door closed and Ilana out of earshot, Richie's sullen silence quickly gave way to something more defiant.

"I really don't know anything," he told them before any questions were asked. "I didn't want to say it in front of Ilana but my relationship with Shasta was almost exclusively sexual. It wasn't like I was paying attention to her routines or who she had catfights with. I don't see how I can help. Having said that, maybe I can help one of you ladies if you're having an issue of a more…personal nature."

At the conclusion of his little speech, he actually winked at them. Susannah looked over at Jessie, borderline dumbfounded at the chutzpah of his guy. The profiler looked back at her with a half-smile on her lips and it was clear what she was thinking without a word needing to be said. It was time to poke the bear.

Susannah smiled back and leaned forward so Richie could get an eyeful of what he'd been sneaking peeks at the whole time they'd been there. While his attention was fixed squarely on her chest, she responded in a playfully coquettish tone that suggested she might be interested in his overture.

"That seems to be how a lot of your relationships go down, huh, Richie?" she posed.

"What do you mean?" he replied, his eyes still locked squarely on her bosom.

"I mean, you said you and Shasta had a mostly physical thing," she continued, "and I don't get the sense that you and Ilana are exactly soul mates."

"We have a good time," he said, finally tearing his eyes away from her torso and looking at her face, "but I bet you and I could *really* connect, soul-wise."

"Would I have to wear the handcuffs to make that connection?" she asked, the sugar in her tone masking the bite of her words.

It took him a second to process what she'd said.

"What?"

"The bruises on Ilana's wrists," Susannah said, still smiling pleasantly, "those are from the games you like to play in the bedroom, same as the marks around her neck."

"Just like the games you used to play with Shasta," Jessie piped in, her tone also conversational, somehow managing to not sound accusatory.

"I don't know what you're talking about," he said cautiously.

"That might come as a surprise to Shasta's assistant, Paisley," Susannah said, letting a little edginess slip in now. "She remembers Shasta telling her very specific stories about the stuff you liked to do to her. Is that what you'd do to me, Richie Boy? Or do you just save that for the older ladies that you like to fleece?"

"What the hell?" he demanded, a look of angry confusion on his face. "I thought you wanted my help with her routine and stuff."

"We'll get to that," Jessie said, "but first, you were tossed out of Shasta's house and told never to return, so why were you there last night?"

"I wasn't—"

"And remember," Susannah interjected, knowing her next words would be especially bear-pokey, "Ilana just told us she went to sleep early so it's not a great idea to lie to us and say you were here with her. We obviously know you were at the party. Why?"

"Look," he said, "yes, I went to the party, okay. Ilana was zonked out. I could hear everybody having a good time and I was bored. There were so many people around, I didn't even think Shasta would notice me. Besides, it had been months since we were together. I thought that was all water under the bridge."

"Did you see her there?" Susannah demanded, keeping the pressure on.

"You know what," he said, popping up, "I don't have to take this crap. I thought I was helping you out but you're treating me like I'm a suspect or something."

"No we're not, Richie," Jessie assured him soothingly. "If you were a suspect, Detective Valentine here would have read you your rights and this would be a much more formal process. We consider you a witness assisting in an investigation. Should we not?"

"This witness is done assisting you," he said haughtily, running his hand through his hair as he stared at Susannah scornfully. "I *will* answer another question you had earlier though. You wanted to know if I would have used handcuffs on you. Here's how it would go down. Your leggy friend here, she's the type I'd marry, you know real-respectable like. Then I'd cheat on her with you. We'd use the cuffs, but I think you'd have put them on yourself. You strike me as the kind of gal who feels like she deserves a little punishment. I'd nail you real good and then never call you again. What I *won't* do is waste any more of my breath explaining myself to either of you."

He got up and started back toward the sliding door. Susannah, fury rising in her chest, shot up and followed him, reaching for her handcuffs as she did. She'd see how *he* liked wearing them.

"You're not going anywhere," she ordered.

"Talk to the hand, bimbo," he said, actually raising one hand as he reached for the sliding door with the other, never even bothering to turn around.

Jessie had stood up now too and was waving her arms wildly, in a pleading gesture for Susannah not to do what she was already in the process of doing. She ignored her partner and snapped one cuff on Richie's raised wrist, then grabbed his forearm and yanked it behind his back.

Whether out of shock, panic, or guilt, the man did something she wasn't expecting: he pressed his right leg against the sliding glass door and flung himself backward, slamming into her and sending them both careening into the patio table and toward the ground. It was all Susannah could do to avoid having him land on top of her as she landed.

She ignored the pain as her hip hit the unforgiving patio surface, and immediately scrambled to her feet. She saw that Richie was doing the same and gave him a sharp kick in the shin before he could fully regain his balance. He yelped in pain but didn't fall. Instead, he took a step toward her.

She was debating whether to reach for her gun or her Taser when a wicker chair appeared out of nowhere, flying across the patio and smashing into the back of Richie's legs, knocking his feet out from under him. He landed flat on his back. Susannah looked in the direction where the chair had come from to see Jessie, standing at the edge of the patio, a pained look on her face.

Susannah nodded and returned her attention to Richie, flipped him over, jammed her knee into his back, and slapped on the other cuff.

"You alright?" she asked Jessie, who was leaning against the patio gate.

"Yeah, I think so," the profiler said unconvincingly. "When everyone hit the ground, I got knocked over too, and I wasn't really prepared for it."

"You didn't hit your head, did you?" Susannah asked, remembering the concussion-related issues Jessie had been dealing with in recent months but had been keeping from the rest of the HSS team. She'd only learned of them because they cropped up while they were investigating a case together, after which Jessie had sworn her to secrecy. As far as she knew, only she and Ryan Hernandez were aware of the problem.

"I might have bumped it," Jessie admitted, "but I don't think it was too bad. I slammed my shoulder pretty hard though."

Susannah wasn't sure if she bought what her partner was selling but now wasn't the time to push the issue. They had to deal with Richie Boy.

"Now I *am* going to read you your rights," she told him, "and depending on what happens after that, we'll see if you get arrested for murder."

"What?" he shouted.

"First things first," she told him, reading him his Miranda warning as she lifted him up and sat him in the wicker chair that Jessie had thrown at him, before asking if he was willing to talk to them without a lawyer present.

"Wait, are you saying that you think I killed Shasta?" he demanded.

"I need an answer to my question before I can answer yours, Richie Boy," she reminded him.

"Yes, yes, I waive my right to be silent and to the lawyer," he said. "Now you gotta know I didn't kill her."

The sliding door opened and Ilana Owens, now with her hair down and wearing a lovely floral sundress, stared at them with her mouth agape. After a large gulp, she managed to form words.

"I just went to change clothes and I come back to…what now?"

"That's what we're hoping to find out, Mrs. Owens," Jessie said. "Now Richie, if you would please answer Detective Valentine's question from earlier: did you see Shasta Mallory at the party?"

"Yes," he said. "I saw her in the kitchen talking to the caterers."

"You were at her party?" Ilana asked.

"Please, Mrs. Owens," Jessie said, "I know this is a lot, but hold your questions for now if you could. Richie, did you interact with her at any point?"

"No way," he said. "When I saw her, I steered well clear. I walked the long way around to stay out of her sight, and then left."

"What time was that?" Jessie asked.

"I don't know for sure," he said, "maybe between eleven-thirty and midnight?"

"Can anyone confirm this?" Susannah asked.

"Sure," he said, suddenly developing a modicum of confidence. "I ran into some buddies at the party, Breezy Ted and JoJo. I left with them and we all went over to Tortoise Tavern on the main drag for a few beers."

"How long were you there?" she pressed.

"We closed the place down at two," he said. "Then we hung out by the lifeguard station near the pier until a cop kicked us out. After that I came back here."

Susannah looked over at Jessie and could see she was thinking the same thing. If Richie Boy's alibi could be verified, it would be near-impossible for him to have snuck back to Shasta's place to kill her within the estimated window of death.

"We're going to need the contact information for Breezy Ted and JoJo," Jessie said with a wince, probably at having to say those names out loud, before turning to Susannah. "Do you want to do the honors?"

"What honors?" Richie Boy wanted to know. "I'm off the hook, right?"

Susannah smiled at her partner. Jessie knew just what a girl needed to make her feel better.

"Richard Vance, you may not end up being charged with murder but you *are* still under arrest for assaulting a law enforcement officer, two of them actually," she said. "Jessie, you want to call Breem and ask him to have some of his people take Richie Boy here in?"

As Jessie pulled out her cell phone, Susannah turned her attention to Ilana Owens, who still looked stunned at the turn of events.

"I'm sorry to throw a wrench in your afternoon, Mrs. Owens," she said, "but I think that all things considered, this day is a net plus for you. You no longer have to be the sugar mama for a guy who burns through your money, leaves you physically bruised, and would have moved on to another divorcee when you got wise to him. Plus, now you can spin the story to say that you helped put an end to his reign of douchebaggery. The truth will be our little secret."

"Thanks?" the woman said, still more dazed than appreciative.

"Don't mention it," Susannah said, shoving Richie Boy off the patio and onto the Strand to wait for the MBPD to show up.

"What happened to toning down the 'bull in the china shop' thing?" Jessie asked as she closed the gate behind them. "It kind of got away from you there at the end."

"What can I say?" Susannah replied with a shrug. "I'm a work in progress."

CHAPTER ELEVEN

He checked his reflection in the Santa Monica Beach restroom mirror.

It was almost a waste of time. The mirrors were so old and dull that he couldn't identify any of his features in detail. Instead of curly blond hair, what he saw was just a blondish mass atop his extremely tall head. His wire-framed glasses were barely discernable on his face. On the other hand, his gangly frame was also blurred by the mirror to give him an unexpectedly imposing appearance. He liked that.

Mark Haddonfield had been working out a lot in recent months and it had paid off in terms of pure strength. It just hadn't made him look any more muscular. But that was okay. His goal wasn't to be a male model. It was to have the functional strength necessary to complete the assignments he'd given himself. And he did have that.

Mark stepped out of the restroom and reestablished his line of sight with the group. They were still where they'd been when he'd left them a minute ago, standing on the Santa Monica Pier, looking out toward the South Bay of Los Angeles, which included Palos Verdes, as well as the beach communities of Redondo Beach, Hermosa Beach, and Manhattan Beach, where Mark's nemesis, Jessie Hunt, was currently hard at work.

As he fell in behind a group of German tourists, keeping an eye on the gang that mattered to him, he wondered how Jessie's case was going. He knew it had something to do with a music manager who'd been killed at her beachfront home while hosting some huge party last night. Other than that, details were scarce.

Frankly, he was surprised, and mildly offended, that she would accept what sounded like a run of the mill murder case when she hadn't made any progress in stopping his handiwork. How she could focus on anything other than the murders of multiple people who had previously nearly been the victims of killers she'd already caught was beyond him.

He'd slaughtered four people over the last few months, each of them in the same style as the original killer who almost took them out, each time without leaving any clues other than the ones he intended for her to find. That she could spend any waking seconds on something other than catching him was another insult in the long list of grievances he had against the woman he once viewed as an inspiration.

It was almost laughable now to think that he'd once held her in such high regard. He'd originally been a fanboy, following her career religiously. He even transferred from Stanford to UCLA last fall when he learned that she'd be teaching a seminar in criminal profiling there.

But he couldn't get into the class, first because of bureaucratic crap, and then because Jessie, without warning, went back to working at HSS full-time. She screwed him over, along with his dreams of becoming her protégé.

As a result of her equivocation and selfishness, he lost his passionate drive and his grades suffered. Without anything to compel him to excel, he couldn't make friends at this new school in this huge, impersonal city.

And everywhere he went, he saw Jessie Hunt's face plastered on screens, staring back at him spitefully, telling him he wasn't good enough. It was like she was challenging him to prove her wrong, to prove that he could steal the headlines from her. But how could he compete with her when she was constantly in the limelight?

First, she was kidnapped by some wacko on her wedding night. Then she got rescued after the LAPD, FBI, and Sheriff's Department teamed up to find her. After that, she saved hundreds of people from being poisoned in a movie theater. Then she caught some pervert using drones to target young women. Next, she solved the murder of some pharma billionaire. No matter where he went, there she was, taunting him.

But somewhere in the middle of all that, despite the odds being against him, Mark soldiered on, refusing to be beaten down by her constant attempts to make him feel "less than."

Somehow, he pulled himself out of his rut, and her silent, judging eyes, and managed to develop The Strategy, which he'd been using for these last few months. And it seemed to be working. He certainly knew he had her attention and that of the rest of HSS. He also knew that he had prospective future victims running scared. LAPD had put protective units on the homes of potential victims who'd survived encounters with past serial killers. They thought they had it covered.

But he'd blown that up when he killed Melissa Ferro. After all, her husband, Richard, wasn't a serial killer. He was just an evil scumbag who murdered his pregnant mistress when she threatened to reveal their affair and who then tried to kill his wife when she became a threat. If he was the new model for the Clone Killer (as Mark had gleefully discovered they were referring to him at HSS) then all bets were off.

There was simply no way to protect that many potential victims. The department would spread itself thin and wear itself out futilely attempting to play whack-a-mole when they had no idea what the mole looked like or where it might pop up. It was delicious. And considering that the next victim on his list would be struck down imminently and hit closer to Jessie than she could ever imagine, all hell was about to break loose.

Mark stayed behind the German tourists as he walked along the far side of the pier, making sure to stay out of the sight line of the gang. As an extra precaution, he put on a baseball cap and sunglasses. He needed to do a better job of blending in.

It wasn't lost on him that Hannah Dorsey had noticed him by the ice cream stand earlier that afternoon. He should have known better. She was Jessie Hunt's half-sister, after all. Of course she would have some of the same skills of perception as her sibling.

That was part of why he was here, in fact. He already knew everything there was to know about Jessie. He was a scholar on the subject. Hell, he could teach his own seminar on her. And he was extremely knowledgeable about Captain Ryan Hernandez as well. The public records on Jessie's husband, former partner, and current boss were copious.

But information on Hannah was harder to come by, partly because until very recently she had been a minor. It was the one real gap in his data set on Jessie. And he needed that data if he was going to fully complete The Strategy. It was all very straightforward.

If he was going to systematically destroy the woman who had ruined him, he first had to kill the people she thought she'd saved. That would terrify those potential remaining victims, while staining her reputation with the citizens of the city that currently adored her. Instead of being the Angel of the City of Angels, she would be the city's Angel of Death.

But he couldn't be confident that would break her. There was a missing piece to the puzzle, and he was pretty sure he was staring at her right now. He needed to understand just how important Hannah Dorsey was to Jessie Hunt and just how devastating it would be to lose her. There was research to be done.

"Sometimes field work is required in order to find answers we can't get in the lab or the lecture hall or the interrogation room, Jessie," he chided sharply. "Not everything is about looking into a suspect's eyes and discerning whether they're lying. You can't always count on instinct to get you where you need to go."

"Who are you talking to?" asked a little boy standing off to the right of him, holding a snow cone.

Mark realized that he'd been speaking out loud, conversing professionally with an imaginary Jessie who wasn't around to respond. He felt a rush of heat come to his cheeks as the kid, no more than six, stared up at him in curious confusion.

"Mind your business and get the hell out of here, you little brat!" he hissed.

The boy stared at him open-mouthed for a few seconds, his eyes welling up. Then he dropped his snow cone and ran off, wailing loudly. Mark quickly turned his back so that he was facing away from Hannah and her friends. He pretended to look up in amazement at the Ferris wheel.

He couldn't believe what an idiot he was. Now there was a small boy about to tell his parent about the mean, tall man who'd yelled at him. The last thing Mark needed right now was attention. As casually as he could, he ambled back up toward the entrance to the pier, making sure not to make eye contact with anyone.

By the time he stepped onto Ocean Avenue and merged in with Friday's late afternoon crowd, he felt reasonably confident that he'd avoided the worst of it. Still, he kept walking north.

That was the direction he needed to be going in anyway. That was where the beach house was, after all, and he had prep work to do. He had to scout the next kill while there was still light. This one was going to be bloody, and he wanted it to go just right.

CHAPTER TWELVE

Jessie knew she shouldn't be annoyed.

Susannah was just trying to help. Moreover, she was doing what any responsible partner would under the circumstances. It was unfair to hold a grudge.

After they handed off Richie Boy to the local officers that Breem sent, Susannah had insisted that before they pursue any other leads, they make a pit stop at MBPD's preferred urgent care clinic to get her head checked out, just to make sure she hadn't suffered another concussion.

After ten minutes in the waiting room without any sign that they were going to be seen soon, Detective Susannah Valentine used her china-shop-bull powers for good, making a scene that got them expedited to an exam room with a doctor, who did a comprehensive workup. An hour later, they left the clinic with an all-clear, which Jessie pretended she expected all along but was secretly relieved about. The grudge was gone.

Just as the sun was beginning to dip toward the horizon in front of them, they returned to Shasta Mallory's place, where according to a call from Sergeant Breem, Jelly was waiting to be interviewed. The member of Chantilly Mace's entourage who had walked into the bedroom just after Paisley discovered Shasta's body was apparently insisting on sharing what she knew. Though Jessie was skeptical that she would be the holy grail of witnesses, they didn't have any other promising leads, so she wasn't about to blow her off.

"Where is she?" Susannah asked Breem after they negotiated their way through the throng of rubberneckers in the sand beyond the police tape and reentered the living room of the mansion. The sergeant, who had been standing on the dance floor, mid-conversation with a young officer, glanced over at her with a stoic half-grin.

"Nice to see you again too, Detective," he said mildly. "I hope you've had a lovely, productive afternoon. Mine has been okay. Thanks for asking."

Susannah looked briefly chastened.

"Sorry," she muttered. "I'm just frustrated by all the brick walls we keep hitting. Please, tell us more about your afternoon, Sergeant Breem."

"Well, the surf was surprisingly strong. It was really tempting to see it and not be able to partake," he answered sincerely. "But those are the sacrifices we make for the job, right?"

"I guess?" she replied uncertainly.

Jessie watched this back-and-forth with unbridled delight. Seeing Susannah Valentine try to restrain her "pedal to the metal" impulses with Breem, even temporarily, made her want to grab some popcorn and settle in for the show. The sergeant was clearly enjoying himself as well, but after a moment, he decided to let the detective off the hook.

"Anyway, enough about the beauty and power of the afternoon waves," he said. "Let's get to the nitty-gritty. I just heard from Pugh in the coroner's office. He wanted me to let you know that he's narrowed Shasta Mallory's time of death down slightly, from twelve-thirty a.m. to two-thirty a.m. Hope that helps."

"At this point, we'll take every data point we can get," Jessie said.

"Well, I wish you luck getting more of those from Jelly. She's in the upstairs office where you did your questioning earlier today."

"And what should we be expecting?" Jessie asked. "Do you really think she has anything material to offer?"

Breem shrugged.

"She was there just after Paisley Sorrento found the body this morning," he noted, "but in my experience, folks who aggressively try to insert themselves into investigations and post about their tangential connections to them on social media probably aren't the most valuable witnesses. But I guess beggars can't be choosers."

"I'm no beggar," Susannah said, already marching up the stairs to the office.

Jessie and Breem watched her go before looking at each other.

"She's always like this, huh?" he said, almost admiringly.

"It's kind of her thing," Jessie acknowledged.

"What does her significant other think of that?" he wondered, his nonchalance failing him for once.

Jessie's lips curved into a smile as she watched him avert his eyes.

"Why, Sergeant Breem—are you trying to probe into the relationship status of Detective Valentine?"

He gave up trying to look cool and returned her gaze.

"Ridiculous, right?" he said. "An old guy like me wondering about the status of some young whippersnapper like her."

"Just how old are you?"

"I turned forty-one last month," he said. "How old is she?"

"She's twenty-nine," Jessie said. "It's definitely an age difference but I know she's not seeing anyone right now, and I also know she's had her fill of eager young bucks who can't see beyond her obvious physical attributes. Do you want me to inquire as to whether there might be interest?"

His expression indicated that he absolutely did, but after a brief pause, he shook his head.

"Nah," he said. "We've got a job to do here. There's a killer out there somewhere. I don't want to complicate finding them by inserting messy interpersonal stuff into the equation. Maybe when this is all done, we can revisit it."

Jessie was about to reply when they were interrupted by a voice from upstairs.

"Jessie, are you planning on joining me any time today?" Susannah called down, clearly agitated.

"Be right there!" she called up before muttering to Breem, "Be careful what you wish for."

She darted up the stairs, where Susannah was waiting impatiently outside the office door. As she walked over, it occurred to her that other than the unfortunate stretch where the detective had flirted with Ryan, aware that he was engaged, but not to Jessie, she'd never seen Susannah Valentine express romantic interest in anyone.

It was hard to blame her. After the trauma she'd suffered as a teenager, followed by years of catcalls and drooling leers, she likely didn't have much faith in most guys. But Drake Breem wasn't like most guys. From Jessie's limited experience, he seemed like an antidote to the jerks Susannah typically dealt with.

"What took you so long?" the detective demanded in her typically charming tone.

"Sergeant Breem and I were just talking about what a ray of sunshine you are, and time got away from us," Jessie teased.

Susannah looked briefly flummoxed, but then regained her composure.

"You ready?"

"Always," Jessie assured her.

They stepped into the office, where Jelly had made herself comfortable behind the desk, with her feet propped up on it. She was typing on her phone. The woman was Latina, in her early thirties, heavyset with short-cropped, dyed blonde hair.

"Jelly, is it?" Susannah asked.

"In the flesh," she replied.

"All right," the detective replied firmly, "I'm going to need you to come over to this side of the desk and have a seat in one of these chairs."

"You got it, boss," Jelly said, hopping up and switching spots. "By the way, The Lady of the Evening wanted you to know that she'll be stopping by momentarily to make her presence felt."

"I'm sorry, what?" Susannah said, walking over to the other side of the desk but not sitting down.

Jessie stayed where she was, standing in between them at the edge of the desk, where she could get a sense of Jelly without being in direct opposition to her.

"You know, The Lady of the Evening, our Diva Queen," she said, and when she got no response, added, "Chantilly Mace? She's on her way to check out how the investigation is going."

"That's not how these things work—" Susannah started to say.

"What's your real name?" Jessie asked, deciding to short-circuit the confrontation she could feel coming on. She was still skeptical that Jelly had anything useful to offer and wanted to find out one way or another as soon as possible.

"Jelina Hernandez," she said defiantly, "but I haven't gone by that in years. I'm only telling you now because I know who you are from the TV and I respect what you do, Jessie Hunt."

"I appreciate that, Jelly," Jessie said, deciding to ride the wave of goodwill. "Actually my husband's last name is Hernandez too, so I think we're getting off to a good start here. Detective Valentine and I don't want to waste your valuable time so we're going to cut to the chase here. Did you see Shasta at all last night?"

"Sure I saw her," Jelly said. "She was all over the place, running around, making sure everything was just so. I even talked to her for a bit. She was asking if Chanti was gonna make it. I had to tell her it wasn't looking good, but that she sent her best."

"When was the last time you saw Shasta?" Susannah pressed.

"Time's not really my thing, Officer," Jelly said. "And especially last night, I was under the influence of a few chemicals, if you know what I'm saying. So I couldn't really tell you."

"Detective," Susannah said.

"What?"

"I'm a detective, not an officer."

"Oh yeah, right, sorry. Sometimes I get my lady cop terms confused," Jelly replied, not winning herself any brownie points. "What I *can* say is that it was exactly eight-oh-nine when I got woken up from a deep sleep on the guest room bed by the sound of Paisley 'nails on a chalkboard' Sorrento coming up the stairs, jabbering away on her cell phone. I came out to tell her to keep her damn voice down but decided to cut her some slack when I saw how frazzled she looked. So I tried to buck her up, telling her what a great party it was, cuz I knew she helped organize it and all, but she just blew me off and went into Shasta's room. Real sweetie, she is."

"So what happened next?" Susannah pressed, trying to keep the woman focused.

"What happened next was—I heard Paisley screaming bloody murder. So I went charging into the main bedroom and saw Shasta all messed up like that. That's how I knew to reach out to Chanti, which is how you fine people got involved. She wasn't gonna let this thing be handled by some Podunk beach police when her best girl was violated, you know?"

Jessie looked over at Susannah. Though the detective still looked steamed at the "lady cop" crack, it was clear that they'd come to the same conclusion: Jelly was not going to be their holy grail witness. It appeared that she'd only been around for the before and the after. Unless her background check showed something suspicious, she was a dead end.

"All right, thanks for your time, Jelly," Jessie said. "You're free to go."

"Seriously? That's all you need from me? You don't want my theories and such?"

"There is one thing we'd like," Jessie said as she opened the office door. "We hear you've been posting a lot about the case with your theories and speculation. It would be helpful if you could limit that for the duration of the case. It might actually be doing more harm than good, and I know that you would never want to do anything that might jeopardize our ability to catch Shasta's killer."

“Damn,” Jelly said as the three of them started down the stairs, “you really think I’ve got that kind of power?”

“You never know,” Jessie said, “but why take the chance? How awful would you feel if you knew that something you posted compromised the case, right?”

Jelly was pondering that possibility when a loud, cascading series of wild, raucous screams pierced the relative quiet of the house. They all looked downstairs, trying to determine the source of the disturbance.

“What the hell is going on?” Susannah demanded, calling down to Sergeant Breem, who was on his radio.

“Come on, *Detective*,” Jelly, said, punctuating the title with emphasis. “That kind of noise can only mean one thing: Chantilly Mace has arrived.”

CHAPTER THIRTEEN

As if on cue, the door burst open.

At first, Jessie couldn't see anyone resembling a pop star. Instead, the living room was suddenly filled with four giant men in jeans and short-sleeved, black T-shirts, along with two MBPD officers. Jessie assumed that the three other well-dressed people trailing the group were part of the entourage.

Once the door closed behind them all, the large men separated like a flower unfurling at time-lapse speed to reveal a tiny woman in cream-colored leisure wear. Her hair was hidden under a baseball cap, and she wore sunglasses, but there was no question who it was.

Chantilly Mace was one of the biggest names in music. Since she exploded onto the scene a decade ago, while still in her late teens, she'd sold millions of albums and later, broken records for music downloads. Jessie didn't know how many Grammys she'd won, but it was a lot. Her tours, which filled stadiums, were among the hottest tickets around.

She was also a brand unto herself. She had her own makeup line, her own athleisure line (which Jessie was pretty sure she was wearing right now), her own fragrance, her own jewelry line, and her own line of organic snacks. She had been married twice and every new beau since was fodder for the tabloids. She'd also gotten into a couple of altercations in nightclubs. One of them, four years ago, led to an arrest and a trial that ultimately ended in a hung jury.

Despite her international fame and outsized reputation, the woman couldn't have been more than five feet tall, but she had the coiled, springy body of a gymnast. Her cocoa skin glowed, even in the dimmed light of Shasta's living room. She took off her cap and sunglasses, handing them to a frazzled-looking blonde woman hovering by her shoulder.

Once they were gone, she ran her hand through jet-black hair, styled in a pixie cut. Her piercing, light brown eyes searched the house until they fell on a familiar face.

"Jelly Belly!" she bellowed in a voice far too out-sized for the person it was attached to.

"Chanti Baby!" Jelly yelled back, barreling down the stairs, scooping up the smaller woman and swinging her around in a circle as they hugged.

The huge security guys around them all stepped back quickly to avoid being clipped by wayward feet, apparently used to this sort of thing. Jessie and Susannah walked down the stairs and waited out the production, which lasted surprisingly long. When Jelly finally put Chantilly safely down on the floor, the singer turned and faced them. Her smile was gone and her stern expression indicated she was all business now.

"Detective Valentine, Ms. Hunt," she said, nodding civilly but not extending her hand, "my name is Doreen Chantilly Mace. As I'm sure you heard, I was the one who pressed for Homicide Special Section to get involved in investigating Shasta's murder."

"Jelly mentioned something about that," Jessie acknowledged.

"Well," Chantilly said, speaking so quietly that they could hardly hear her, "you should also know that woman was like a mother to me, way more than my real one ever was. When I moved here from Oakland at seventeen with nothing but four hundred and twenty-two dollars and a voice, no one gave me a shot. The only people interested in me didn't want to hear me sing, that's for sure. I got lucky when I met her. She believed in me. She helped me hone my craft and my image. She taught me to trust my instincts and not to take any crap. She wasn't all cuddles and hugs, but she got the job done, and she was always there for me. So now I'm going to be here for her. I'm not going to let this stand, you hear me? I'm not going to let her murder go unavenged!"

By the time she was done speaking, her voice had risen from a near whisper to a crescendo, filling up the entire room. She stared at the two of them with eyes blazing, pumped up on her own righteous fury.

"It's clear that this is very personal for you," Susannah said, though her tone suggested she wasn't bowled over by Chantilly's speech, "but in the LAPD, we don't operate based on vengeance. Justice is our guiding principle. *That's* what we can promise you."

"Call it what you want," Chantilly Mace said dismissively, "what *I* want is an update on the status of your investigation. Your unit was called in this morning. The sun's fixing to set in the next hour or so. I could record a whole album in that time. Tell me you've made some progress."

Jessie could feel Susannah stiffen beside her. Being given instructions by any civilian was bound to rub her the wrong way, but when they came from someone who carried herself with such a sense of egotism, even if it came from a place of genuine concern, it was going to amplify the rawness.

"We're very sorry for your loss, Ms. Mace," Jessie said, doing her best to smooth over the rising tension, "and we certainly understand your desire to know what happened to someone you were so close to. Anyone in your position would feel the same way. But you surely understand that in an ongoing murder investigation, we simply can't share everything we know without compromising the case. But we can assure you that we're pursuing every avenue available to us. Along those lines, maybe you can help us. If you'd be willing to answer a few quick questions—?"

"Are you accusing her of something?" the harried blonde next to Mace demanded angrily, stepping forward.

Jessie looked at her in confusion, then at the singer, who seemed on the verge of getting offended too.

"What—no," she said quickly. "We just thought that you might have some unique insight into Shasta that we don't, considering your long history together. Maybe you'd know if there was anyone who might want to harm her, anyone she mentioned being afraid of?"

Mace's face briefly took on an expression that Jessie couldn't initially identify. Only when the singer opened her mouth to respond did she realize that it was a muted variation of shame.

"Here's the thing about Shasta," Mace explained, "she never talked to me about her troubles. That's what made her such a great manager. She always stayed focused on mine. You probably think that makes me selfish, that I never asked about what was going on in her life."

Jessie was about to offer a bland reply but before she could, out of the corner of her eye, she saw Susannah shrug. It took everything she had not to visibly wince. She saw that Chantilly Mace had noticed it too and it was clear that she didn't appreciate the gesture. Her brow furrowed and she seemed to coil even more tightly than she already was. Then Drake Breem stepped forward.

"People on the outside don't always understand what makes a relationship between two folks tick on the inside," he said quietly, his tone suggesting personal experience with the subject. "It sounds like you and Shasta had a symbiotic, synergistic thing going on that seemed to work for both of you. Who's to judge how people connect, am I right?"

Jessie wasn't sure if Breem believed everything he said or if he was just playing up his surfer vibe to serve as a peacemaker. Either way, she was impressed. Chantilly seemed to be as well.

"See," she said, looking around at her collection of hangers-on, "bargain bin silver fox here gets it."

Upon hearing those words, Jessie found her patience for the star suddenly wearing thin. She'd put up with a lot of rich, famous jerks while pursuing cases, but rarely had she encountered such random, undeserved cruelty from a person whose persona was all about a hardscrabble, "fight the power" everywoman making good.

Chantilly seemed oblivious to how her comment had been received. To his credit, Breem simply smiled, as if the jibe had made no impact on him at all. When the woman continued on, he said nothing.

"So I answered your question about Shasta," the singer said, "which I know was really just a way to distract me from *my* question, but it didn't work, so here it is again: how close are you to catching this bastard?"

Jessie looked over at Susannah, worried she might explode. But the detective had a surprisingly calm expression on her face, all things considered. When she spoke, her voice was equally restrained.

"Ms. Mace," Susannah said, "despite what you may think, we don't answer to you personally. We are trying to solve a crime and we simply won't reveal information about our investigation to you until we release it to the rest of the public. Until then, you're welcome to get updates from Jelly's social media feeds."

Chantilly Mace's face twisted into a grimace that Jessie had never seen on TV or on the cover of a magazine. She leaned forward and pointed her finger at Susannah as she replied archly.

"Let me tell you something, girl. I didn't come all the way down to this backwater beach town to get the runaround from anyone, definitely not from some top-heavy tart who looks like she's about to leave here any minute because she's got a stripper gig at a bachelor party in the valley later tonight. I had your giraffe partner over there brought in special on this case. But you should be on your knees thanking me for this assignment. Otherwise you might be on your knees somewhere else, you follow? I can break you with a snap of my fingers—both of you, to be honest. So start talking, you brunette Barbie bitch!"

Jessie rested her hand gently on Susannah's forearm, partly as a show of support, but mostly as a stop sign. She didn't want her partner to make a mistake she'd regret. If anyone was going to do that, it would be Jessie.

"Snap your fingers," she said softly.

"What did you say to me, you mutant Amazon?" Chantilly demanded angrily.

"You said you could break both of us with the snap of your fingers," Jessie said, stepping forward, "so let's see you back up those big words, Doreen. I'd love to see you try."

One of the singer's security guards took a half step forward to meet her.

Jessie held up her hand in his direction but kept her eyes on the singer.

"Careful there, Gigantor," Jessie said. "You sure you want to take that next step? Remember who you're dealing with. This 'top-heavy tart' next to me won the police academy's hand-to-hand combat competition going up against a guy roughly your size. She's also a deadeye target shooter out to three hundred yards without a scope. Considering that you're less than two away from her, I don't know if you want to lay a hand on me and test that itchy trigger finger of hers. And I can't be responsible for how these beach police will react if you or one of your muscle brothers does something stupid. I know your boss lady there called their department Podunk. I can't imagine they loved that or getting bigfooted on this case."

She took another step forward so that she was just inches away from Mace, staring straight down at the woman she dwarfed by nearly a foot.

"As to me," she said sweetly, "I'm not some giddy fan who's going to be intimidated by a tiny tot who pays her bills by singing real loud. Don't come at me with threats of breaking me. I've stared down serial killers for a living, including my own father. If I was going to be broken, it would have happened a long time ago, and not by the likes of you. You're very talented but you are out of your depth. Go sing a pretty song and let the professionals do their job."

Chantilly Mace, perhaps for the first time in years, appeared speechless.

After a few seconds, she seemed to regroup. Turning to the blonde beside her, she extended her hand and was immediately given her cap and sunglasses, which she promptly put back on.

"We ready?" she asked of her security team.

"Give us a second to make sure the route is clear," one of the previously silent members of the entourage said. No one else spoke for the next ten seconds as he murmured into a microphone attached to his collar and listened to a voice in his earpiece. Then the guy announced, "We're good."

Chantilly started to walk away, surrounded by her human bowling ball collection, then stopped and turned around. She focused her attention on Susannah. Jessie felt her neck muscles tense up.

"I'm sorry—I shouldn't have gone after your looks," Mace said under her breath. "Truth is, if I had your body, I'd be rockin' it too. You do you."

Then she spun on her heels and rushed out, disappearing into the protective envelope of her giant security detail just before stepping outside. Jessie watched the circus navigate through the shrieking mass of fans, which seemed to have doubled in the short time since Mace had first arrived. Susannah sighed next to her.

"I think it's going to take a while to process being insulted and complimented by one of the biggest stars in the world, all in less than a minute."

Jessie had to admit that even for her, this was one of the wildest celebrity interactions she'd had. She'd dealt with entitled superstars in many cases, but none who packed as much arrogance and genuine passion into such a small package.

"I wouldn't give anything she says too much weight," Jessie said as she shook her head, still watching the Mace train shove its way through the crowd to the limo that was parked on The Strand, proudly ignoring the prohibition on vehicle traffic. The fans followed along, grabbing, squealing, hoping for any chance to see or touch the singer.

Not all the fans, though. Jessie noticed one guy standing amid the crowd, whose attention wasn't focused on the chaos of the departing superstar and her entourage. Instead, his gaze was fixed on the mansion. In fact, he seemed to be staring through the open front door directly at Jessie.

"Not even the rockin' body part?" Susannah asked.

"You were pretty secure about that long before you met Chantilly Mace," Jessie reminded her, still staring at the guy on the sand. Tall and skinny, he was wearing black board shorts, an unbuttoned, short-sleeved maroon shirt, and had long brown hair and a scraggly-looking beard that reminded her of a lost member of one of those 1970s bands like Lynyrd Skynyrd or the Allman Brothers Band. She was debating whether his intense focus on what was going on in the house was just curiosity or something more.

"Anyway," Susannah said, "I just wanted to thank you for sticking up for me. Considering that I once tried to hook up with your husband, admittedly before I knew you, you've turned out to be a pretty damn loyal friend-type person."

Jessie glanced over at her briefly in disbelief before returning her attention to the scraggly guy.

"Susannah," she replied, "you have an amazing facility for taking what should be a heartwarming moment and making it super awkward and uncomfortable. Having said that, you're welcome. Also, don't be obvious about it, but if you look toward the front door, there's a seventies Southern rock band–looking guy on the sand staring at us."

"Okay," Susannah said. "Is that a big deal? There's police tape up everywhere, and we *are* conducting a murder investigation. Shouldn't we expect stares?"

"That's true," Jessie conceded. "I just found it odd that when the global music megastar and her entourage came within a dozen feet of him, he never even glanced her way. He just kept watching us."

"What are you thinking?" Sergeant Breem asked from behind them, not looking in the direction of the guy but rather turning away and bending down, pretending to tie his already tied sneaker. "Do you want me to have one of my officers outside engage him? I have someone a couple of blocks over who could go down to the beach and approach him from behind."

"That's not a bad ide—" Jessie started to say.

Before she could complete the sentence, the guy seemed to sense something was up and turned around, heading in the opposite direction.

"I'll call my officer," Breem said.

The scraggly guy glanced over his shoulder, then without warning, started running.

"Go for it," Jessie told the sergeant, "but we can't wait. Have him meet us."

She leapt down the stairs and out the open front door, with Susannah right behind her.

CHAPTER FOURTEEN

The guy was fast.

Maybe it was the head start. Or maybe it was that he was barefoot, which was an advantage when running on sand. But for whatever reason, by the time Jessie left the cement walking path of the Strand and started chasing the scraggly guy onto the beach, he had a good fifty yards on her. Susannah, who wasn't as long-legged as her and didn't run five miles every morning like she did, was well behind.

It didn't help that with so many people spread out on the Friday evening of Labor Day weekend, the beach was an obstacle course of humanity. She dodged rows of folks lying out, hoping to catch the last rays of the fading sun, as well as multiple umbrellas, along with picnic tables and chairs, and even a few sand castles.

The crowds didn't thin out until they reached the wet, packed-in sand close to the water. With fewer people to worry about stepping on and a better grip on the firmer sand, she began to close the gap on the guy, who kept looking back, sensing he was in trouble.

After what she guessed was nearly half a mile of non-stop sprinting, pumping her legs relentlessly in the stultifying early evening heat, she could almost reach out and grab him. She was about to do just that, to try to tug at his shirttails and knock him off balance, when she saw him reach for something in the pocket of his board shorts. Realizing that she didn't have time to go for a weapon of her own, she leapt at him, tackling him right as a wave crashed in to shore.

They landed just as the water came rushing in over them. Despite the heat in the air, the water was bracingly cold as it swallowed her up. She tried to hold her breath, but after running for several minutes without a break, she couldn't help gasping for air and some water got in. She began to cough and gag. The wave briefly pushed them toward the beach before sucking them out into the deeper water.

Jessie did her best to scramble to her feet while attempting to regain her breath. Just as she felt the ocean's surface below her toes and took her first uncluttered breath, another wave slammed into her, shooting her back toward the beach face first. This time the force was so strong that she landed on the sand, too far to be sucked back into the water. She pushed herself up onto all fours just as Susannah arrived.

"You good?" the detective asked.

Jessie nodded breathlessly.

"Good, because he's not. I'm going in after him."

Jessie turned her head and saw the scraggly guy flailing about desperately in water that looked to be about five feet deep.

"Be careful," she wheezed. "He has something in his pocket."

She pushed herself upright and stumbled over to the water, where Susannah was dragging the guy out. He looked panicked.

"I can't swim!" he shouted.

"You don't have to," Susannah shouted at him, annoyed, "this water's two feet deep. You already nailed me in the face once with all your thrashing about. If you do it again, I'm going to punch you back, got it?"

The guy stopped fighting her and she dropped him in the sand on his back.

"Roll over," she ordered.

"Why?" he asked.

"So I can cuff you."

"Why?"

"Just do what I tell you, man," Susannah said. "You are not in a position to be asking me questions right now."

The man rolled over and she cuffed him.

"You want to check his pocket, Jessie?" she asked.

Jessie kneeled down and carefully felt around, pulling out a piece of hard plastic. It was his driver's license.

"Is this what you were going for when I was chasing you?" she asked.

"Yeah," he said.

"Why didn't you stop running?" she demanded. "I thought it might be a weapon."

"I was scared," he said in a thick southern accent that she hadn't picked up on before. "You were chasing me."

"I was chasing you because you were running away after staring at us while we were conducting an investigation," she said, looking at his license. "Do you care to explain yourself…Trey Killian of Nashville, Tennessee?"

"Yeah," he said, sounding miserable, "but can I do it inside? I'm cold."

"You think you're cold?" Jessie shot back. "At least you're dressed for the beach. I just got drenched in clothes I'd wear to the supermarket."

As they spoke, a lifeguard SUV pulled up next to them. The driver, shirtless and muscular, leaned out the window.

"Need a ride, ladies?" he asked. "Officer Timms here tells me I'm to chauffeur you and your guest to the police station."

Timms, who was sitting in the passenger seat, grinned at them.

"I'd offer you a hand but it looks like you've got everything under control here," he said.

"Maybe you could offer us some towels," Jessie suggested.

"Sure thing," he said, hopping out and popping the rear door.

While he did that, Jessie turned her attention back to Killian. Looking at him up close, now removed from the adrenalized situation earlier, she got the distinct sense that this wasn't the kind of guy who had returned to the scene of the crime to admire his handiwork. He had an eager, puppy dog energy that didn't usually match up with killers. But she needed to operate from more than just instinct.

"Why did you run, Trey?"

"I guess I just panicked a little bit," he replied unconvincingly.

"That's not going to fly," she told him as Timms handed her a towel. "You were *way* too interested in that crime scene. Either you know something, or you did something. Does Detective Valentine here need to read you your rights or are you going to answer our questions in a forthright manner?"

Timms threw a towel over Killian's shoulders. That, along with the threat of a potential arrest, seemed to tip the scales for him.

"The latter, ma'am," he told her.

"All right," she said, "let's get you warm, and you can start talking. Why were you at the house?"

"I was just curious to see what progress had been made," he answered as he slid into the middle of the back seat, with Jessie on one side of him and Susannah on the other. "I was at the party last night when Shasta got choked. I wondered if she was killed by the same guy."

"You saw her get choked?" Susannah repeated, saying aloud what Jessie was thinking.

This was the first time that anyone other than Mary Mary, whose credibility as an eyewitness was dubious at best, had claimed to actually see the attack on Shasta. It meant that pursuing that angle wasn't a total waste of time, even if Richie Boy had turned out to be a dead end.

"Yeah," Killian said, "I didn't just see it, I helped stop it. It was really weird. This fat guy with a long beard who was wearing a top hat and white tuxedo was on the dance floor with Shasta and he was just choking her out. It took a few seconds to realize what was going on. But eventually a group of us started pulling him off her. Even then, he tried to go after her again. This big, strapping blond dude had to punch him in the chest a few times before he went down. After that, the guy kind of scurried off through the crowd and got away. I saw him run off down the Strand."

"And no one called the police?" Jessie asked as their SUV careened bumpily along the beach.

"Shasta insisted that we not," Killian said. "She said that they would just shut down the party. She didn't want that because she had clients coming. She kept saying she was fine, so no one called. I didn't think anything of it until today, when I heard she'd died. Even then, I thought maybe she OD'd or fell down the stairs or something. But then someone told me that she was choked to death. When I heard that, it was just too freaky. So I came over. I was even thinking of volunteering what I saw. But then I saw you guys and got cold feet. Sorry about that."

Jessie looked over at Susannah and could tell from her partner's expression that they were drawing the same conclusion: Trey Killian was going to end up being useful, but almost certainly as a witness and not a suspect.

"Why were you at the party in the first place?" Susannah asked, making sure not to let their shared assumptions prevent her from doing her due diligence.

"I'm a session guitarist," Killian explained as the SUV finally left the sand and returned to solid pavement, "and a buddy of mine got an invite—"

"Sorry to interrupt," Officer Timms said from the front seat, "but I'm getting a report over the radio of someone—an older male—claiming to have killed Shasta Mallory. He was spotted holding some kind of weapon in the alleyway just outside Hercule's Bar a minute ago. You want to make a pit stop over there? It's literally a thirty-second drive from here."

"Let's do it," Susannah said before turning to Jessie. "I assume you're cool with that."

"I am," Jessie told her. "You want to uncuff our Southern fried buddy here?"

"Good point, I might need them," Susannah agreed before fixing Killian with a hard stare. "Do you promise not to run back to Nashville if I do that?"

"Yes ma'am, but I'm actually originally from Lake Charles, Louisiana, just for the record," he told her. "I know that's not the point, but I'm trying to be completely forthright."

"We appreciate that," Jessie said as her partner uncuffed him. "Just stay in the vehicle. "We'll want you to see if this guy in the alley matches the man you saw last night, okay?"

Killian nodded.

"We're here," Timms announced as the car came to a stop in front of the bar. "Other units are en route but we're first on the scene so stay alert."

"I'm always alert," Susannah told him.

Jessie didn't love her partner's cockiness but said nothing as she jumped out of the car, her eyes scanning the area for a potential killer.

CHAPTER FIFTEEN

They dashed over to the front entrance of Hercule's.

Jessie did her best to ignore the wet, sandy clothes rubbing uncomfortably against her skin in the sticky heat and stay on the lookout for any older men holding weapons claiming to be killers.

"He went that way," the bouncer standing out in front of the bar said, pointing around the corner the second they arrived. They peeked around the alleyway, which led steeply down toward a beachside parking lot, but the street was empty.

"He could have gone either way to the next block," Timms said. "Do we each want to take one?"

"Sure," Susannah agreed as the sound of sirens in the distance got closer. "Why don't you go one block to the left? I'll go one back to the right. Jessie, you okay going down this one just to make sure he doesn't double back?"

"Sounds good," Jessie said, removing her weapon and starting down the alley. She had to lean way back to counter the steepness of the narrow road as it descended down toward the beach. The sun was now really starting to dip in the sky ahead of her, making it hard to see. Since she didn't have any sunglasses, she moved to her right, along the side of Hercule's, to block the blinding rays and to avoid feeling so exposed.

The sirens were getting closer now and she was about halfway down the alley, nearing the side entrance of the bar, when she thought she heard a loud groan coming from the doorway. Suddenly concerned that their suspect may have attacked someone else, she pressed her back up against the wall next to the entrance, took a deep breath, and then spun to her left, pointing her weapon at the door.

On the ground in front of her was an older man, probably in his sixties, splayed out on the steps in front of the door. He had a tangled beard and wore the remnants of a disheveled suit. The strong odor of alcohol wafted off him.

"I killed her," he moaned mournfully, his eyes clenched tightly shut as he reached for something in his slacks pocket. "I killed the lady in the house."

"Stop!" she ordered, training the gun on his hand as he fumbled around. "Put your hands where I can see them!"

"I'm the killer!" he screeched, his voice rising above the sirens that now sounded only a block or two away. "I did the dirty deed!"

Then his hand gripped whatever he'd been reaching for in his pocket and he ripped it out. Jessie's finger rested on the trigger of her gun, a twitch from pulling it. The man lifted his item high in the air and she saw what it was: a flask.

She relaxed her finger as she heard shouts and footsteps approaching. She glanced over to see both Susannah and Timms running up the hill toward her, both huffing heavily. She returned her attention to the man, who was now unscrewing the flask top and taking a glug from it.

"I think I found our suspect," she told them.

When they joined her, it took several moments before either could speak. It was Timms who finally managed to respond first.

"I should have known," he gasped.

"What do you mean?" Jessie asked.

"That's Red Henry," he said.

"Red Henry?" Susannah asked incredulously.

"His real name is Walter Falk," Timms explained. "He's the male version of Mary Mary, only he's not independently wealthy. He's a homeless alcoholic. We've tried to place him in shelters countless times, but he always ends up back down here. I didn't realize he'd returned so soon. He also has a bad habit of confessing to every crime in town."

A squad car appeared at the top of the alley and two officers jumped out, hands on their holsters.

"It's just Red Henry," Timms yelled up to them. "Can you call it in?"

They nodded and returned to the vehicle. A moment later, the siren cut out.

"Why does he confess to crimes he didn't commit?" Jessie asked.

"Usually it's when he's hungry or doesn't feel like sleeping on the street that night," Timms said. "He'll show up at the station and confess to whatever crime he read about in the local paper. He likes to do it later in the evening, when it's too late for investigators to prove otherwise, or for him to appear in court. So he ends up getting a night in a cell with a bed, dinner, and breakfast. He must have heard about Shasta Mallory and figured that for an unsolved murder, there was no way we could turn him away if he was confessing to it after five on a Friday night."

"How often does he do this?" Susannah asked.

"At least a couple of times a month," Timms said. "We may as well take him in tonight, just in case. But—and I don't want to overstep here—I'm extremely skeptical that he's your man."

"Why is that?" Jessie asked, already in agreement but curious to hear Timms' reasoning.

"Well," he said, "even at a party as crazy as the one last night, I'm pretty sure Red Henry would have attracted attention if he had walked in. The man doesn't look like her kind of guest, and he doesn't exactly smell like a field of daisies either, you know?"

"It's a good point," she said. "Let's have Trey Killian come down and take a peek at him. If he doesn't recognize him, you can take him in for the night, but obviously don't actually charge him with anything connected to the case. The second that word gets out that someone is in custody on anything related to Mallory's death, even if it's on a technicality, this thing will blow up, especially with Chantilly Mace on the war path."

"It's not just her," Susannah noted. "I checked. Jelly has over a million followers on some of her feeds."

They brought Killian down to the bar's side entrance, where he immediately shook his head upon seeing Red Henry.

"The guy who attacked Shasta was a lot younger and stronger," he said. "Not to be rude, but this gentleman doesn't look like he would have survived one punch from the big guy I told you about."

"Okay," Susannah said, visibly shaking despite the warm weather, "here's what going to happen, assuming everyone's on board. Officer Timms, you are going to escort Mr. Killian and Red Henry back to the station, where Henry can get his dinner and cot but otherwise be kept off the radar. Our witness here can give a detailed description of Shasta's attacker to your best police sketch artist. Once that's done, please have that sent to both me and Ms. Hunt. At that point, after giving you his contact information, Mr. Killian is free to go. Sound good?"

"Sure," Timms said. "What will you be doing?"

"I'm glad you asked," she said, with just the slightest edge in her voice. "You may have noticed that the sun is close to setting, at which point these damp, salty, sand-covered clothes will go from uncomfortable to unbearable. Unless she objects, L.A.'s best known criminal profiler and I will be hitching a ride in one of your squad cars back to Shasta Mallory's place, where my vehicle is parked. Then we will be braving rush hour traffic in said damp clothes back downtown to our station to update our boss on the status of this case, which is basically, 'we got nothing.' Then, if we are lucky, we'll get to go to our respective homes to rest and regroup before seeing you bright and early tomorrow morning to start fresh, when we'll hopefully have more luck than we did today. That, Officer Timms, is what we will be doing. Did I get anything wrong, Jessie?"

"That sounds about right to me," Jessie said. "Sorry to leave you with the dirty work, Timms, but I can already feel the chafing, and I'm not loving it."

Timms held up his hands in surrender, clearly hoping she wouldn't elaborate.

"That was pretty good," Susannah whispered as they waddled up the steep alley. "I didn't know the word 'chafing' held such power. You really amped it up there."

"I only wish I was exaggerating." Jessie winced.

CHAPTER SIXTEEN

"How's she doing?" Ryan asked.

Jessie, who had been lying on the living room couch with her head in his lap, sat upright and looked at her husband. She had just hung up after talking with Kat, and the expression on Ryan's face indicated that he was more than a little concerned.

"You heard my side of the conversation," she said, surprised at the question. "Couldn't you tell?"

"Jessie, you're pretty good at hiding your emotions," he said. "So if you thought that Kat was struggling, you wouldn't let her know that you had those doubts. And if you could keep them from her, you might be able to keep them from me too. So I thought I'd just ask directly: how do you think she's doing?"

Jessie had to concede that he was right. She was adept at concealing when she thought something was awry. It was a skill she had developed so she didn't tip off suspects that she was on to them. But in this case, there was no deception involved.

"Kat's good," she said. "According to her, technically she's fully recovered from all the injuries. She can breathe clearly through the broken nose now. The fractured kneecap has fully healed, as have all the stab wounds. She said there's still a twinge in the right shoulder when she raises it above her head, but it doesn't prevent her from achieving full range of motion."

"So she's still on track to come back next week?" Ryan reconfirmed.

"She and Mitch are bringing all her stuff down from Lake Arrowhead in his pickup on Monday. She still intends to reopen Gentry Investigations on Tuesday. In fact, she reminded me of Hannah's offer to squeeze in a few days of interning before she started focusing exclusively on getting ready to start college. She wanted to know if she was still up for it."

"What did you say to that?" he asked curiously.

"I know that Hannah is still onboard, but I promised I'd reconfirm that when I called her, which I was planning to do right now."

"Before you do that, do you have any more updates for me on the Mallory case?" he asked. "Chief Decker was asking."

"I don't think so," she said. "I told you about Trey Killian, the witness who provided the description for the sketch artist. We had that sent to Jamil, who put it in the database. I'm not optimistic that we'll get a match though. The look of the guy in the sketch is so weird, it's almost like he was wearing a disguise to throw people off."

"That suggests that the initial attack might have been premeditated, right?" Ryan noted. "If he thought far enough ahead to put on a disguise?"

"Possibly," Jessie agreed. "But why attack her in public if he knew he could come back later to do it in private?"

"I think that if you can answer that question, you'll be well on your way to catching your killer."

"Right now, it feels like we're a long way from that," she said with a heavy sigh. "Just like I get the impression that the rest of the team wasn't making much progress on the Clone Killer."

"To be honest Jessie," he admitted, "other than what you have Jamil and Beth doing—contacting all those potential victims and warning them to be alert—we're at an impasse. All the other HSS detectives are working their own cases. No one has had time to follow up on it today."

"Wonderful," Jessie muttered, "so we're nowhere. Jamil didn't say it, but I could tell my request to contact all those people was pretty overwhelming, and that was *before* I told him to put the sketch of Shasta Mallory's attacker in the database too."

She adjusted herself on the couch beside him and felt a twinge in her own shoulder, though she doubted it was anything like what Kat had suffered after her stabbing at the hands of Ash Pierce. Still, the pain reminded her of how she'd gotten hurt and that she owed Ryan an additional update.

"I meant to tell you this earlier, but there was a little incident today," she said, before quickly adding, "nothing major. Susannah and I were apprehending a suspect and he got rowdy. I got knocked over and hit the ground."

Ryan tensed up but said nothing. She continued.

"I landed on my shoulder pretty hard and bumped my head," she said. "Even though it didn't feel like much, Susannah insisted that we go to urgent care to get it checked out. They did multiple tests, which confirmed that I didn't suffer any head injury and I've felt fine ever since. But I didn't want to keep it from you."

She'd had a bad habit in the past, which Ryan had called her on, of underplaying and even disregarding past close calls after her concussion in the mineshaft collapse last March. Now she was trying to turn over a new leaf and this was part of it.

"Thanks for being honest with me," he said, taking her hand and squeezing it softly.

"Sure," she said, glancing away, realizing that her revelation didn't in any way resolve the larger trust issues that had been plaguing them for months. She felt a sudden need to change the subject, even awkwardly. "You said Decker was asking for updates on the Mallory case? How come? Was he getting blowback from Chantilly Mace?"

The look in Ryan's eyes indicated that he knew she was desperately trying to steer the conversation away from their personal travails, but he apparently decided not to push the issue.

"Not from her," he said. "In fact, Decker said that when Mace called him, she referred to you and Valentine as 'a couple of badass bitches,' which he understood to be a compliment. However, the response was less flattering from some of Mallory's other big-name clients. He said a group of artists are unhappy with the pace of the investigation and are going to say so in a press conference tomorrow morning in front of police headquarters.

"Great," Jessie muttered sarcastically, "that won't turn things into even more of a circus. I guess we'll just have to deal with it."

"If you don't like that, I've got an unrelated update for you that's going to make you equally unhappy," he said, his jaw clenching as he spoke.

"Okay," Jessie said, trying not to visibly react.

She was still getting over his last big, unexpected revelation, the one where, for months, he hid from her the fact that a mental patient had made threats against him, Hannah, and Kat because he didn't want her to worry; the one that led to hitwoman Ash Pierce causing the injuries that Kat was just now recovering from and almost led to both her and Hannah's deaths.

You're making a super duper effort to let that go, Jessie. Keep up the good work.

As she silently chastised herself for her inability to forgive, she prayed that what he was about to tell her wouldn't compound the problem. While outwardly she remained placid, inside, she braced herself.

"I just got word that Ash Pierce's trial has been moved up," he said, looking at the TV, even though it wasn't on. "Apparently, she's prioritizing the 'speedy' part of the trial, so she's being transferred from Lompoc Penitentiary down here to Twin Towers in L.A."

"When is that happening?" Jessie asked, doing her best to ignore the pit that had suddenly developed in her gut.

"No exact word yet," he said. "I was just told that it's going to happen 'imminently.' I don't know if that means two days or two weeks."

"Which means that Hannah needs to emotionally prepare to testify earlier than she expected," Jessie noted.

"Yeah," Ryan said, "that was the main reason I thought you should know. Sorry for bringing you down."

"No, thanks for telling me," she told him. "I'll break the news to her."

"This weekend?" he asked.

Jessie thought about that prospect. Ash Pierce, even shackled and in a prison jumpsuit, was what nightmares were made of. Though she was petite and far from physically imposing, the former marine and CIA assassin turned contract killer was adept at deception and, as Kat learned the hard way, torture. Though Hannah had managed to just barely outwit and outmaneuver her, the experience had left internal scars, including nights when she woke up screaming, her body covered in sweat.

"No," she said, "that would really mess her up. She deserves to have one weekend of fun, free from anxiety about this crap. I'll tell her after the holiday."

Ryan gave her a look which he immediately tried to erase, but it was too late. She recognized it. It was his "so you're keeping something from her to protect her?" expression. He didn't say a word to that effect, which would have been relationship suicide, but it lingered there between them.

"Have you heard anything from her today?" he asked quickly, clearly trying to move past the moment.

"She's texted me throughout the day," Jessie answered. "Sent me a few photos too, lounging on the beach, that kind of thing. But like I said, I was going to call just to check in, if that's cool."

He hadn't even responded when her phone rang. She looked at it and then held it out to show him, unable to keep the smile off her face. Then she answered.

"Speak of the devil," she said, "we were just talking about you. How's it going?"

***

"Why were you talking about me?" Hannah asked as she stood, leaning against a wooden fence overlooking a cliff in Santa Monica's Palisades Park. "Have I done something wrong without knowing it?"

"No," Jesse replied. "I was just telling Ryan that you were texting me updates, but I wanted to actually hear your voice."

"That's very sweet," Hannah said. "Well, to answer your question, I'm with the Wildpines crew, of course. We're just admiring a cliffside view of the pier and the ocean while we wait for our dinner table to be ready. Patrice got reservations at a seafood place across the street that supposedly has amazing lobster rolls, so I'm pretty excited."

As she spoke, she and the others stood side by side along the wooden fence overlooking the cliff, with her at one end. Chris, at the other end, was playing peek-a-boo with her, poking his head out from behind Carlos and then darting behind him again.

"You sound excited, maybe even a little giddy," Jessie said. "Are you sure it's about the lobster rolls?"

"What do you mean?" Hannah asked, feeling her face flush in the darkness.

"I guess I'm just wondering if there's one particular lobster roll that you're more excited about than the others?"

Hannah wanted to plead ignorance to Jessie's real reference but knew it was a waste of time.

"How did you know?" she asked in a hushed voice.

"I can profile voices too, little sister," Jessie told her.

Even though Annie, who was standing next to her, was deep in conversation with Doug, Hannah turned and leaned away from her.

"Chris and I are really hitting it off," she whispered into the phone. "I wasn't sure if the connection I felt up in the mountains would still be there, but we picked up right where we left off."

"That's awesome, have fun with it," Jessie said, sounding genuinely excited for her. Then there was a brief pause in which Hannah knew the caveat was coming. "But not *too* much fun."

"Jessie, I'm eighteen," Hannah started to protest.

"No, that's not what I mean," her sister said quickly. "I trust you to make the best decisions for yourself when it comes to what you do with

Chris. I just mean, don't let the fun get in the way of staying alert. I hate to be a bummer, but with everything that's happened to us lately, I feel like I have to give you the obligatory reminder: be vigilant. Keep your eyes open. If something feels off, trust your instincts. And don't hesitate to call me if things go south. Deal?"

"Deal," Hannah said.

"I'm really sorry I had to go there," Jessie told her.

"It's okay," Hannah assured her. "I would have almost been disappointed if you hadn't. Almost."

"Glad I could live up to expectations," Jessie said. "Now I'm going to stop being such a downer and let you go. Have fun and give Chris a kiss for me."

"Goodbye," Hannah said firmly.

"Goodbye, little sis," Jessie said.

Hannah could hear her chuckling as she hung up. When she turned back around the rest of the gang was still engaged in their various conversations, save for Chris, who was looking at her curiously. He walked over.

"Is everything okay?" he asked. "Your energy kind of changed there after you got that phone call."

"No, I'm good. I was just checking in with my sister." she told him. "I think I'm getting a little peckish though. Any word on how much longer before our table might be ready?"

"Let me check with Patrice," he said, stepping back over to the group.

With his attention elsewhere, Hannah took the opportunity to look around. She tried to be as casual about it as possible, but as she made a leisurely turn around the park, she scanned everyone in the area, looking for anybody who appeared suspicious or whose gaze lingered on her longer than it should have.

She recalled the gangly guy from earlier this afternoon at the beach, who'd stared at their group unusually long, and kept watch for anyone behaving similarly this evening. But there was no one. Everybody seemed involved in their own activity, focused on enjoying their own Friday night, just as she was supposed to be doing.

Mildly annoyed with her sister for putting the anxiety in her head but aware that it was likely a good thing, she returned her own focus to her friends and the fun they had in store for her the rest of the night.

CHAPTER SEVENTEEN

Three-quarters of a mile north of Hannah, Mark Haddonfield stood in the darkness outside the beach house, studying it, reviewing his plan of attack.

He knew that, while the place had a security system, it hadn't been activated for this weekend. With all the chaos of moving in, it apparently just wasn't a priority, which was understandable. But it also worked to Mark's advantage.

It meant that he'd be able to slip inside to scope the place out and determine the best place for the attack. Would an open space like the kitchen or living room be the best choice? That would make quite a statement, but it came with obvious risks, the most noteworthy of which was that he might be seen during the big moment.

He could always do the job in the bedroom. That was the most logical spot for any number of reasons. It was more secluded, of course. But it was also more in keeping with the spirit of the exercise. This victim was special after all, and the circumstances of the death needed to be treated with the appropriate reverence. If he was going to honor the purpose of the endeavor, The Strategy required that the mission be completed there.

Mark picked the lock of the side door and entered the house. He pulled out his digital camera and began taking photos. He could have used his phone for the task, but that would have geo-tagged his location and cost him an alibi. That's why his phone was currently hidden in a movie theater in the Santa Monica Place mall a mile south of here.

He'd bought a ticket to the movie, hidden his phone in the theater, then left through a back exit, leaving the door slightly ajar, and caught a cab here. Now he snapped as many pictures as he could, well aware that he was on a tight timeline. He had to get back to the movie theater before the film ended, collect his phone, and be seen walking out, preferably by doing something memorable, maybe tripping into someone holding a bucket of popcorn.

But that could only happen if the first part of the plan went off without a hitch. He knew his intended victim was out to dinner tonight.

But the restaurant was just up the road, and without his phone, there was no way for Mark to be sure they were still there.

What if there was a problem with the reservation? What if there was an upset stomach or a simple change of heart and a desire for homemade grilled cheese sandwiches instead of an overpriced meal? He would never know until the car pulled up in the driveway, leaving him no time to escape.

Mark put those thoughts out of his head. He couldn't control what happened outside of this beach house. All he could do was take his photos, get out of here, retrieve his phone, and go back to his hotel to prepare for what was to come. The rest was out of his hands.

He had to believe that justice and destiny were on his side. If they weren't, he would have been caught by now. If they weren't, Jessie Hunt would have discovered his identity. If they weren't, Hannah Dorsey would have pulled out her phone this afternoon and snapped a photo of him. But none of that happened.

Those were all signs—signs that fate was on his side; signs that the vengeance he sought was justified, even necessary. Blood would be spilled. The city would turn on Jessie Hunt. And she would regret not giving him a chance, not taking him seriously, not recognizing his brilliance.

"You had your chance," he scolded. "But you were more interested in glory-hunting than in actually doing the hard work of educating the next generation of criminal profilers. You wanted to be adored by the news anchors—another day, another report calling you the Angel of the City of Angels. It's your sustenance, isn't it. You can't live without it!"

He stopped, realizing he was yelling. His voice echoed through the cavernous house. For a moment, he feared that someone outside might have heard him. But then he calmed down. The house had thick walls and it was set far apart from any others. He actually liked how he sounded, like a professor calling out a lackluster student in front of the entire class.

It was unfortunate that another innocent would have to pay for her to learn the lesson. But education comes at a price. Hers would be steep.

CHAPTER EIGHTEEN

This party wasn't quite as big as last night's, but that didn't matter, at least not for his purposes.

In fact, because Nicole Boyce's house wasn't as spread out as Shasta Mallory's mansion, the event still felt vital. People were more tightly packed together, and it was harder to move around, giving the festivities a sense of size and energy, even if he guessed that there were no more than half the people here than he'd had to navigate last night. It was still only 10 p.m. He suspected that the crowd might reach 300 in another hour.

He was glad that he'd chosen a different outfit for tonight. The white tuxedo and fat suit would have been extra challenging in tonight's close spaces. This evening, he'd gone with a dramatically different look.

He had on a sparkly black leather jumpsuit, open midway down his chest, along with black boots and black gloves. His scruffy, longish black wig went past his shoulders in the back and covered his forehead in the front. He wore large sunglasses and had a press-on mustache, along with a spray-tan that he worried might start to drip off in the combined heat of the evening and the crowded house. He thought he looked a little like late-era Elvis, only tanner, in better shape, and with facial hair.

He easily slid past chattering pockets of people until he found Nicole in a corner of the living room, having an animated conversation with a group of friends. They had to shout to be heard over the music pounding through the overhead speakers.

Clearly tipsy, she was holding court, animatedly waving her muscular arms to make her point. Even though she was retired now, she still looked like she could go out right now, hop on her board, and ride a big wave. She had on a pink bikini top and a sheer, white sarong over the bottoms. In between, her washboard abs rippled as she moved. He knew that she was the same age as him, thirty-six, and he was jealous that he couldn't maintain that level of abdominal firmness. Then again, he couldn't afford to spend all day staying in shape.

Much like others he passed by earlier, Nicole and her friends were discussing Shasta Mallory's murder, how she'd been found dead in her bedroom this morning. But infuriatingly, just as in those other exchanges he'd overheard, no one was mentioning the attack that Shasta had suffered earlier in the evening. It was as if that hadn't even registered with people.

As usual, all they wanted to talk about was the rich person who'd been wronged. Once again, he was being dismissed, ignored. No one acknowledged the unusual-looking man who'd accosted Shasta on the dance floor earlier in the evening. It was like he didn't exist. Only the rich, powerful woman was worth their time. It was typical. They were so self-involved that not even a fat man in a white tuxedo and top hat choking the party hostess could earn a moment's notice. Well, maybe they'd remember this.

He stepped over so that he was right behind Nicole and reached up, putting his gloved hands on her shoulders. He began gently massaging them as he said, using his best Elvis impression, "You look like you need a hunka hunk of burning massage love."

One of the women across from him and Nicole put her hands to her open mouth in shock and another started giggling as a third asked, "Did you hire Elvis to do massages and why does he have a mustache?"

"No," Nicole said, glancing over her shoulder with a mix of surprise and amusement, "but I can't say I'm upset."

"What would Lachlan say?" another friend asked.

"Maybe Lachlan should be here instead of halfway across the globe getting his rocks off with Lady Afulu," Nicole replied bitingly.

"Oooh!" all three women said in collective glee as they high-fived each other.

As they did, none of them noticed that he had suddenly switched from massaging Nicole's shoulders to squeezing her neck. He heard her gasp and felt enormous satisfaction at the sound. His one regret was that he couldn't see her face.

But a moment later, he got a thrill when he saw something almost as great—the shocked faces of her friends. And then, when Nicole swung her elbow back into his rib cage, hoping to break free of him, those shocked expressions turned to horror, especially when they realized Nicole wasn't able to break free. He might not have washboard abs like her. But he was work-strong, and no amount of swung elbows or stomped feet was going to deter him.

He was actually a little disappointed. Had he wanted to, he could have broken her neck right then, but that wasn't the goal. He was waiting for one of them to scream for help and had to soften the grip around Nicole's neck in the interim.

It wouldn't do to hurt her so badly that she had to go to the hospital. He wanted her scared but not incapacitated. He wanted her frazzled but not enough to call the cops or cancel the party. Were these idiot friends of hers going to ruin that? What would he do if they just continued to stand there in open-mouthed senselessness?

"Help!" one of them finally screamed. "He's choking Nicole!"

That broke the dam. All three of them started screaming and within seconds there were four people on him, tearing his hands off Nicole's neck. None of them were as big as the blond guy from last night and no one looked like they were ready to punch him. But two guys, both smaller than him, did muster up the courage to shove him toward the side door.

A woman standing nearby quickly opened it and they pushed him out. He stumbled down the two steps, losing his balance and nearly falling onto the pavement before catching himself. The door slammed closed behind him. He heard it lock as one of the guys yelled, "Get out of here or we'll call the cops!"

He looked around. This side of the house, with just a narrow walkway dividing it from the one next door, was devoid of people, probably because it was dark with limited access to the house. He waited there for a second, wondering if a group of guys would burst out, with fireplace pokers in hand, ready to beat him to a pulp. But other than one woman who peeked through a curtain to see if he was still there, there was no reaction at all.

Unsure whether to be relieved, angry, or disappointed, he turned and walked down the path to where it ended at a small gate that connected with the Strand. He hopped the gate and found himself among a swarm of people milling about in front of Nicole's house, some waiting to get in, others just loitering.

About thirty yards away, he did see an MBPD officer approaching the house, shouting futilely for people to clear the Strand so pedestrians could get by. Not wanting to push his luck, he adjusted his jumpsuit, turned the other way, and began walking in the opposite direction with a smile on his face.

He wasn't stressed. After all, he knew he'd be back.

***

He returned an hour and a half later, in fact. Just after 11:30, he wandered into the house the same way he had before, through the front door. Only this time he was wearing jeans, a T-shirt, and a baseball cap pulled low to cover much of his face. He looked like half the other guys at the party, which as expected, had swelled in size from before. The only difference was the latex gloves he wore, which no one noticed.

Unlike earlier in the evening, this time he made his way through the crowd without any fanfare, drawing as little attention as possible. He took the stairs to the second floor, where he pretended to wait in line for the bathroom until the hallway was empty. Then he jimmied the locked door of the bedroom that Nicole shared with her husband, who she'd revealed was not in town tonight. He poked his head in.

"Anyone in here?" he called out. "All the other bathrooms are full. Is it okay if I use this one?"

There was no reply. He quickly stepped inside, closed the door, and locked it again. Then he moved to the bathroom, and from there into the walk-in closet. He found a spot in the dark left corner in the back, behind some of Nicole's long dresses, where he could sit down and still remain hidden.

It might be quite a long wait and he didn't want to stand up for what might end up being hours. He settled in, resting his back against the wall. Then he took a long, deep breath, finally allowing himself to relax. The hard part was over. Now there was just anticipation, followed by the fun stuff.

The party was just getting started.

CHAPTER NINETEEN

"You're kidding, right?" Jessie asked in disbelief as she sat in the passenger seat of the car.

"No," Susannah told her. "Check my bag if you want to."

Jessie did just that, grabbing the small backpack from the backseat and unzipping it. Sure enough, her partner had brought a set of spare clothes along for the day. Susannah had generously offered to pick her up and they were on their way to Manhattan Beach, hoping to beat the heat by arriving earlier than they had yesterday.

"Do you really think you're in danger of having another ocean-related incident?" Jessie asked, stifling a laugh.

"Who's to say?" the detective replied. "All I know is that if something does go down, I'll be prepared, and you'll be stuck traipsing around in some soggy slacks."

"You do know there's this thing called 'stores,' Susannah?" Jessie asked, unable to control her giggles now.

"Stores are for the weak, Hunt," the detective replied, trying to keep a straight face.

At that, they both broke out in laughter. Jessie was happy for the emotional release. Though she didn't say it, she was relieved to be driving to the beach, pursuing this case with Susannah, despite the woman's quirks, and even if they hadn't made much progress.

At the very least it was a way to take her mind off how little progress they were making in the Clone Killer case. If she wasn't trying to solve Shasta Mallory's murder in Manhattan Beach, she'd just be spending her Saturday morning staring in frustration at the corkboard in the Central Station bullpen. Here, she felt *some* forward momentum.

When their laughter finally subsided, Jessie decided that now was as good a time as any to test the Sergeant Drake Breem waters.

"I know we didn't have a ton of success getting answers yesterday," she said, "but what did you think of the MBPD folks we worked with?"

"Solid team," Susannah said with a shrug. "That's where Jamil came from, right?"

"Yep."

"You'd never know he worked there," Susannah noted. "He's a lot more straitlaced than some of them."

"Compared to who?" Jessie asked, following the path the detective was laying out for her.

"That Sergeant Breem for one," she said. "When he was trying to smooth things over with Chantilly Mace, I thought he was going to try to get us all into a sharing circle or something."

"What were your impressions of him, other than being in touch with his emotions?" Jessie pressed.

"What do you mean?" Susannah asked, glancing over at her suspiciously.

"I mean, do you have any general thoughts about a law enforcement type that Chantilly called a 'silver fox,' who gets his job done in a professional manner, but still likes to catch a sweet wave from time to time, *and* seems to have lived through enough stuff not to let his eyes bulge out of his head when a detective who looks like a lingerie model walks through the door?"

Susannah quickly returned her eyes to the road and Jessie noted that her grip on the wheel had suddenly gotten tighter.

"I hadn't thought about it," she said unconvincingly.

"Wow," Jessie said with a laugh, "I don't have to be a criminal profiler to see through you."

Before she could tease her partner any more, her phone rang. It was Ryan. She put the call on speaker.

"What's up?" she asked. "You're on speaker."

"I wanted you both to hear this from me before you started getting news alerts," he said. "There's been another murder in Manhattan Beach. The victim was also strangled to death, also after a huge party at her house. Have you ever heard of Nicole Boyce?"

"I don't think so," Jessie said, looking over at Susannah, who shook her head no as well.

"Well, apparently she's pretty well known down there," Ryan said. "She's a former model and professional surfer who has her own surf wear line now. Apparently she owns a boutique in the area. That's all I really know at this point, other than that she's a big deal in the surfing community and ESPN is already running stories about her death. That, coupled with the press conference later this morning involving Shasta Mallory's other music clients, could make this a very complicated day. I'm sending you the address now."

After he hung up, Jessie turned to Susannah.

"I guess the time for casual girl talk is over," she said. "We should get down there ASAP. Maybe you should turn on your siren."

***

Jessie stood on the sand in front of Nicole Boyce's house.

It was still technically in Manhattan Beach, though it was right on the border with Hermosa Beach, where the Strand was briefly broken up by a set of stairs. The house was more akin to Ilana Owens' than to Shasta Mallory's in size and design.

Two stories high and fairly narrow, with homes on either side that boxed it in, it also looked to be on the older side, and very well-worn. Even before going inside, Jessie got the impression that Boyce was less interested in residential upkeep than some of her neighbors.

"You ready?" Susannah asked. "I want to get cracking before news crews show up and make our lives hell."

"Let's do it," Jessie said as they approached the front door. She couldn't agree more. This was already bound to be a circus once the media got involved. When they learned she was handling the case, that would only up the ante.

They were both better prepared for a day spent beachside than they had been yesterday. Though each of them still wore pants, they were looser and more casual than those they'd have employed on a case in downtown office buildings. Jessie had on a cream, button-up top to deflect the sun and Susannah had gone with a restrained-for-her lavender, polo-style shirt that was only half a size too small.

They passed under the police tape, showed their IDs to the officer at the front door, and went inside, looking for Sergeant Breem. He was nowhere in sight, but Jessie saw another familiar face making notes on a pad by the kitchen counter, and immediately walked over.

"Officer Shaw?" she said.

Looking up to meet her gaze was a young woman in her mid-twenties. Though physically unimposing—about five foot two and 110 pounds soaking wet—Jessie knew that the appearance was deceiving. Officer Carrie Shaw was not to be trifled with.

A former gymnast, Shaw was athletic and wiry, which had come in handy when she'd helped subdue the killer Jessie had been tracking when she was last in this neck of the woods. Back then she had been the newest cop in the department, not even experienced enough to stand guard at crime scenes. But perhaps because of her assistance in that case, she now carried herself with a clear confidence that she'd lacked just a year ago.

"Ms. Hunt," she said with a smile, pushing her short brown hair out of her eyes, "it's good to see you again."

"You too," Jessie said. "It looks like you're moving up in the world. Are you in charge of this crime scene?"

"Yes ma'am, temporarily," she said. "There was a fatal accident at the corner of Marine and Sepulveda that required multiple units, so Sergeant Breem asked me to hold down the fort here until you arrived."

"Well, it looks like you've got everything under control," Jessie said. "You can update us in a minute but first, let me introduce you to Detective Susannah Valentine from HSS. I'm partnering with her on…whatever this is."

"Nice to meet, you, Detective," Shaw said, extending her hand.

"Likewise," Susannah replied, shaking it.

"Susannah," Jessie explained, "Officer Shaw here was just a rookie last summer when she noticed suspicious activity in a home here on the Strand. Her assistance led to the apprehension of the suspect we were looking for. Not only that, but she also actually helped me physically take him down. If not for her, it might have gone very differently that night."

"Impressive," Susannah said, and it sounded like she meant it, before dispensing with the pleasantries. "So what have we got here?"

Shaw nodded, understanding that compliment time was over.

"Our victim, Nicole Boyce, started out as a model in her teens before becoming a pro surfer," she began. "She's a local legend around here. I actually went to her surf camp when I was a kid. She was throwing one of the many Labor Day weekend parties last night. It ran until about four a.m. this morning."

"You guys let parties run that late?" Susannah asked, surprised.

"Normally, we'd shut them down earlier than that," Shaw acknowledged, "but like I said, Nicole is a local legend, so the rules are a little different for her. Anyway, she was supposed to meet some friends to go surfing this morning around six but didn't show up. They figured she was just hung over, so they let it slide, but they stopped by after they were done to tease her about being a wuss. They were going to wake her up and drag her out of bed. That's when they found her on the floor in the bathroom."

"They just came into the house unannounced?" Jessie wondered.

"Yeah," Shaw said. "She and her crew are pretty chill. You can tell from looking around the house that they lead a pretty relaxed lifestyle. There's sand on all the furniture. No one locks their doors. They don't have any security systems or video cameras. Friends come and go whenever they want. It wouldn't have been weird for them to just jump in bed with her. They've all known each other since they were preteens."

"Okay," Jessie said. "Are the crime scene folks up there right now?"

"Yes," Shaw said. "And Pugh from the medical examiner's office too. He's waiting for you, but I already heard him say that he thinks she was only killed in the last three to five hours, which makes sense, considering that I have witnesses who said she was seeing people off when the party ended at four."

Jessie looked at the time on her phone. It was still only 8:37 a.m. Had the killer lain in wait in Nicole Boyce's bathroom for hours until her last guest left, only to strangle her when she finally retired for what was left of the night?

"There's something else," Shaw said hesitantly.

"What is it?" Jessie asked. She could tell the young officer was nervous, worried that she'd made a mistake of some kind.

"I hope you won't be upset with me or think that I've overstepped my bounds," she said, her words starting to tumble out, "but I was just waiting around here, and I didn't want to waste what seemed like a good use of my time."

"Officer Shaw," Susannah ordered firmly. "What the hell did you do?"

"A few of Nicole's friends came by a little earlier," she explained. "They were very upset and mentioned that they were at the party last night. They were reluctant to give formal statements on camera, but I got them to agree to speak to me. I was writing down my notes from our conversation when you came in. Would you like to hear what they said?"

"Yes, please," Jessie said quickly before her partner could chastise Shaw for not being more forceful in demanding video statements. The officer was about to begin when a voice called down to them from the second floor.

"Are the HSS people here yet?"

It was deputy medical examiner Carl Pugh.

"We are," Jessie yelled back up to him.

"You want to see the body before we remove it?" he asked with a hint of testiness.

"We'll be right up," Jessie said, before returning her attention to Shaw. "Please continue."

"Okay," the officer said as they started up the stairs, "they told me that they were all hanging out at the party, just talking with Nicole, when this guy came up behind her. He was dressed in a black leather jumpsuit. One of them said he looked like Elvis Presley in his later years, but with a mustache. He had long dark hair that fell into his eyes, which they couldn't see anyway because he was wearing sunglasses. He was wearing black gloves. And he was very tan."

"Okay, a tan, mustached Elvis impersonator," Susannah said as they reached the top of the stairs. "That doesn't sound that odd for one of these parties so far."

"No," Shaw agreed, "but then he started massaging Nicole's shoulders, without asking or anything."

"Did she know him?" Jessie asked.

"Not according to them," Shaw said, "but at first she didn't mind. They were even joking about how her husband would be jealous. But then the guy suddenly started choking her, out of the blue, for no reason. They said they started yelling for help and some guys came over, pulled the man off her, and shoved him outside."

"They didn't try to subdue him or hold him until police arrived?" Susannah wanted to know.

"I asked the same thing," Shaw said. "They claimed they were too in shock to think about that, and that they were focused on making sure Nicole was okay. By the time anyone thought of going after him, the guy was gone. And besides, Nicole didn't want to call us anyway. They said she was worried that we'd shut the party down because of all the illicit substances being consumed on the premises. She claimed she was more scared than hurt and that a few shots of bourbon would have her all better. So that was the end of it, at least that's what they thought until this morning."

They had stopped outside what Jessie assumed was Nicole Boyce's bedroom.

"I assume you got all their names and contact info?" she said.

"Yes, and I told them they should expect to be called in later for more formal interviews with the investigative team. I just didn't want to try to corral them *and* keep tabs on the crime scene when I wasn't sure when you'd be arriving."

"That's okay," Jessie said, speaking before Susannah could contradict her. Technically, the officer should probably have insisted on keeping the women there, but her notes were comprehensive and under the circumstances, she'd made a judgment call. Jessie didn't want her to get a tongue-lashing over it. "Why don't you head back downstairs? We'll be fine from here."

Shaw nodded and returned the way she'd come.

"Getting soft in your old age?" Susannah asked once Shaw had retreated down the stairs.

"She's clearly already beating herself up for not following protocol, Susannah," Jessie said. "Sometimes you don't have to dress down an officer. She's a good cop and she'll be an asset on the case, assuming we don't push her away."

"Fine," Susannah muttered as they walked into the bedroom, "maybe you can get her a lollipop later, too."

Jessie didn't respond. When Detective Valentine got like that, there was no point. They walked through the bedroom, with its open sliding door leading to the balcony overlooking the tiny first-floor courtyard, and joined Pugh in the bathroom, where Nicole Boyce lay on her back.

Her eyes were closed, and her sun-bleached blonde hair was messy, as if it had gotten tangled when she tried to break free from her attacker. She was wearing a pink bikini. A white sarong rested just off to the side of her. Jessie wondered if it had come loose during the struggle.

If she'd been wearing clothes, Nicole Boyce would have looked like a normal thirty-something woman. She was of average height. And though she was quite attractive, the constant exposure to sun and saltwater had given her a slightly weathered appearance that had perhaps aged her prematurely.

Her body, however, had battled the years impressively. She might have been retired, but she looked like she was still capable of competing in her sport. Her arms and legs, even hours after death, were incredibly toned, and her stomach was flat and hard.

Jessie kneeled down next to the body of Nicole Boyce, and somehow felt that even though they'd never met, she understood her. This was a woman who, even after wrapping up a party at 4 a.m., had so much passion for what she did that she planned to go surfing that same morning at six. This was a woman who got a kick out of making her husband jealous, who liked a few shots of bourbon, who didn't mind friends leaping into her bed at all hours, who was willing to sacrifice skin care for sun and sand and sea spray.

Nicole Boyce was a "live life to the fullest" kind of person and now she was lying lifeless on her bathroom floor. Seeing her like this made Jessie's gut churn with rage. She stood up.

"We've got to get this guy," she said quietly to Susannah. "This won't stand."

"I know," the detective agreed. "I get that we're about justice but right now I feel like dishing out some of that vengeance Chantilly Mace was talking about yesterday."

Jessie nodded.

"Speaking of yesterday's victim," Jessie noted, "we may as well say out loud what we both know to be true after looking at these two women."

"What?" Susannah asked.

"We're dealing with a serial killer."

CHAPTER TWENTY

Jessie could feel her partner's frustration rubbing off on her.

They were in a small conference room at the Manhattan Beach police station, which had been set aside for them. And after four hours of reviewing notes, adding possible leads on a whiteboard, and making calls, Susannah Valentine seemed to be near her breaking point.

"No video cameras at the house," she said irritably, "in fact, no security of any kind. No one saw this Elvis guy leave. No one saw him come back in, at least not in the same get-up. But people could come and go whenever they wanted so he could have just wandered in at any point if he liked. But according to Pugh, there were no fingerprints or DNA on Nicole Boyce's neck, just like with Shasta Mallory. And since he wore gloves during the neck massage, that's a dead end too. So we've got nothing."

"That's not necessarily true," Jessie reminded her. "Don't forget, we have Jamil and Beth checking for possible connections between the two women. They've only been at that for a couple of hours. Maybe something will pop. This is an insular community, and they didn't seem to travel in the same social circle. One was a music manager, and another was a surf legend. If there's a link, it should become clear soon, whether it be past boyfriends, shared business relationships, overlapping service providers, mutual friends, or something else along those lines."

"I guess," Susannah said. "I would have thought they'd have found something by now."

Jessie didn't say it out loud but so did she. Jamil had found much more complicated connections in far shorter times. She couldn't help but wonder if he and Beth were being spread too thin. Her other request, for them to call all potential victims of past killers she'd caught and warn them that they might be in danger, was a massive undertaking. And it wasn't like they could just say "hey, be careful out there." They had to be diplomatic in how they alerted people. In retrospect, the ask may have just been too much.

She had another concern too, one she was hesitant to bring up, though she suspected it was silently eating away at Susannah too and was likely part of why she was so irritable. This was two murders in two nights. Did that mean this guy was planning another one for tonight?

"Let's get out of here," she said, standing up. "I need to clear my head, and I think it would probably do you some good too. You look like you could explode at any minute."

"Do we have time for that?" Susannah asked.

"We can still discuss the case," Jessie assured her. "We'll just do it while we get some coffee and walk by the beach. We're down here. We may as well take advantage of our surroundings."

"It's too hot for coffee," the detective grumbled.

"Iced coffee then," Jessie said, feeling like she was dealing with a petulant child.

That seemed to satisfy Susannah. They walked outside and made the short jaunt down to the main drag along Manhattan Beach Boulevard. It seemed that the moment they rounded the corner, and the ocean came into view, the cloud over the detective's brain cleared.

"Didn't your little buddy, Officer Shaw, say something about Nicole Boyce's husband being jealous?" she asked.

"She did," Jessie recalled as they stopped at a small coffeehouse and got in line.

"Maybe we should look into that," Susannah suggested. "Is it crazy to suggest that he might kill Shasta Mallory one night in order to establish a serial killer situation when all along his real plan was to kill his own wife the next night?"

"It's not crazy at all," Jessie said, pulling out her phone and calling Shaw. "I only wish I'd thought of it first."

Shaw picked up on the first ring.

"Shaw here," the officer said promptly.

"Hey," Jessie said, putting one AirPod in her ear and handing the other to Susannah so they wouldn't be overheard by other folks in line, "it's Jessie Hunt. I'm here with Detective Valentine. We had a question for you. You said earlier that Nicole's friends were joking about how her husband would be jealous about her getting that massage from the Elvis guy. Do you know what the story is there?"

"Oh yeah, they were just teasing her," Shaw said. "It's kind of an inside joke around here. Nicole and her husband have a notoriously stormy relationship. They're like the South Bay's own personal soap opera, sort of a beachside *Days of Our Lives*. They both get jealous all the time because hot-looking fans are always hitting on them."

"Both of them?" Susannah pressed.

"Yeah, her husband is Lachlan Restrepo," she explained. "He's a big wave surfer who's almost as famous as she is. But if you're thinking he might be a suspect, I looked into it. He was doing Indicators and Afulu."

"I don't know what that means," Susannah said, annoyed.

"Sorry," Shaw said sheepishly. "He was in Indonesia for a surfing competition. Those are both surf spots in the region. But I checked around and one of his long-time buddies told me that someone already called to break the news about Nicole and he's currently on a flight back. His buddy gave me Lachlan's direct number. I reached out but it keeps going straight to voicemail, which makes sense if he's over the Pacific."

"Okay, thanks," Jessie said. "Can you send that number to us please?"

"Sure thing," Shaw said. "I'll do it now. Oh, and one more thing."

"Yes?"

"Camera crews from multiple sports networks have arrived out front here," Shaw said. "I just thought you'd want to know. I figured that if they see you, they'll know something is up and this will go from being a sad sports celebrity death story to something much bigger. You might want to steer clear."

"Thanks for the heads-up," Jessie said.

She hung up as she looked over at Susannah's scowl and could tell what she was going to object to.

"Come on," she said before her partner could go there, "I know you're bummed that your theory about the husband being the killer didn't pan out. And yes, Shaw should have passed along the info about him being in Indonesia to us so we could reach out to him directly. But you can't tell me that you didn't do the same sort of stuff—follow up on leads without authorization—when you were an ambitious beat cop trying to make a name for yourself. Cut the kid some slack. She's doing half the work for us. Plus, that warning about the press presence at the house was big. The longer we can avoid a media firestorm, the better chance we have of solving this thing before it gets out of control."

Susannah seemed to relent slightly.

"I will admit that Shaw's notes from her interview with Boyce's friends were damn comprehensive. She does good work."

"There you go," Jessie teased as they got close to the front of the line, "doesn't it feel good to be positive?"

"Yeah, but positivity doesn't get us any closer to catching this killer."

"I know," Jessie conceded, "and I think we both need to admit what we were hoping we could avoid if Lachlan Restrepo was a credible suspect: that we might be facing another attack tonight."

"Why the hell do you think I was hesitant to come get coffee, Jessie?" Susannah growled under her breath. "I feel like we're wasting valuable time here."

Jessie shook her head vehemently.

"No way," she insisted. "I've always found that I have my biggest breakthroughs come when I get out of the same tired headspace. This is good for us."

"If you say so," Susannah grumbled as they moved up in line.

"Besides," Jessie added, trying to channel the optimist in her, "maybe the descriptions Nicole's friends are giving the sketch artist right now will help. If there's sufficient overlap between the new ones and what Trey Killian gave us from the attack on Shasta Mallory yesterday, it might be enough to actually narrow the suspect list in the database for Jamil and Beth."

"Speaking of those two," Susannah said, "we still haven't gotten any hits on connections between our victims. At this point, I'm starting to doubt we will."

"Let's check in again," Jessie suggested as she silently noted that the guy in front of them, who had just ordered a candy bar and paid with cash, was shaking like a leaf.

She was immediately suspicious of him and not only because he looked extremely nervous for someone involved in a simple retail encounter. He also wore his baseball cap so low that it covered the entire top half of his face and he had on an olive-green army jacket when it was easily ninety-five degrees outside. As Susannah started to order, he shuffled off to the left.

"Will you order for me?" Jessie asked her partner. "Just a large iced coffee."

Susannah nodded and Jessie moved over so that she was right next to the man, whom she realized up close was actually a teenage boy, probably no more than fifteen.

"Hi," she said, making sure to keep her voice conversational so as not to scare him off, "that candy bar looks good."

"Um, yeah," he muttered, clearly attempting to adopt a deeper voice.

"I'd ask if I could try a taste of it," she whispered, borderline flirtatiously, "but I know you can't rip the wrapper open *and* hold on to the tip jar you just slipped under your jacket."

He immediately froze.

"It's okay," she said, still talking in a quietly lilting voice. "You still have time to fix this. But there's really only one way to do it. Running away right now would be a bad move, considering the lady ordering drinks right now is a police detective. But if you slide back over to the counter, casually put the jar back where it was, and walk out of here, I'll keep your momentary bad judgment between us."

The kid looked over at her and she realized that he was closer to thirteen than fifteen and had used a black pen to draw stubble on his face. His eyes were wide with terror, and he was starting to hyperventilate.

"How do I know this isn't a trick to bust me?" he squeaked.

"If I wanted to do that, it would have already happened," Jessie told him. "Now I know you don't really want to rob these hardworking people of the tips they've spent all morning earning. So go ahead and put the jar back before they notice it's gone, and we'll forget this happened. What do you say?"

He nodded anxiously and shuffled back over next to Susannah, who was now staring at him suspiciously. She glanced over at Jessie, who winked at her. The kid turned around to face her and held his jacket out to indicate that he wasn't hiding anything. Jessie nodded and then indicated that he should leave. He scurried out without another word. Susannah walked over.

"The drinks will be ready in a minute," she said. "How much do you think was in the jar?"

"Maybe seventy-five bucks?" Jessie guessed.

"You were nicer than me," Susannah said. "I'd have him in cuffs right now."

"He was so young that he had to draw hair on his face," Jessie told her. "I figured I'd try scaring him straight instead. Besides, it gave me an idea."

"What's that?"

Let's wait until we get our drinks and can talk outside," Jessie said. "I don't want anyone to accidentally hear me and choke on their lattes."

CHAPTER TWENTY ONE

Jessie waited until they were down near the pier, away from any passersby, before she let Susannah in on her theory.

"I started thinking about what this guy is doing," she said. "Not just the murders, but the lead-up. He comes to these parties and attacks the hostesses in front of large groups. He scares them, but then makes them think they're safe because others come to their rescue. Later he comes back and strikes again, using the same method. It's like he gets off on creating a false sense of security in them. He gets the initial thrill of frightening them, then another rush by terrifying them again, only the second time around both he and the victim know that there's no hope of escape. It's doubly cruel."

Susannah nodded along in agreement.

"So what's your idea?" she asked. "You still haven't told me."

Jessie pulled out her phone and called the HSS research office.

"I want to focus on the disguises," Jessie told her as the phone rang. "White tuxedos, black leather jumpsuits—this guy has a flair for the dramatic. That can't have come out of the blue."

"Hello?" Jamil said, answering.

"Hey, Jamil, how's it going?"

"Still no connections between the victims to speak of," he said, sounding mildly irritated. "I would have called if anything had come up."

Jessie was a little taken aback by his tone but understood why. He must be feeling seriously under the gun.

"That's not actually why I'm calling," she told him.

"If it's about reaching out to all the Clone Killer's potential future victims, that's a slog too," he informed her sharply. "I had to hand that over to Beth exclusively while I focus on your new request. And it's not like it was a quick job to begin with."

Jessie saw the look in Susannah's eyes and could tell she wanted to clap back at the guy for his snappishness, but she shook her head adamantly. Jamil Winslow wasn't short with people unless he'd been pushed to near the breaking point. The fact that he was speaking this way was more of a reflection of the pressure she'd put on him than how he was handling it, and having a detective call him out wouldn't help. But that didn't stop his fellow researcher from doing it in her own way.

"Jamil," they heard Beth say soothingly over the speakerphone, "maybe you could try *not* to bite Jessie's head off first thing when she calls. What do you say?"

There was a moment of silence on the line before Jamil responded.

"I'm sorry, Ms. Hunt," he said. "I'm just a little frazzled. I shouldn't have taken it out on you like that."

"Don't worry about it," she said. "I'm actually having second thoughts about how realistic it is to expect you guys to reach out to every potential victim. I'm not sure it actually helps them if they don't have the resources to protect themselves. We may need to consider how we approach their safety."

"Well, realistic or not," Beth said with clear pride in her voice, "I think it's possible that we may be able to contact everyone on the list sometime today."

"Wow, that's amazing," Jessie told her, feeling a modicum of relief at the potential good news before remembering the reason she'd reached out. "But as I said, that's not why I'm calling. I want to talk to you guys about disguises."

"I'm sorry?" Jamil said, obviously confused.

"With both of these murders," Jessie explained, "it looks like the killer attacked the women earlier in the evening while in disguise. Can you check the database for violent crimes committed while wearing disguises? I don't mean robberies, but more personal, intimate acts of violence—sexual assaults, home invasions, and murders, of course."

"I'm searching now," Jamil announced and, after a long pause said, "There's nothing that matches very closely. I do find a home invasion where clown masks were worn, but that was three suspects. And it was in Altadena, over two years ago. It doesn't seem like a match and nothing else I see feels as personal as what you're dealing with."

Jessie sighed, looking out at the waves rolling in toward shore and trying to channel their mellow unflappability.

"Well, it was worth a shot," she said, hoping she didn't sound too deflated.

"Um, I might have a suggestion that doesn't totally fit your parameters," he said hesitantly.

"Go for it," Jessie said. "We're worried that there may be another attack tonight, so we're not overly concerned with parameters."

"Okay," he said, sounding more confident. "I recall a case from back when I was researching for the MBPD. It involved a Peeping Tom who was accused of looking into multiple homes on the Strand."

"I searched through all recent convictions for the last two years," Susannah said, "even for misdemeanors. I would have noticed that. Why isn't there a record of it?"

"Because this guy was never charged," Jamil said. "He always wore disguises so the victims who saw him through their windows couldn't positively identify him. But we had a suspect in mind. Give me a minute to locate my old files and I'll pull up his name. I'll be right back."

"He's getting out his laptop," Beth said after a brief silence. "While you're waiting, do you want an update on how that press conference outside headquarters went this morning?"

"Oh yeah," Jessie said. "We've been so focused on this that I totally forgot about it. Tell us."

"It wasn't great," Beth said. "There were three high-profile singers, all clients of Shasta Mallory, on the front steps, railing against the department, saying that if she was more famous, we'd have already solved the case, but that because she worked behind the scenes, we were dragging our feet. They called it a travesty of justice."

Next to Jessie, Susannah shook her head at no one in particular. A gust of ocean breeze blew hair into her face, and she angrily brushed it aside.

"They do realize that we're only involved in the case in the first place because of celebrity hectoring," she said, frustrated. "This beach town isn't even in our jurisdiction, and until this second murder added a potential serial killer element, her death wouldn't have fallen under HSS's purview."

"Actually, they never specifically mentioned HSS *or* the second murder," Beth said. "They were so intent on attacking the police department in general that those things never came up."

"I'll take that as a win," Jessie said. "Once HSS gets mentioned, the media's ears always prick up. We lucked out on that front."

"Not only that," Beth added. "From the news reports that I've seen, the press hasn't made the connection between the two cases yet. None of them focus on where Shasta Mallory was killed. They're all about her famous clients. And the stories about Nicole Boyce spend so much time on her surfing and modeling careers that they barely reference her being killed in her South Bay home. I haven't heard a single word about Manhattan Beach, strangulation, or house parties."

"That won't last long," Jessie said. "Someone is bound to make one of those connections soon. And if there's another attack tonight, this place will be ground zero for the media. Speaking of which, do we know how many of these big house parties there are along the Strand every night?"

Susannah's eyes got wide, clearly remembering her personal experience.

"Back when I was coming here a decade ago, it seemed like there was something going on every few houses," Susannah recalled, before adding, "Then again, my faculties were a little fuzzy at the time."

"It depends on the night," said Jamil, who was apparently back. "As they get deeper into the weekend, there are more parties, and they get bigger. Tonight is Saturday, so I'd guess that there will be at least half a dozen major house parties along the Strand, maybe as many as ten. A few of them will likely be even bigger than Shasta Mallory's."

Jessie squinted in the early afternoon sun, looking down the long stretch of beach from the Manhattan Beach Pier to the Hermosa Pier and beyond. The entire stretch was littered with enormous homes as far as the eye could see. The sight was daunting.

For half a second, she considered asking Sergeant Breem if there was any way to just cancel all the house parties this weekend. But then she thought better of it. The small beachside police department didn't have the resources to enforce such a draconian measure, even if it was willing to try. And it was unlikely that the wealthy denizens of the community would stand for that kind of restriction anyway. These parties were going to happen, regardless of the threat.

"Then we really need to find this guy quick," she said. "If we've come up empty by this evening, that's multiple potential crime-scenes-in-waiting."

"Here's hoping I'm about to help with that," Jamil said. "Our prime suspect in the Peeping Tom case was a guy named Cyril Currie. He was found in the immediate area of three of the five reported incidents soon after they were called in but could never be tied to any of them so he walked every time."

"That's promising," Jessie said. "What else do you have on him?"

"He fits the basic description of your choking attacker in the two incidents," Jamil replied, "which was 'white, medium height, in decent shape, under fifty.' Obviously, because of the disguises, we can't narrow it down much beyond that. But Currie is Caucasian, thirty-three years old, five feet ten, and 180 pounds. It's not a total reach."

"It's better than what we had two minutes ago," Jessie told him. "Where can we find Cyril Currie?"

"According to the info on file, he works at a branch of First Coastal Credit Union on Sepulveda, just south of Rosecrans," Jamil said.

Jessie turned away from the ocean view to see if Susannah was ready to go meet their latest lead. She shouldn't have been surprised by what she saw. Her partner had already started sprinting back to the police station and the car.

"Thanks, guys," Jessie said.

Then she hung up and started running too.

CHAPTER TWENTY TWO

Hannah could feel the eyes on her.

She and the rest of the Wildpines crew were at an outdoor beachside café, all seated around a large circular table. The others were digging into their food, and she pretended to be just as interested in her strawberry-banana smoothie and the big basket of truffle fries they were splitting as everyone else. But her attention was elsewhere, on the man at the small table thirty feet away from her.

It was the first time today that she'd felt uncomfortable. The morning had been delightful, with a late morning wakeup, a light breakfast at the beach house, and the next several hours spent either on the sand or in the water. She'd napped in the sun, played keep-away with the waves, tried her hand at building a sand castle, boogie-boarded, and sat under a big umbrella, discussing fall college plans with everyone.

But now, getting a mid-afternoon snack in the shaded café with everyone chatting around her, she couldn't enjoy the moment. All she could think about was Jessie's warning from last night and how potential danger lurked around every corner. She wasn't mad at her sister for reminding her. That was her job. She was just pissed that she had to constantly be on alert. And in that moment she decided to do something about it.

Hannah took one last sip of her smoothie, stood up, and walked over to the guy's table. As she did, she took a moment to study him more closely than she could when she was taking furtive half-glances at him.

The guy, who was sipping a beer and nibbling at a salad, had curly brown hair, fair skin, and wire-rimmed glasses. Though he was seated, she could tell from the way he was sprawled out in the plastic chair that he was lanky in an awkward, baby giraffe kind of way. She stopped at his table and glared at him. To her surprise, he met her eyes, unembarrassed.

"Why do you keep staring at me, man?" she demanded.

"Am I?" he replied, as if he genuinely hadn't been expecting the question. "I guess it's because you look really familiar to me, and I can't quite place where from."

"That's no excuse," she said, taking a step closer into his personal space. "You need to stop. Don't you know that it's rude and creepy to stare at young women? I mean, what are you, thirty?"

"I'm twenty-seven actually," he said. "Listen, I'm sorry. I didn't mean to weird you out. I was so focused on trying to figure out why I know you that it didn't occur to me that it might come across the wrong way."

"Is everything okay here?" Melina asked, coming over. She put her hand on Hannah's wrist gently and gave a little squeeze of support. "Is this guy bothering you?"

"I don't know," Hannah said, taking Melina's hand in hers and squeezing back. "Are you?"

The guy suddenly snapped his fingers.

"I know how I recognize you now," he said, a wave of relief flooding across his face. "You're Jessie Hunt's little sister, right?"

"So what?" Hannah said, a little shiver forming at the base of her spine.

"It's just that I know her, I mean kind of," he said. "It's a little complicated to explain but your sister really helped me out of a jam once. The next time you talk to her, will you tell her that Andy Gelman says 'hi' and 'thanks again'?"

"Why didn't you just tell her yourself?" Hannah wanted to know.

"Well, at the time she helped me, I was a little out of it, and then I left the country for a while," he said. "But you're right, I should reach out to her to let her know how much I appreciate what she did for me. Maybe I'll look her up."

"Great," Hannah said, "and in the meantime, you'll quit boring a hole in the back of my head with your eyes?"

"Scout's honor," he said, holding up his fingers.

"You satisfied?" Melina asked, sounding dubious.

"We'll see," Hannah said as they turned and headed back to the table. Once they were out of earshot, she leaned over and whispered in Melina's ear, "Thanks for having my back."

"Of course. Glad I didn't have to cut him."

Hannah fought back a giggle. The truth was that she was fairly confident that Andy Gelman wasn't a serious threat to her well-being. He seemed more clueless than dangerous. But all the same, once she sat back down, she readjusted her chair so she could keep tabs on him, just in case.

CHAPTER TWENTY THREE

First Coastal Credit Union was deathly quiet.

Jessie didn't consider it a huge surprise. The branch normally closed at 3 p.m. on Saturdays and they were walking in at 2:47 on the Saturday of a holiday weekend.

She didn't see Cyril Currie when they first entered the building so Susannah went to speak to the branch manager, a fifty-something man in a sports jacket and Hawaiian shirt with patchy gray hair. While she did, Jessie looked around.

There were actually more tellers in the branch than customers. Including them, the manager that Susannah was speaking to now, and the banking associate who was clearly playing some kind of game on her desk computer, the joint was definitely *not* hopping. And yet there was no sign of Currie.

Jessie walked over to the personal banking area, wondering if he might be hiding in a cubicle behind one of the partitions. She heard the faint squeak of a distant door being opened as the bank manager replied to Susannah's whispered question with a painfully loud, "I think Cyril's in the restroom."

Jessie cringed, first at his booming voice, and then at the possibility that popped into her head: what if the squeak she'd just heard was the men's restroom door opening as Cyril Currie came out? She spun around just in time to see the back foot of someone disappear down a hall out of sight, followed by a soft beep and that same squeak a second time. Quickly, she joined Susannah and the manager.

"Is the men's room over there?" she asked, pointing to where she's seen the foot hurry off.

"Yes," he answered, startled by the unexpected question from a second interrogator.

"This is Jessie Hunt," Susannah said. "She's my partner. Jessie, this is Mr. Tranter, the branch manager."

"Nice to meet you," he said.

"You too," Jessie replied, before quickly moving on. "Do you need a key card to access the restroom?"

"Yes," he said.

"We need to borrow your key card, Mr. Tranter," she told him. "I think our guy heard his name and retreated to the little boys' room. We need to have a chat with him."

"Is that absolutely necessary?" Mr. Tranter asked. "We have customers in the building."

"It is," Susannah said. "Are there any windows or possible exits via the restroom?"

"No," he assured them. "It's completely enclosed."

"Great," Jessie said. "Key card, please. And you may want to close the branch a bit early today."

With his jaw open, Tranter handed over the card. Jessie took it without another word and immediately went down the hall where she'd seen the retreating foot. Susannah, right behind her, pulled out her weapon and positioned herself to the left of the door. Jessie stood to the right, removed her gun, and looked at her partner.

"You ready?"

"Always," Susannah said. "You unlock and open. I'll go in first. You follow behind. Sound good?"

Jessie nodded, swiped the key card, and pushed the door slightly ajar. Susannah leaned in and kicked it open with her foot, stepping inside. Jessie followed her, pressing up against the open door. No one was visible in the restroom, though two feet could be seen in one of the three stalls.

"Cyril Currie," Susannah announced, "this is the Los Angeles Police Department. We need you to open the door and come out with your hands up."

There was a brief moment of silence before a voice responded shakily.

"Um, my name's not Cyril. I don't know what this is about, but I'll do whatever you say. Can I just take a second to finish up in here and then I'll come out?"

Susannah looked over at Jessie, perplexed, then shrugged.

"You have twenty seconds," she told him.

The man did what he needed to do, then spoke again.

"Okay, I'm going to flush the toilet, then open the door, and come out. Please don't shoot me."

"Move slowly," Susannah instructed.

The man did exactly what he said. When he emerged from the stall, it was clear that he wasn't Cyril Currie. The guy in front of them was short, Latino, and in his mid-twenties.

"Who are you?" Susannah demanded.

"My name is Ronaldo Silva," he answered. "I came here to deposit some cash from some contracting work I did this morning. I just decided to use the bathroom before I left. Is that not legal? I swear, one of the employees let me in."

Jessie offered the guy a tight smile.

"No, Mr. Silva, that's not illegal," she said. "You're free to go."

"Can I wash my hands first?"

She nodded and he hurriedly cleaned up before darting out of the bathroom.

"I guess I had it wrong," she said after he left.

"Maybe he's already left for the day," Susannah suggested, heading for the door.

That didn't sit right with Jessie.

"But Tranter didn't seem to think so," she pointed out. "He thought he was in here. And this doesn't seem like the kind of place where you just bail without keeping your boss looped in, even on the Saturday of a holiday weekend."

She turned around and looked back at the stalls, then at Susannah again. Her partner got the hint.

"I guess we should go ask Mr. Tranter what's up then," the detective said.

"Agreed," Jessie added, walking deliberately toward the squeaky door, opening it, and then letting it close again. After ten seconds, two feet appeared, stepping down from the toilet seat in the last stall at the far end of the bathroom. They heard a click and the stall door opened outward.

Susannah, closer to it, barreled forward. Currie must have heard her coming because he tried to pull it shut again. As he yanked it closed, she tried to pry it open.

"Wait!" Jessie yelled, worried that her partner was opening herself up to a clear shot from Currie once the metal door was wide open. But it was too late.

Before she could move to help, Susannah ripped the door open. It hit the wall so hard that it appeared it might break off at its hinges. Her gun went flying from her hand, landing under the row of sinks. She ignored it and made a move toward the stall before stopping in her tracks.

No!" she shouted.

Jessie, her heart beating fast, hurried forward, gun raised, just in time to see the detective get splashed with water. She looked into the stall, where Cyril Currie's hands were cupped in the bowl, after having apparently tossed toilet water onto Susannah Valentine. He started to raise them a second time. Jessie pointed her gun at him.

"So help me god, if you toss that water on me, I will shoot you in the kneecap."

The man froze, his hands just shy of emerging from the bowl.

"Let it drain from your hands," she ordered.

He did as he was told. Next to her, Susannah was moaning, more in disgust than anger.

"Step out of the stall," Jessie instructed. "Keep your hands extended at your sides, *way* out at your sides. Can you search him, Detective Valentine?"

"I guess," she said, like a teenager who'd been asked to wash the dishes. When she was done, she said, "All clean—not literally, obviously."

"Wash your hands," Jessie told Currie.

As he did, she looked him over. The man was wearing a navy sweater vest over a powder blue dress shirt, along with tan slacks and black loafers. That was seriously committed bank attire for a summer afternoon. She got the sense that Cyril Currie was wound pretty tight.

"Cyril Currie," she said. "Your work day is over. My wet colleague here is going to read you your rights. Then we're going to take you back to the police station to ask you a few questions. Do you understand?"

Currie nodded silently. She wasn't entirely sure that he grasped the magnitude of the situation and decided to make it clear for him.

"If you have satisfactory answers for us, today will just prove to be embarrassing for you. If you don't, this will be the end of your life as you know it. Either way, here's some advice for you: when she's arresting you, I wouldn't do anything else to piss off Detective Valentine. Do we understand each other?"

"Yes," Currie said in a voice barely louder than a whisper.

Despite his acquiescence, Jessie stayed close by as Susannah took him into custody, just in case her partner lost her cool and tried to drown him in the toilet bowl.

CHAPTER TWENTY FOUR

"Let me go at him one more time!"

Jessie shook her head, hoping that by staying calm, she could somehow settle Susannah down too.

"There's no point," she insisted. "I get that you're upset. But going back in there again won't change the facts."

"You don't get it, Jessie," Susannah insisted. "I've been frickin' interrogating that bastard while wearing toilet water clothes. It can't have been for nothing."

Jessie knew that her partner wasn't really upset about clothes. Or at least that they weren't the main source of her frustration. She was upset that if Cyril Currie's alibi held up, as it looked like it was going to, their last good lead was about to go up in smoke when they were only hours away from more house parties getting under way.

"I *do* get it," Jessie assured her. "This guy is a total pervert. It's clear to me, just from the way that he deflected during the interview, that he was the one peering into those homes a few years back. And it's frustrating that he's walking around consequence-free. But for the time being, there's not much we can do about that. And based on the evidence that he's willingly given us from his phone, he was in San Diego for work training until yesterday evening. That eliminates him in the Shasta Mallory killing and makes him very unlikely to be responsible for the Nicole Boyce murder."

"Damn it," Susannah grumbled. "I thought we finally caught a break."

"I know," Jessie said. "Listen, Timms is still in there with him. Why don't we let him finish up with the guy. You can change out of your toilet clothes, take a shower, and we'll start fresh. In retrospect, it looks like it *was* a good idea for you to bring that change of clothes after all."

Jessie grinned broadly, hoping her partner would take the comment in the spirit it was intended.

"How long have you been waiting to bust that one out?" Susannah asked, trying not to smile.

"A while," Jessie said. "I really wanted to 'bowl' you over."

"Oh my god, stop," Susannah pleaded. "Fine, I'll go shower. Anything to get away from your awful jokes."

"Good," Jessie said as they headed toward the women's locker room. "Meanwhile, I'll check in with Jamil and Beth. You know how they love it when I ask if they've discovered anything on matters they've been looking into all day."

"Good luck with that," Susannah said, grabbing a towel and heading off.

Once she was gone, Jessie, against her better judgment, did exactly as she said she would. After pacing back and forth along the row of lockers, holding off for all of thirty seconds, she called the research office.

"Don't get mad at me," she said, still pacing when Jamil picked up, "because I am definitely *not* calling to see if you found any connections between Shasta Mallory and Nicole Boyce."

"Good," Jamil said. "Because that would be insulting, since I would have called you immediately if we had found anything."

She was about to apologize when, to her surprise, he launched into the update anyway.

"We still haven't, by the way," he said. "No mutual business connections. No intersecting social circles that we can discern, no shared, previous romantic relationships. There is of course some overlap in service providers, considering that they live in the same small community. They used the same hairdresser at one point. They frequented the same bakery. They get their internet service, water, and electricity from the same companies, but so do ninety percent of the residents on the Strand."

Jessie, who had finally stopped walking back and forth between the lockers, was about to raise an issue on that last point, but Jamil beat her to it.

"And before you ask, we checked every time they had a service call from a provider in the last year. None of the workers who serviced Mallory's home went to Boyce's or vice versa and none of the workers who went to either place have a criminal record for anything violent. We'll continue to look, but as of now, we've got nothing."

"Well," Jessie replied, slumping down on a locker room bench but otherwise keeping her deflated spirits out of her voice as best she could, "it's a good thing I didn't call about that then."

"Oh," he said guiltily. "Why then?"

Amused and a little amazed that she'd managed to snow him, she moved on quickly.

"I wanted to let you know that Cyril Currie didn't pan out," she said. "He had an alibi for the first murder, and we think he's going to end up having one for the second as well. But don't get down about it. It was still a good lead. Way to think outside the box."

Jamil's silence told her he was indeed getting down about it.

"Hey," she said forcefully, "this is the kind of thing we talked about in group. If you carry *all* the burdens of the world on your shoulders, it's not reasonable to fall apart when something eventually drops. You have to expect it to happen from time to time and then cut yourself some slack when it does. Either that or hand off some of your burdens."

She was referring to the survivors' group meeting that she and Jamil attended every Saturday, along with Hannah, a meeting they were all missing today.

"I remember," he said. "I was just hoping I might have had the key to cracking the case this time."

"So did I," Jessie said. "By the way, are you going to try to make tomorrow's meeting, since you're missing today's?"

"Are you?" he challenged.

"I'll go if you do," she told him, "assuming we get a one-hour lull in this case."

"Deal," Jamil said, though he still sounded a little bummed.

Beth cleared her voice softly to remind Jessie that she was still on the line too.

"What have you got, Ms. Ryerson?" she asked.

"I didn't expect it to turn out this way, but it's looking like I'm the one with good news to share," she said in her best "cheer everyone up" voice.

"What's that?" Jessie asked, happy to help change the subject and keep Jamil from going back to a negative personal place.

"Will you allow me a moment to explain?" she asked cautiously.

"By all means, take your time," Jessie said.

"Okay, we here in the research department determined that since you joined Homicide Special Section as a criminal profiler almost two years ago, you've helped stop eighty-two killers. Thirty-four of them verifiably intended to kill another potential victim if they hadn't been caught or killed. Some were serial killers who had multiple additional victims in mind. Those eleven intended victims are under police protection."

"Jessie knows all this, Beth," Jamil muttered impatiently.

"She said I could take my time," Beth objected. "Don't ruin this for me just because you're in a sour mood, Jay."

Jessie bit her tongue. She had never heard Beth refer to Jamil, who was technically her supervisor, as "Jay" before, nor talk to him so sharply. She wondered what was up with that.

"Sorry," he said quietly.

"You're forgiven," Beth whispered back, before returning to her normal voice. "Anyway, these other killers weren't intentionally pursuing multiple victims. In some instances the next target was just inconveniently in their way or was someone they feared might rat them out in the future. Regardless, we calculated who each of those potential victims was and came up with a total of one hundred fourteen people who were at risk of being killed if you hadn't caught the murderer in time."

"I didn't realize it was that many," Jessie said in quiet amazement.

"Yeah, that's a lot of people you saved, Jessie," Beth replied, "and that's not even counting all the people in that movie theater last April who weren't killed because you uncovered Zoe Bradway's plan to poison their popcorn. We don't know their names because they all ran out of the theater complex in a panic. That was hundreds of people. But we do know the names of *these* hundred fourteen people. And that's what I'm getting at. I just got off the phone with the last of them. Between Jamil and I, we have contacted and warned every single one of them, as you requested."

For a moment, Jessie couldn't find the words to respond. After swallowing the lump in her throat, she did her best.

"That's incredible," she said, standing up again. Suddenly she was very glad that she was all alone in the small MBPD women's locker room. "You should be so proud of yourselves. That's an amazing accomplishment, one I wasn't sure was even capable of being achieved. Thank you guys so much. It lifts a huge weight off my mind."

"I'm only sorry we couldn't do more," Beth said. "Obviously all we could do was tell folks to be on guard, not take unnecessary risks, try to stay in group settings, that kind of thing, until we get this resolved."

Jamil spoke up at that point.

"We did also tell them that if they felt unsafe, they should reach out to the department or go to a police station. Some of them asked for officer check-ins, but we told them that resources were just too limited right now. Beth was great about reminding them that they still need to live their lives, just with a little more awareness. She's much better at public-facing interactions than I am."

"You don't say," Jessie teased before adding, "It sounds like you both did great work. You should give each other a pat on the back, or a neck massage, or something."

The lack of a response from either of them told her she'd hit a nerve. Just then, Officer Carrie Shaw walked into the dressing room, giving her the perfect excuse to extricate herself from the uncomfortable situation she'd created.

"Hey, guys, I've got to deal with something here, but you let me know if anything else pops, okay? Great. Bye!"

"That sounded awkward," Shaw said as she came over, opened a locker, and began to undress. "It reminded me of one of those painful high school phone calls I had with the guy I accidentally revealed I had a crush on."

"Yeah," Jessie said, "I think I may have stirred up a situation like that and left other people to deal with the emotional fallout. It's quite possible that I'm Cupid, if Cupid was terrible at his job."

"Good thing you're pretty decent at your day job then," Shaw said, looking completely exhausted as she peeled off her uniform, baring the small, lean figure that Jessie knew was capable of unexpected physical strength under duress.

"Not so great at it today, actually," she conceded. "None of our leads have panned out. I was thinking of just going back to Nicole Boyce's house in the hope that it might trigger something useful for me, but I'm worried that I might get spotted by the press after what you said earlier."

Shaw grabbed a sundress off a hanger in her locker and ran her hand along it to smooth out a wrinkle.

"It would be a risk," she warned.

"What would be a risk?" Susannah asked, as she emerged from the showers, drying herself off with a towel flung over her shoulder, but otherwise completely nude.

"Going to the Boyce house," Shaw said, quickly looking away as her cheeks turned bright red. "There are at least three camera crews posted out there with reporters doing standups every hour or so. It'd be hard for you to get back inside without being seen."

"Is that even the best use of our time?" Susannah asked, oblivious to the rookie cop's discomfort as she turned around and reached into her backpack for the clothes she'd brought with her. "Shouldn't we be focusing on where he'll hit next rather than where he's already been?"

Jessie couldn't help but ache slightly as she watched Carrie Shaw do her best not to stare, open-mouthed, at Susannah. The young officer tore her eyes away, and instead looked down at her own far less curvaceous form, before hurriedly throwing on her sundress.

"What do you think, Carrie?" Jessie asked with a supportive smile, using the officer's first name to try to redirect her attention away from whatever insecurity she was feeling. "Should we be concentrating our attention on the house parties tonight?"

"Um, that's going to be hard," Shaw said, trying to focus on the question. "There are going to be a lot of them."

Susannah, now in a bra and underwear, turned back around.

"You're younger than either of us," she said to Shaw, "in addition to being local, so tell me if I'm way off base here, but when I used to crash parties here a decade ago, we would always look for the big ones, sure. But we'd also try to scope out the ones with the least security and the easiest access. You know, the ones that were the friendliest to party crashers. I'm wondering if maybe our suspect is looking for the same thing—a party he can slip into unnoticed, and where, if he attacks someone, he's not going to get taken out by hired pros. What do you think, Shaw?"

The young officer seemed to have found her bearings again. Her cheeks had returned to their normal color, and she had regained most of her confidence.

"I could throw out some options for parties," she said, "but the truth is, my intel would have been better about four years ago when I was just a civilian with a red Solo cup looking for a good time. Now that I'm a cop, people don't share as much as they used to. I wouldn't trust that anything I give you is the latest, greatest information."

"Well, we're running out of options here," Jessie said. "We don't have a suspect and afternoon's about to turn into evening. We need to know where this guy might go. If you don't have a solid guess as to where he might be headed, do you at least have a suggestion for who might?"

At that question, Shaw's face lit up.

"I might actually," she said. "There's a guy who's always in the know. The problem is getting him to open up."

"Why?" Jessie asked.

"Well, he's kind of a local legend—" Shaw started to say.

"It seems like everyone around here is a local legend," Susannah interrupted, still mostly undressed.

"She was about to give us a lead," Jessie chided. "Are you going to let the woman talk or not?"

"Go ahead," Susannah muttered apologetically.

"Anyway," Shaw said, pleased to have the upper hand for once, "his name is Curly Duff. These days he likes to give the impression of being this burnout beachcomber. He spends half his days wandering the sand looking for trinkets that might be treasures. The other half of the day he hangs out in local bars, talking about nothing to all the other layabouts and slackers."

"So why exactly is he a local legend?" Jessie asked.

"Because he's not as chill as he seems. He used to rob houses back in the day, right here in Manhattan Beach," Shaw explained. "He even stole some expensive art, which was never recovered. He had a whole crew and everything. But some of the robberies got violent. Eventually he got busted. On one job, the homeowner tried to fight back and a guy in his crew started beating the poor man in the head with a fireplace poker. Curly told him to stop but the guy wouldn't so Curly shot him dead. The rest of the crew scattered but Curly stayed behind to help the homeowner. The cops arrived. Curly was left holding the bag for the robbery, the homeowner's assault, and the death of his crew member. He ended up serving nine years of a twenty-year sentence. When he got out, he went into the home security business. The homeowner he saved was his first client. He ended up making millions. Then he retired and just started bumming around."

"That is a fascinating story," Susannah said, "but how does it help us?"

"Because," Shaw said, with a gleam in her eye, "he knows everybody. He still keeps his ear to the ground on both sides of the law. He's always on top of what's happening. He can't help himself. It's in his blood. And he likes to party. He may wander the beach or sit in bars during the day, but he loves these house parties as much as everyone else, and if anyone knows which ones are the easiest to access, it'll be him."

"Sounds great," Susannah said. "Where is he now?"

"It's not as simple as that," Shaw reminded her. "Remember how I said the problem is getting him to open up? He hates cops. We tried to turn him into an asset multiple times without success. He won't even talk to Sergeant Breem and you've met him. There's not a more chill law enforcement officer out there. If Drake Breem can't win the guy over, no one can."

"I don't know," Susannah said with a grin, "Jessie here can be a real charmer when she tries."

"Plus, he's volatile," Shaw added, undeterred. "His history of robbing homes, plus his time in prison, did something to him. He seems all mellow on the surface, but I've seen him turn dark real quick when he's set off. I know of at least two people who ended up battered and bloody in alleys after disagreements with him. Neither would press charges but there was no doubt who was responsible. He's a scary guy."

"We'll take the cautions under advisement," Jessie said, "but considering our ticking clock and limited options, he sounds like just the guy we need to talk to. Why don't you show us where we can find him at this time of day?"

"Okay," Shaw said with a shrug as she slid into her sandals and threw her backpack over her shoulder.

Jessie turned to Susannah, who was still dressed in just her bra and underwear.

"And unless you've decided that's the outfit you're wearing for the interview, maybe you could put some clothes on, Detective Valentine?"

"Hey, you never know," Susannah replied with a smirk. "Based on what Shaw said about the guy's bad attitude, this might be our most effective interrogation technique."

Jessie shook her head in amazement.

"How about we start with 'good cop, bad cop,'" she suggested, "before we move on to 'good cop, naughty cop?'"

Jessie had to admire her partner's bravado, even if deep down, she was starting to worry that no amount of confidence would help them get to the bottom of this case.

CHAPTER TWENTY FIVE

Curly Duff's place was a shack.

At first, Jessie wasn't even sure they had the right address. She had to check the map on her phone twice and text Shaw again just to make sure it wasn't a mistake. It was hard to believe that a retired millionaire who made his money in home security lived in a broken-down cottage the size of a two-car garage.

"This is definitely it," she said as they stepped off the Strand and dodged the dilapidated patio furniture on the tiny patio in front of his door. The glorified shed was bordered on either side by three-story houses that not only dwarfed their neighbor in the middle but seemed to actually look down on him with contempt.

The front door was pulled nearly but not completely closed and they could hear a television in the background. Jessie looked over at her partner and spread out her palms, extending the invitation for the detective to knock. Susannah grimaced but did the honors. When her knuckles rapped on the wood, bits of sand and debris crumbled off and fell to the ground.

"Who is it?" called out a raspy-voiced male.

"LAPD," she announced, "we'd like a word, Mr. Duff."

"Here are two for you," he shouted back. "Screw off!"

Susannah's face immediately twisted up into a grimace, but Jessie winked at her.

"We knew he was going to be a tough nut to crack," she whispered before barking, "Just kidding about that. We're with Publishers Clearing House. You may already be a winner, sir! Don't you want to claim your prize?"

There was a moment of silence, followed by what was clearly someone getting out of a creaky chair. Seconds later, she heard a sliding sound and a rattle. Then the door opened to reveal a fifty-something-year-old guy in pink board shorts and an unbuttoned, short-sleeved yellow polo shirt.

Everything about him was gray, from the mop of frizzy (some might even say curly) hair on his head to the copious hair on his chest to the stubble on his face, which had several scars. Even his eyes were gray. He wasn't good-looking exactly, but he had a rough, battle-tested hardness that Jessie could imagine being attractive when it wasn't terrifying.

He was holding a beer in one hand and a cigarette in the other. He eyed them both as he took a long drag, wiped the sweat off his brow, and offered a grim smile.

"I gave up on ever getting what was mine when Ed McMahon died," he said solemnly. "Nice to know your organization meets its obligations."

"We pride ourselves on our credibility," Jessie said, willing to play along as long as he was. "There are just a few perfunctory questions we're required to ask before we can determine definitively if you are in fact, already a winner."

"How did you find me?" he demanded.

"How did the Clearing House find you?" she asked, unsure if he was still participating in their little charade or not.

"No, how did *you*—Jessie Hunt, criminal profiler for Homicide Special Section, and your stern-looking partner—find me?" he wanted to know. "How did you know I wouldn't be at the beach or at one of a dozen bars? How did you know to look me up here instead of at the fancy mansion where my mail gets sent? How did you find me?"

As he spoke, Jessie couldn't help but notice that despite his shack's humble appearances, it wasn't as ramshackle as it first seemed. The interior doors were much more secure than the one they stood at now. And while there were no exterior cameras, she counted at least three mounted in the visible areas of the living room and kitchen. She also saw a high-tech security keypad just inside the entrance.

Suddenly, it occurred to her that the sliding and rattling sounds she'd heard when he'd "opened" the already slightly ajar door were a chain lock and a swing bar door guard. Both were designed to allow the door to be opened just a bit to see who was there. But they provided an additional feature for someone who cared: they gave the illusion that the resident was a casual, devil-may-care type who didn't bother to close his door when in fact, getting inside was no easy feat.

"Officer Carrie Shaw told us where you'd be," she answered, deciding it was time to be direct. "She thought you might be able to help us out and we're in a bit of a time crunch, so we figured we'd dispense with standard procedure and just stop by."

"I'm surprised Shaw knew my schedule," Duff said, sounding impressed. "I thought I was a little harder to peg than that."

"She called it your 'regrouping' time," Susannah said. "You've finished the important work of wandering the beach and completed the business of afternoon barhopping but you're not quite ready to begin the task of the early evening pub crawl. Personally, what she called 'regrouping' sounded like 'nap time' to me."

Duff stared at her for a moment before returning his attention to Jessie.

"Your partner's not great with people, is she?" he noted dryly. "All your carefully cultivated Publishers whatever humor flushed down the drain with one nasty old-guy dig. We're done here."

He started to close the door.

"We need your help, Mr. Duff," Jessie said, more plaintively than she'd intended.

He held the door open just enough for her to see his face.

"Why the hell should I care about what kind of help the cops need from me?" he pressed bitterly. "They didn't cut me any slack when I needed it."

"I heard about that," Jessie said, "and it sounds like you got a raw deal for doing the right thing. But don't let that stop you from being decent now. You can make a difference. You can save a life."

"You think I care about that?" he demanded, with a caustic laugh.

"Sure I do," Jessie shot back. "I think you care about saving your own life, for one. And I think you're scared, way more scared than you're letting on."

"What the hell are you talking about?" he asked, pulling the door open again, his nostrils flaring angrily. Next to Jessie, Susannah stiffened noticeably.

"I think you try to project this image of cool," Jessie said, "living in this hovel, leaving the door slightly open. But we both know you've got locks on the inside in case anyone tries to smash through. I see cameras everywhere in there. Your bedroom door is heavily reinforced. I recognize the brand. It probably cost over five grand. And based on the alarm panel next to the door, I'd say your security system is more advanced than most of the mansions along the Strand. You act casual but you live paranoid, Mr. Duff."

He looked like he wanted to argue but after a moment the nostrils stopped flaring and he seemed to calm down.

"What's your point?" he asked.

"You lost nine years of your life to save a guy you didn't know but you've been running away from that ever since," she told him. "You made millions. You act the tough guy. You don't let anyone get close. You lived behind bars for nearly a decade but even now, when you're supposed to be free, you still have bars on your home and your life. I'm giving you a chance to change that. You know who I am. You know why we're down here."

"The choking murders?"

"That's right," Jessie said. "We're asking for your help with them. You know they're connected, don't you?"

He paused, sensing that if he answered this question, he was opening the door to all the others that would follow. Then he sighed and quite literally opened the door, motioning for them to come inside.

"I'm surprised everyone doesn't get that they're connected," he said.

"They will soon," Jessie said. "We think there's going to be another attack tonight."

"Jeez," Duff muttered under his breath, closing the door behind them.

"That's why we're here," Susannah said. "We don't have any suspects and there are so many parties on the Strand that the killer might show up at. We need to find the right one—a huge one with the easiest access and the least security where he'll feel confident that he can get in and out safely."

Duff shook his head forcefully and his mess of gray hair flopped violently atop his head.

"That's the wrong criteria," he said.

"What?" Susannah retorted, clearly trying not to sound put off and failing miserably.

"No offense," he said, holding up his hands in a show of peace, "but that's not how it works around here. Look, there are a bunch of parties each night, increasing in number as we get closer to the holiday. There may be as many as two dozen of decent size along the two-mile stretch of the Strand from El Porto Beach south to the Gateway Parkette tonight. But less than a third of those will really be jumping."

"That fits with what Jamil told us earlier," Jessie said.

"Sure," Duff said, "Winslow, right? The research guy who left MBPD for HSS. Smart kid. Knows his stuff. You're lucky to have him. He's consulted for me on several occasions."

"Wait. What?" Jessie said, stunned.

"Who can get by on a city salary these days?" Duff said. "I hired him to provide detailed neighborhood crime stats for some client work I did. Don't worry. It was totally aboveboard. Let's stick to the point here, which is that, of those few parties that are really rocking, only a few *matter*."

"What does that mean?" Susannah asked.

"Ah, that's the important question," he said, showing real enthusiasm for the first time since their arrival, "and that's what really jumped out at me about these murders. They were both at the 'It' party."

"The 'It' party?" Jessie repeated.

"Yeah," he said, "you know—the one people are talking about, at least the locals. It's like the cool kids' table in the cafeteria at school. There's usually only one of those parties a night, maybe two at most. Thursday night, Shasta Mallory had the 'It' party because people were hoping for a star sighting. It also happened to be the biggest of the night, but that was just a coincidence. It doesn't always work out that way."

"And Nicole Boyce was last night's 'It' party?" Susannah asked.

"Right," Duff confirmed. "It wasn't the biggest one by a long way, but it was the place to be because everyone wanted to be around Nicole."

"This changes things," Jessie said. "We knew these women were hosting parties, which made their homes more easily accessible and themselves vulnerable. But I don't think that we understood that they were 'hostesses' of the parties in such a formal sense. That makes me wonder if the hostess element isn't just a convenient way for the killer to access potential victims—but the reason they're being targeted in the first place."

"You think he's specifically going after the hostesses of these 'It' parties?" Susannah pressed.

"I don't know," Jessie said, "but it's worth considering. We've been asking Jamil and Beth to find connections between these two women. Until now, I didn't even realize this was a thing that constituted a legitimate connection."

"I'd say it is," Curly told them. "Hosting a major summer holiday Strand 'It' party is a big deal. The list of folks who do it is pretty exclusive."

"So you're saying we need to be at tonight's 'It' party?" Jessie asked. "I assume you know what it is and who's hosting?"

Curly Duff looked first at Jessie, then over at Susannah.

"I do," he said, "and I have to tell you something—ladies, you're not dressed for it."

CHAPTER TWENTY SIX

"You've got to be loving this," Jessie muttered under her breath.

She didn't even need to wait for Susannah to reply to know the answer, but she got one anyway.

"I'm not *hating* it," her partner said, flashing a mega-watt smile as they passed the horde of people milling outside Daphne Klein's house and entered her expansive front yard. Mixed in among the crowd they left behind were two news crews, one from a local station and another from a national sports network. While reporters and producers from both outlets eyed Jessie and Susannah closely as they went by, no one said anything to them.

That might have been because of how they were dressed. Like everyone else at the party, they were in costumes, as if they were attending a Halloween party in early September. According to Curly Duff, that was Daphne Klein's thing, which was part of what made her bash an "It" party. But these weren't standard costumes. Because of the stifling heat and the beach locale, guests were expected to wear more revealing outfits.

That's why Jessie—in defiance of every fiber of her being—had made a last-second stop at a sportswear shop and picked out a halter tennis dress with an apricot-colored bodice. The outfit wasn't really a costume, but with the way it hugged her so tightly from the waist up and cut off near the top of her thighs, it sure felt like one.

Then again, that was the point—to look completely different than she normally would, partly to fit in at the party, but also to avoid detection by the media. To further that latter goal, after getting her outfit, she'd joined Susannah at a costume shop, where she'd bought a blonde wig, which was currently resting on her head, tied in a ponytail, so the long hair wouldn't get in her way if she got in either a long rally at the net or a knock-down, drag-out fight with a murderer.

Susannah, as Jessie had predicted, had embraced the assignment. At the costume shop, she found an outfit that seemed tailor-made for her. It was a naughty cop costume, complete with a police cap, a navy, buttoned cropped top, and a miniskirt, which likely made her one of the few law enforcement officers currently operating with a bare midriff.

Cleverly, the outfit also allowed her to wear her holster and real gun without it seeming strange, although she did remove the clip, just in case some drunk idiot tried to grab for it.

"I feel ridiculous," Jessie whispered just after nine, as they walked through the main doors of the enormous beachfront home and into the cavernous front room, which was filled with dozens of people.

"Well, you look fabulous," Susannah assured her while they slithered through the dancing throngs, until they finally found an open space near the fireplace. "The key is to believe you are and everyone else will too. Besides, look around. You can't tell me you feel *that* ridiculous."

Jessie had to admit that she had a point. Just like the two of them, most people here had committed to the bit. Some were simply wearing conventional swimwear, but others had gone all out. Two young ladies nearby had created handmade, barely-there bikinis out of seashells. Another woman had wrapped herself in rainbow streamers that were covering a solid five percent of her body. An attractive couple walked by, wearing only diapers and matching sashes that read respectively "Mr. South Bay" and "Miss South Bay." A man dancing on the second-floor balcony appeared to be covered in gold paint, a well-placed sock, and nothing else.

"I'm just going to look at it as an undercover assignment," Jessie said. "Incredibly, in this environment, wearing this outfit will draw less attention than my normal clothes would, so I can watch everyone without seeming suspicious."

"I know you've secretly been dying to pour yourself into a getup like that, Hunt," Susannah teased. "But whatever justification gets you through the night."

Just then, two guys in their early twenties adorned uncreatively in swim trunks and neckties came over.

"Can I get you ladies a drink?" the taller of the two asked them.

"Thanks, but we're good for now," Jessie told him.

"Hey, has anyone ever told you that you look like that tennis player, Maria Sharapova?" the shorter guy asked. "You're not really her, are you?"

Jessie looked over at Susannah, who was smirking because on the way over, she'd predicted that someone would make that exact comparison. The urge to offer a snarky comeback was huge but she fought it off. Creating even a small scene was the last thing she wanted right now.

"No, but thank you," she said with a sweet smile.

"Actually," Susannah said, "now that you mention it, some drinks sound great. It's getting pretty hot in here. I saw that there's a bar toward the back. Could you guys get us some mojitos?"

"Yes ma'am, officer!" the taller guy said, saluting. "Whatever you say. I don't want to disappoint you and make you take me in. Or maybe I do."

Susannah giggled as she tossed her hair back, then gave him a coy smile.

"I guess it all depends on the quality of those drinks, young man," she said. "Better get to it."

The guys scurried off enthusiastically.

"That ought to keep them busy for a while," Susannah said, shifting back to her normal voice. "The line at the bar is excruciatingly long."

"You're scarily good at turning that flirty girl thing on and off," Jessie said.

"Survival technique," the detective said wearily. "Do we want to do a lap around the house to see if anyone leaps out at us before we call Daphne down here?"

"Good idea," Jessie agreed.

Because Curly Duff knew everyone in town, he'd called Daphne Klein earlier that evening and put her on the phone with Jessie and Susannah. Klein was the socialite wife of a big-time Hollywood studio executive. They explained their concerns and suggested she cancel the party. After she finished laughing at them, they all came to a compromise: Daphne would remain upstairs with friends until the two of them arrived around nine. Based on the prior attacks, it seemed unlikely that the killer would show up that early. After they got to the house and gave her the go-ahead to come downstairs, they'd stay discreetly close to her for the rest of the night.

But independently, Jessie and Susannah had agreed that before they risked calling the hostess downstairs, they wanted to at least try to get the lay of the land, and maybe, if they got lucky, unmask the killer before he could act. Thus the lap around the house.

They started moving but it was slow going. The whole place was essentially one huge dance floor and even in the short time since they'd arrived it had gotten more crowded. It was hard to see what was going on amid the writhing mass of bodies. And with the relentlessly thumping music, it was difficult to hear much of anything either. Jessie leaned over and shouted into Susannah's ear.

"With everyone wearing costumes, they *all* look ridiculous and suspicious," she said. "Until someone does something overtly violent, we're going to be hard-pressed to discern between wild party behavior and something more disturbing."

Susannah nodded but didn't respond. Her eyes were darting everywhere as the two of them skirted around the edge of the living room and pushed through a hallway into another, smaller room that was equally packed. Jessie knew what her partner was thinking because she had the same thoughts.

The charm of the silly outfits was fading. The reality of staking out an enormous home filled with hundreds of people was settling in. The killer might be here among them right now and they would never know it.

He could be standing right next to her, and she'd have no clue.

CHAPTER TWENTY SEVEN

He stood amid the crowd, with a friendly smile plastered across his face, hoping that no one could hear his heart beating through his chest.

As far as he could tell, everyone was oblivious to the giddy anticipation he was feeling, as they danced to the boisterous music, shouting to be heard over it. He put the martini he'd been handed on a table and politely squeezed through a group of people blocking the doorway he needed to navigate.

"Cool outfit," one of the women said.

"Thanks," he replied, before moving on quickly.

It was reassuring to get the compliment because it meant he wouldn't seem like the odd man out. He was wearing an old-timey 1920s-style men's bathing suit, comprised of a ribbed wool onesie that buttoned at the crotch and had a scoop neck. In addition, he wore a pair of mid-thigh swimming shorts fastened with a white, webbed belt and a metal buckle. He was also wearing a wig that gave him tightly cut black hair that looked like it had been doused in pomade.

He stepped into the larger room and scanned the area again. He'd already been here for twenty minutes, looped through the giant house twice, and yet he still hadn't seen the hostess. He was starting to get antsy. How was it possible that she wasn't at her own party?

And then he saw her. She was in front of him, walking down the stairs, wearing a silver, fringed flapper skirt with her hair tied back. He tried to catch up to her so that he could meet her just as she reached the main level, but it was difficult with so many people in between them.

He almost lost sight of her completely as she darted into the cluster of people at the base of the stairs, who greeted her warmly and guided her to an area near the massive French doors leading to the front yard. He was all for that, as it made for an easier exit once he was pried off her. He saw her again and methodically resumed his march toward her, sliding on his latex gloves as he moved.

She began dancing with her back to him, and the sparkles on the fringe of her dress drew him in like a homing beacon. He saw a small opening amid the churn of bodies and headed directly for her, extending his hands, reaching out for her neck, which seemed so slender and fragile.

Then he was there, squeezing tight, but not too tight. It was a challenge to maintain even pressure with his blood pumping so hard. She tried to wriggle free, but she was no match for him. He wanted to turn her around to let her see his eyes, so that later tonight, she would make the connection between the two attackers in the moment before she died. But that would require twisting her and he feared he might break her neck in the process.

Suddenly, they were on him. Two people tearing at his hands as several others went for his body. He felt himself falling to the floor along with her. She was being yanked away from him as multiple bodies tried to pile on top of him.

And then, as he felt the weight of them about to collapse down upon him, he made eye contact with her. But instead of giving him satisfaction, the sight caused a completely unexpected reaction: shock. His mind suddenly a sea of confusion, he fixed on the one clear thought that emerged from the muck: he had to get out of there.

He stopped fighting gravity and allowed the swell of people above him to fall down into a pile. In the ensuing chaos, he shot up, tore free from their grasp, and hurtled out of the house, through the French doors, and off into the night.

He could hear the angry shouts behind him for about a block before they faded away. Still, he kept running for several more blocks before he slowed to a walk. Five minutes later he was in his car, heading home to clear his head, take a shower, and change.

But he'd be back in a few hours. There were errors to correct and wrongs to right. The real work was still to come.

***

Jessie pushed her way through the morass of humanity, trying to get back to the front room, where the chaos they could hear but only barely see was coming from. Beside her, Susannah had taken to stomping on people's feet to make them move.

"I don't want to ruin our cover, but we have to get over there," the detective said desperately. "Should I just pull out my gun?"

Jessie shook her head.

"I've got a better idea," she said. "Follow my lead."

She put her head down, started groaning, and began barreling forward into people.

"Hey, watch it!" some guy yelled.

"I think I'm gonna throw up," she moaned loudly, "let me through!"

The guy immediately hopped out of the way, as did the other people nearby.

"Look out—she's gonna puke!" the guy bellowed.

The crowd parted like the Red Sea.

"Clear a path," Susannah ordered, grabbing Jessie's shoulder and guiding her in the direction of the commotion they'd heard. "She's feeling sick. You've got to let her get outside now."

Jessie kept her head down, letting her partner direct her through human traffic as she focused on making noisy retching sounds. After ten seconds of that, Susannah tapped her on the back.

"You can stop now."

Jessie looked up to see that they were near the front of the house, where it opened out onto the yard. It looked like a fight of some kind had just been broken up. Several people were holding one guy with long blond hair back from another dude with a crewcut, who was sitting on a couch, holding a bloody napkin to his nose. Susannah didn't waste any time trying to get answers and walked up to the blond guy being held back.

"Why did you punch him?" Susannah demanded. "Was he trying to choke someone?"

"What?" he said, stopping his struggle to get free long enough to look simultaneously confused and annoyed by her question. "Are you here to arrest me, Officer Chesty?"

Jessie, no longer faking nausea, slipped past the collection of guys assembled nearby who all said "Ooh!" in unison, and grabbed the forearm of the blond guy, twisting it behind his back as she kneed him in the back of his leg. He dropped to his knees, wincing in pain.

"That was a very rude way to talk to my friend," she said, tugging his forearm upward slightly. "She asked you a simple question and you responded in an offensive manner. Apologize!"

"Sorry!" he grunted.

"Now answer her question—did that guy over there try to choke someone out?"

"No," the blond guy muttered. "He knocked over my beer."

"It was an accident, man!" the bloody-nosed dude objected.

Jessie leaned over and whispered in the blond guy's ear.

"So this altercation involved no choking of any kind?"

"Uh-uh," he gasped.

"Okay," she said so only he could hear as she gave an extra little tug. "I'm going to let you up. I suggest you go outside and take a breather. If you bother me or my friend or anyone who inadvertently bumps your beer, I'm going to reach out to my good friends in the Manhattan Beach Police Department and get you tossed in a cell for the night. Got it?"

He nodded. She let go and stepped back. As he stood up and scurried outside, desperately avoiding eye contact with her, she heard a loud voice behind her.

"What the hell is all this?"

She turned around to find a voluptuous, dark-haired woman in her mid-forties wearing what was essentially a black negligee stomping toward them. She recognized her immediately and walked over, as did Susannah.

"Hi, Daphne," she said quietly. "I'm Jessie Hunt. This is Detective Susannah Valentine. We spoke earlier. I thought you were going to stay upstairs until we gave you the all clear to come down."

"I couldn't wait any longer," Daphne said. "The music and the happy voices were just too much. And then I heard about this ruckus. I had to check on it. So now I'm here and you can keep me safe. If this person you mentioned tries anything, you'll stop him, right?"

"Yes ma'am," Susannah said.

"Frankly," Daphne said, "I'm flattered that Curly thinks my party is choke-worthy. But all things being equal, I'd rather everyone just run around half-naked and have the evening end without incident."

"So would we, Daphne," Jessie said.

Unfortunately, all her experience told her that the chances of that kind of happy ending were remote. Whoever killed Shasta Mallory on Thursday night and Nicole Boyce on Friday night was unlikely to take Saturday night off.

Whether he was already inside the house or still out there somewhere, waiting to get in, he wasn't done. He would strike before the night was out. But at least when he did, they'd be here, waiting for him.

CHAPTER TWENTY EIGHT

Hannah could feel it coming.

This was the night. Something was going to happen. She was almost sure that Chris would try to kiss her tonight.

There wouldn't be a better time. They were ambling along the beach after a big group dinner. Once the meal was done, everyone else had headed to an outdoor market to do some window shopping. The two of them had said they'd catch up later and decided to take a leisurely stroll where the wet and dry sand merged together.

It was dark out now, with only the moon to guide their path. The crowds had long since abandoned the beach, leaving only a few late-evening wanderers like themselves and a few surfers catching some late-night waves. At some point, Hannah felt her fingers brush Chris's and then they were holding hands.

The fluttering butterflies in her belly reappeared suddenly and she swallowed hard, hoping to contain them. She'd done more than hold hands with other boys in the past, but not since her life was ripped apart by the slaughter of her adoptive parents two years ago. For a long time, she hadn't even entertained the possibility that she could feel this way again. But the last few days with Chris had changed that.

"What's going to happen in the fall?" he asked, raising the unspoken subject that had hovered over the otherwise magical weekend.

As they'd teeter-tottered on the edge of romantic moments, in the back of Hannah's head, and apparently Chris's too, had been curiosity about what it might lead to, if anything at all. Oddly, it was hearing him pose the question aloud that clarified the answer, in that moment, for her.

"In the fall, which basically means in a few days," she said, "you'll go off to RISD to wow them with your incredible talent with a paintbrush. I start at UC-Irvine in two weeks, and I'll see how that goes. Beyond that, who knows? I say we play things by ear and not get too stressed. But don't you think we ought to have something tangible to *not* get stressed about?"

"What do you mean?" he asked.

She turned to face him. Because they were the same height, five foot nine, she could look directly into his sky-blue eyes. The butterflies were everywhere now, careening off each other as they flapped their tiny wings, threatening to burst out of her. She decided to let them.

"I mean this," she said, leaning in and brushing her lips gently against his.

His eyes grew wide in startled delight.

"What's the point of worrying about what happens next if we don't do anything now, Chris?" she asked, before moving in again, now with more confidence.

This time, when her lips met his, he reciprocated enthusiastically. He cupped her cheeks in his hands, and she ran her fingers through his hair as they lowered the protective barriers that had been holding them back until now.

They lingered like that, silhouetted in the moonlight, lips locked, torsos clutched tight together, bare feet cold in the frothy surf that bubbled up to cover their toes, for what felt like forever. At least, that is, until the gang of surfers waiting to catch a wave just down the beach caught sight of them and began to engage in some extremely suggestive heckling.

"Maybe we should get out of here," Chris suggested with a goofy smile.

"I think that's a good idea," Hannah agreed. "Those guys sound a little rowdy."

They turned and headed back up toward the drier sand, away from the water and toward the shortcut path that led back to the market and their beach house. In the distance, Hannah caught a glimpse of a far-off figure next to a dune near the path.

In the dim light it was hard to be sure, but she thought it looked a lot like the gangly guy she'd noticed staring at her earlier. A cloud passed over the moon and she squinted to get a better look. But by the time the cloud had moved on and she had a clear view again, the figure was gone.

"Let's take the long way," she said suddenly.

"Why?" he asked, perplexed as they put on their shoes. "If we take the path, we can avoid the catcalls and save five minutes getting back."

Hannah didn't want to sound paranoid by mentioning what would sound like a Slender Man sighting in the dunes. But there was no way she was walking along a darkened path with terrible sight lines right near where she was pretty sure she'd just seen the guy who'd been staring at her creepily just yesterday.

"Personal experience," she said, deciding to keep it vague. "You just never know who might be hiding back there waiting to take advantage of two unsuspecting teenagers. I'd rather deal with the obnoxious surfers I can see rather than the potential knife-wielding meth-head I can't."

Chris studied her, unsure whether to laugh or be horrified.

"Okay—dark but fair," he said. "Let's take the long way."

They walked about halfway up the beach, far enough away from the water to avoid hearing the surfers amid the crashing waves. But their position still allowed decent distance from the dunes so that they would have fair warning should someone leap out and come running in their direction.

Chris talked giddily about what activities the rest of the weekend might hold but Hannah was only half-listening. Her senses were on high alert as she listened for any unusual sound and kept her eyes moving, scanning for unexpected movement. They were nearing the point where the beach met up with the boardwalk and overhead lighting would offer the moon some help. Just then both their phones buzzed.

"Who is it?" Hannah asked, not taking her eyes off the dunes.

"Patrice," Chris said. "Everyone's sick of window shopping. They're going for gelato at that spot near the greasy spoon joint we saw earlier today and want to know if we're in. Are we?"

"I think so," Hannah said. "We can get some more solo time later, but I think some gelato and late-summer evening group merriment sounds nice right about now."

"Okay, I'll let them know we're coming," Chris said, beginning to text back as they stepped onto the wooden boardwalk and were bathed in artificial light.

Hannah immediately felt more secure, though she knew that the sensation was an illusion. Danger could come in the light as often as in the dark. Still, she could feel the tension in her neck ease slightly.

"Actually," she said, "why don't you go ahead? I'm going to run back to the beach house really quick to stop by the bathroom. I'll catch up."

"You sure?" he asked. "I can come with you."

"No, it's cool. I'll only be a minute."

"Okay," he said, leaning over and giving her an awkward kiss that got teeth as much as lips. "I'll work on that."

"You better," she teased.

He darted off toward the gelato shop and she headed in the direction of the beach house, making sure to stay in the lighted areas as she went. She did in fact need to use the restroom, but that wasn't the main reason she was heading back. Her pepper gel and Taser were in the backpack in her bedroom and right about now, she was feeling pretty naked without them. It was dumb to have left them behind in the first place, but she'd let herself slip into complacency as the weekend had worn on. Plus, it was hard to find a place to put them when half the time she was only wearing a bikini.

She switched from a brisk walk to a jog, not wanting to be without her little fighting friends any longer than necessary. By the time she rounded the corner and saw the beach house, she had a little sweat on her brow. She considered slowing down but then thought better of it. She could throw some cold water on her face at the beach house.

Besides, she didn't get the sense that Chris would complain about a little perspiration. The thought made her smile to herself.

CHAPTER TWENTY NINE

By the time Mark Haddonfield got back to the beach house, he was both breathing and sweating heavily.

Part of it was because he had to rush to make sure he was there first. But he knew that a bigger part of it was because he was trying to foolishly outrun the idiocy that had put the entire Strategy at risk.

He was sure that Hannah had seen him at the edge of the dunes. It was his own fault. Instead of staying focused on the task of the evening, prepping the beach house, he'd gotten cocky. Because his prey wouldn't be back at the house for a while, he figured he could keep tabs on Hannah from afar, then leave with more than enough time to do the deed.

He watched her and her friends at dinner and imagined himself at the table with them, laughing, sharing stories. He'd been doing a lot of imagining lately. Ever since yesterday, when he'd locked eyes with her at the beach, he'd allowed himself to picture what life might be like if he could parlay that moment of connection into something deeper and more lasting.

Originally, he'd intended to spy on Hannah Dorsey with one primary goal in mind: to learn how he could use the younger sister to hurt the older one. First, he would discover more about Jessie's weaknesses through someone she loved. And eventually, once he'd learned all he could, he would simply destroy the person she loved. But now, he was starting to have doubts.

Mark wondered if there might be another way. Hannah was only three years younger than him. She was clearly smart as a whip, sharing Jessie's intellect, although hopefully not her corrupt self-righteousness. With her blonde hair, flashing green eyes, and statuesque figure, she would be stunning by his side.

What if he asked her out on a date? And if she said yes, what if he could win her over? What if they became a couple? It seemed crazy, but was it really? The more he thought about it, the more plausible it became in his mind.

He hadn't been caught. Jessie Hunt had no idea who was committing these "Clone Killer" crimes. If he stopped now, they would remain unsolved. He and Hannah could fall deeply in love, perhaps get married, and Jessie Hunt would stand there at their wedding, having no idea that she was happily beaming at the man who had murdered multiple people she had tried to save.

Maybe he and Jessie could end up working together after all, once she saw how intelligent he was; how talented he was at profiling too. Perhaps his original dream of having her mentor him could work out after all. It didn't seem so far-fetched.

And then Hannah had kissed that pretty boy by the beach and all his fantasies were blown to smithereens. That's when, like an idiot, he stood straight up by the dune, spotlighted by the moonlight, and she'd seen him. After that, he'd had to change course. No more casual observation.

It was straight back to the beach house to prepare for the job at hand. The silly notions of marriages and reconciliations had interfered with the important work before him and now he was rushing, rather than being methodical. That was how mistakes were made. That was how unintended clues were left.

As he moved quickly around the house, preparing everything for his victim's imminent arrival, he tried to stay focused. All that mattered now was The Strategy. All that mattered was punishing Jessie Hunt.

"That boy isn't right for her," he muttered to himself, as he moved into the bedroom where he intended to snuff out a guiltless life just minutes from now. "You know it and I know it, Jessie. After the first romantic rush has passed, he'll bore her to tears with his easel and his watercolors. He might as well wear a beret and smoke a clove cigarette. She'd be better off dead than trapped in a lifeless relationship like that, don't you think?"

There was no response, but he knew that she agreed with him.

He snapped on the gloves and pulled out the long shard of broken glass that would be his murder weapon for this evening. Then he slid into the bedroom closet and waited. His prey would be here soon.

He didn't want to do this. With all the prior victims, he had managed to find a way to justify eliminating them. Admittedly, sometimes those justifications were dubious, but he could cling to them at the final moment, when he had to snuff out their existence.

But this one felt different, like he was crossing a line into arbitrary cruelty, like he was no longer just using the knife, but twisting it too. There was no way around the truth: tonight's victim was just a means to an end. Despite any poor romantic judgment in the past, tonight's victim didn't deserve what was coming.

Then he heard the side door of the beach house creak open. A moment later it slammed shut, and along with it, so did the doubts Mark had been feeling. He had an obligation to do this, not just for himself, or for The Strategy, but for history.

It would hurt, but true growth required pain and sacrifice. And in this case, it also required blood.

CHAPTER THIRTY

Jessie felt herself slipping.

It was hard to stay alert, even under these intense circumstances, after hours without anything happening.

She and Susannah had been at Daphne Klein's party since nine. It was just after 11 p.m. now and no one had made an aggressive move toward Daphne. That is, unless one counted the dancing balcony man in the gold paint and solo sock costume, who had briefly, jokingly, faux-humped her on the dance floor, before focusing his attention on a gentleman more to his liking.

But other than that one, fleeting moment when there seemed to be a potential threat, the only excitement of the evening had come from seeing which guests were most likely to lose their outfits entirely, and how many of them would do it accidentally or by design. Jessie was considering sneaking into the kitchen to brew herself a cup of coffee when she saw Officer Carrie Shaw step through the front door. The young cop looked around, made eye contact, and motioned for Jessie to meet her outside.

"Stay with Daphne," Jessie told Susannah. "Carrie Shaw just showed up. It looks like she has news."

The detective nodded and Jessie weaved her way through the now-less-crammed living room and out into the yard. She joined Shaw in a darkened, secluded area off to the side, where other guests wouldn't take note of a cop talking to a tennis player.

"What's up?" Jessie asked.

"I tried to text you, but I didn't hear back," Shaw said.

"Sorry," Jessie said, pulling her phone out of the small purse she'd been holding. "There was nowhere to keep it or my gun with this outfit, so I had to carry a bag. With all the noise in there, I guess I didn't hear any texts or calls. Want to fill me in?"

Shaw dived right in.

"Despite what Curly Duff told you, this might not be the right party," she said. "I've been doing the rounds up and down the Strand and I just found out that a woman at a different party was choked earlier tonight. Apparently, it happened a few hours ago but just like with the other women, she didn't call it in because she was worried that we'd shut the party down to do a big investigation and she didn't want the thousands of dollars that she'd spent on catering and decorations to go to waste. It's a Prohibition-era Roaring Twenties party."

"Who is she?" Jessie asked.

"Her name is Maya Easton," Shaw said. "I didn't close the party down, but I called Timms and told him to stay in sight of her while I went looking for you. I figured you'd want to stop by."

"You figured right," Jessie said. "I'm going to get Detective Valentine. Contact Sergeant Breem. Then you can take us to this party. We may have finally caught a break."

***

It could have gone worse.

Maya Easton could have freaked out or been unreasonably stubborn or difficult, but to Jessie's surprise, she had taken their firmly worded "request" in stride. It was all the more impressive, considering that they'd told her in the guest bathroom of her own home, with people banging on the door to get in.

"It's not the end of the world," she had told them when they informed her that she needed to wrap up her festivities early without drawing suspicion. "I got some quality revelry in, and I can just send them all to the party next door anyway."

She had been less enthused when they explained the rest of their plan to her, which involved using her as bait. Sergeant Breem, along with Officers Shaw, Timms, and Oldmeyer, would be outside, officially keeping tabs on the other parties in the area but available on short notice if needed.

"We want you to leave your house open and accessible," Susannah had explained to her, "so that this guy can get inside and make his move. We don't want him to suspect that he has anything to worry about. Ms. Hunt and I will be here, acting like passed-out party guests, but in general, we don't want to alert him to our presence. So, after we do a search of the house, we'll have you hang out in your bedroom and we'll keep in constant contact with you via text, okay?"

Maya, who was divorced and hadn't met anyone tonight that made the plan a romantic sacrifice, had reluctantly agreed. That led them to their current situation, with Susannah lying on a couch in the downstairs living room, Jessie in one of the upstairs guestrooms, and Maya nervously texting away from her main upstairs bedroom.

Jessie settled in, unsure how long they'd be waiting. The coroner had estimated that Shasta Mallory was killed between 12:30 and 2:30 a.m. Nicole Boyce was murdered between 4 a.m. and 6 a.m. It was now 11:24 p.m.

They were coming up on peak killing time.

CHAPTER THIRTY ONE

Wade Cronin wasn't going to make the same mistake as before. When he returned to the house, he would attack the correct woman.

Even as he parked his car a block away and got out at 11:42 p.m., he shook his head at the absurdity of the evening's events. How could he possibly have known that the woman he intended to strangle to death, Lola Dorman, was having a *joint* Roaring Twenties party with her next-door neighbor and friend Maya Easton? How could he have known that they would decide to wear matching flapper costumes and do their hair the same way?

And how could he possibly have known that Maya would have been visiting Lola's party at the same time he was there, walking down the stairs, with her back to him, so that he would assume she was Lola and grab her neck in front of multiple guests, only to discover he had the wrong woman while he was being attacked by her rescuers? What were the chances?

But everything was cleared up now. The double-party confusion was resolved. The error would be corrected. And soon, the wrongs that he suffered would be righted.

As he walked to Lola's he was wearing a simple, button-down, short-sleeved striped shirt and a pair of matching striped drawstring shorts that were casually '20s-era appropriate but would draw little attention. In fact, no one gave him a second look as he walked through the front door of the party, which was still hopping, and wandered back to the kitchen to grab a beer.

"This is a great party," he said to one of the catering servers, keeping his straw boater hat low to cover his face. "Is the hostess around? I'd like to congratulate her."

"I think she may have retired for the evening," the server said. "Her husband said she had a few too many martinis and took her up a little while ago."

"That's too bad," Wade said, trying to sound disappointed. "Maybe I'll go thank him instead then."

Wade did indeed go look for Steve Dorman, but not to thank him. He needed to make sure that Lola's husband was nowhere near the bedroom. Only when he was confident of that could he go up there to do the work. It was especially important that tonight went well.

After the last two nights, he knew that the police would be out in force. He'd already seen more officers than usual patrolling the Strand. He'd made the calculated risk that it was wiser to deal with Mrs. Dorman earlier rather than later in the night and use the party crowd to his advantage. Leaving a house around midnight with a crowd of people would look a lot less suspicious than skulking out alone at three or four in the morning.

Of course, that meant a greater chance of someone walking in on him. It was a chance he'd just have to take in order to make Mrs. Dorman pay for what she'd done. Just like the others had been made to pay for what they'd done. It was a matter of honor more than anything else. And Wade Cronin was nothing if not a man of honor.

As he pushed through the crowd, looking for Steve Dorman, he reminded himself that it didn't have to be this way. When he first signed on with Beach Plumbers after moving south from Bakersfield three months ago, he thought it would be a fresh start. He had hopes of getting a tan, learning to surf, and generally leaving behind the unpleasantness of life in the San Joaquin Valley, where he'd spent all his life.

He'd extricated himself from his domineering single mother, his sneering, abusive older sister, Wanda, and from Jem, the on-again, off-again girlfriend he'd been seeing since high school, who only called him when she was pissed at her husband, sick of her kids, and three vodka and cranberries in.

With the $7,100 he'd saved over the last five years working plumbing jobs, along with some construction on the side, he'd loaded up his pickup and moved south, with the confidence that he'd find a place to live and that his skill set would get him work. It only kind of worked out that way.

He did find a place to live, but it was crashing on the couch in an old high school friend's one-bedroom apartment in Gardena and paying half the rent for the privilege. He couldn't get a full-time position with Beach Plumbing, but they let him fill in when other guys were sick or didn't show up, which was often. The same was true with South Bay Plumbing Systems. And Beach Cities Pipe Masters. He filled in whenever there was an opening, hoping to be offered a permanent position with any of them. It never came.

What *did* come was the arrogance and the abuse. While the customers he dealt with in Bakersfield generally lacked the wealth of the people in these beach communities, they also lacked the attitude. It seemed that almost every job he went on here required the homeowner to make a sarcastic or belittling remark. It got to the point that, when a customer was plain old nice, he was genuinely surprised.

He probably would have just kept his head down and dealt with it if not for a series of events in the last few weeks that made him realize that life was too short for him to put up with all the crap. First, his mother, admittedly a shrew of a woman, got a severe case of pneumonia and died within a day of being admitted to the hospital.

Not long after that, he learned that his sister had recently convinced their mom to change her will and cut him out completely as punishment for leaving town and "abandoning the family." As a result, he lost his half of their inheritance. It turned out that it was only $12,000 and her trailer, which sold at auction for $6,000. But still, that money would have come in handy. And it was more the principle of the thing. His only remaining relative had intentionally screwed him when it came to their mother's death.

Lastly, he'd learned just last week that the husband of Jem, the old girlfriend he'd been intermittently sleeping with, had discovered her infidelity, though not that Wade was her partner. He'd come home and shot her four times, then turned the gun on himself, leaving their three children orphaned. It had been a rough few days.

With all that bouncing around in his head, he'd gone to the home of Shasta Mallory on Monday of this week, along with two other guys from Beach Plumbing, to deal with a clog in her kitchen sink. She was particularly anxious because she had a huge party on Thursday night. One of the other plumbers told him that it was part of a whole thing that went on around here, where the super-rich who lived along the Strand threw massive blowouts over long summer holiday weekends.

But no party justified Mrs. Mallory screaming at him for putting his gloved hands on her butcher block after removing a corroded pipe. The exact phrase she had used was "Keep your goddamned E. coli mitts off my food prep area, you filthy sewer rat."

She had actually grabbed a kitchen dish towel and swatted at his hands with it, as if he was a fly that had snuck in through a window and needed to be squashed.

"Sorry," he had muttered in the moment, glad that neither of the other plumbers was in the kitchen at that moment to see the incident and report his error to the day manager, which could have resulted in him losing work.

But later that evening, when he had time to mull over what happened, the rage started to ferment inside him. What kind of person reacted that way to an honest mistake, especially by someone who had come to her home to try to help her with a problem that she couldn't solve on her own? What made Shasta Mallory think she could treat another human being this way?

When he got back to his place—really just his couch— he did a little research on Mallory and discovered that she wasn't just this way with service people. She was a surly, hateful person with just about everyone she interacted with, save for her famous music star clients. She reminded him a lot of his sister, Wanda, who never met a person she didn't try to make feel small.

Wade spent that whole night lying on the couch, staring up at the stained ceiling, thinking about how Mallory had wronged him, just like Wanda had wronged him. It occurred to him as he tossed and turned on the uncomfortable couch that Shasta Mallory was far from the only customer who had been abusive to him.

There was Ed Koftic, who had gotten pissed that their work fixing his overflowing toilet interfered with watching the Dodgers game. Milton and Reyna Craig didn't like how slippery their recently installed water-softening system made their dishes and pestered him relentlessly for a discount he wasn't authorized to give. But those bits of obnoxiousness were within the bounds of normal customer behavior. Shasta Mallory's was not.

Neither was the behavior of Nicole Boyce, who never said a single word to him the entire time he was there helping a guy from South Bay Plumbing Systems unclog an outdoor shower station that had become so blocked up with sand that the water was gurgling up and spilling into the living room. She had simply pointed out the issue to him and his partner, never bothering to get off the phone to greet them or explain the particulars. She didn't even make eye contact. It was as if direct communication with the help would somehow infect her.

The whole time they were there, she remained on the phone, involved in an intense argument with someone who Wade later determined through his research was her husband, whom she apparently had a volatile relationship with. She yelled at him almost every minute that they were there, and only acknowledged their existence with an occasional, dismissive pointing or waving gesture.

She wasn't as overtly hostile as Mallory but she still made Wade feel less than a person. Lying on the couch that night, he added her to his list.

Lola Dorman's conduct was also not acceptable. She had been one of the first customers he'd helped service. Her husband was a city council member, and she was a prominent real estate agent, as he would later learn. But at the time he joined the team from Beach Cities Pipe Masters, which re-piped her guest house, he was just "stubble boy" who needed to be "spoken to" about tracking sand into the house and reminded that if the workmen's port-a-potty was occupied, then he should "go in the ocean or piss his pants, but he can't use the facilities in my home."

It was when Wade did a quick web search at 3 a.m. on the couch that late Monday night/early Tuesday morning, that he learned that each of those women usually hosted a Strand party over Labor Day weekend. The rest of the plan sprouted from there. Oddly, the decision to kill them wasn't that momentous. It felt like a no-brainer.

If they treated him like this, he could only imagine how many other people they stomped to dust over the years. They were like his sister, Wanda, only with real power and money. Each of them deserved it. He moved almost immediately past that to the planning.

He only had a few days to prep. To hide his identity he had to get disguises, and in some cases, literal costumes. He had to buy latex gloves so he wouldn't leave fingerprints. He had to review his plan of attack.

That was easy for Shasta Mallory, whose house he'd just visited. But he was at Nicole Boyce's place two weeks ago. And he hadn't been to Lola Dorman's home in three months, and even then, he'd only entered the main house on that one ill-fated visit to use the bathroom.

And yet, so far it had all worked out. The Shasta Mallory killing had been perfect. He'd spent so much time ensuring everything would go smoothly that when he finally got to wrap his hands around her neck in her bedroom and stare into her eyes, he was unprepared for the rush of excitement it would give him as her eyes bulged in panicked terror.

As she tried desperately to gasp for air she couldn't get, he had whispered to her, "I'm the plumber."

He thought he saw a moment of recognition on her face just before the light left her eyes, but he couldn't be sure. Either way, it was more satisfying than he could have possibly hoped for. As a result, he could barely contain himself the next day waiting for the chance to teach Nicole Boyce the same lesson.

For her, death had come in the bathroom rather than the bedroom, which made for a different kind of excitement—dirtier and rawer. It helped that she was an athlete. She was stronger than Mrs. Mallory and fought back hard, which was thrilling. But in the end, he was much bigger and stronger and had the element of surprise. She was no match for him.

When he whispered, "I'm the plumber," he didn't see the same recognition in her eyes, which was a little disappointing. He didn't know if that was because it had been several weeks since his visit and she'd already forgotten how she'd wronged him, or if the horror of this moment had made all other thoughts flee from her head. In the end, it didn't really matter. She was dead, and just like Shasta Mallory, she would never treat someone "beneath" her so badly again.

Wade snapped out of the memory at the sight of Steve Dorman, who was standing in a corner of his expansive living room, holding court as he talked to two buddies, with his back to the stairwell. It couldn't have been more perfect. As casually as he could, Wade shuffled up the stairs, weaving past several folks who were chatting at the top of the landing.

He moved down the hall, which was empty other than two women giggling in an open bathroom as they checked their makeup. Then he arrived at the main bedroom, which he'd identified from checking real estate websites earlier in the week. He wasn't surprised to find that the door was locked. Of course it was. Steve was a good husband and wouldn't want to leave his inebriated wife vulnerable in a home filled with partygoers, some of whom they didn't know.

Unfortunately for the Dormans, Wade Cronin was adept at overcoming simple residential bedroom door locks. He snapped on his latex gloves and defeated it in seconds.

When he stepped inside the bedroom, closed and relocked the door, it was 11:53 p.m.—time to teach his final lesson.

CHAPTER THIRTY TWO

Jessie wasn't sure he was coming.

As she sat on a chair in the guest bedroom across the hall from where Maya was serving as bait, doubt began to nibble at the corner of her mind. Not because they'd been waiting a long time. They hadn't.

But she started to wonder if it was a mistake to clear out so many of the guests. The goal had been to make it easier to spot someone suspicious, but the downside was that it might, for the same reason, have made the killer skittish. He likely used crowds to sneak in and get to his victims. Had they inadvertently scared him off?

She looked at her watch. It was 11:49 p.m.

For the briefest of moments, she was tempted to use this otherwise wasted downtime to text Hannah to see how things were going with Chris. But she fought back the urge. First of all, it was too late. Either her sister was asleep, or things were going extremely well. In either scenario, Hannah wouldn't appreciate the intrusion. More importantly, Jessie needed to keep her focus on the current situation. A sudden buzz interrupted her thoughts.

"*We're going to have to bail,*" Sergeant Breem texted abruptly over the shared chain that they'd all been using. "*There's a big bar fight down at Hercule's and they're asking for help. I need to pull Shaw, Timms, and Oldmeyer. You guys okay for a bit?*"

"*Yes,*" Susannah texted back.

"*Let us know if you need us back here,*" he replied. "*We can be back in under two minutes.*"

"*Will do,*" Jessie texted, before adding to Susannah separately, "*I'm going to go check in on Maya for a minute. You still good down there in the living room?*"

"*If by 'good,' you mean 'bored as hell,' then yes, I'm good.*"

Jessie texted Maya that she was coming over, walked across the hall, and knocked on the door. The woman quickly let her in and locked the door again.

"Is this happening or not?" she asked.

"We honestly don't know," Jessie admitted. "But everything suggests that it will. Like we explained earlier, the last two murders happened later on the same night that the hostess was attacked. Unfortunately, because the times of the killings varied so widely, we can't be certain when he might try to come after you."

"And you don't know why he's picking particular people?" Maya asked.

"No," Jessie acknowledged, frustrated that they had made so little progress on that front. "Other than that both victims have been women who hosted Strand holiday parties, we don't have much. The first was on Thursday night. The second victim had her party last night. She didn't know the first victim. Your party is on a Saturday and you told us you don't know either of the other women."

"Like I said, I've obviously heard of Nicole Boyce," Maya said, "and I've seen her around. But I didn't know her personally And I didn't know the other woman at all."

"Right," Jessie said. "So, we're still trying to find that connection among the three of you."

They stood there in silence for a few seconds before Jessie decided that she'd stalled long enough.

"I better get back to the guest bedroom," she said. "I wanted to check in on you but you're not much good as bait if I'm in here with you."

"Okay," Maya said, standing up, ready to lock the door. "I wonder why this guy picked me and not Lola."

"What do you mean?" Jessie asked. "Who's Lola?"

"Lola," Maya said as if she was discussing the President of the United States. "My next-door neighbor, Lola Dorman. We're hosting this themed party together. That's the only reason I didn't completely lose it when you had me kick most folks out of the party I'd been planning for weeks—because I could send them all next door."

"I thought you were just sending them to the party next door to politely get them out of the house," Jessie said, feeling strangely unsettled. "You're saying the parties are affiliated?"

"Sure," Maya told her, "through the Roaring Twenties theme. We even wore matching flapper costumes. We had different decorations, food, and drinks at each house, but the vibe was the same. In fact, I was over at her place earlier, trying some of the hors d'oeuvres she was serving when the guy jumped me."

Jessie's whole body surged with a tingling sensation that started in her chest and shot out to her fingertips and toes.

"You're saying that you were attacked at your neighbor's house and that the two of you are dressed exactly the same tonight?" she repeated.

"Uh-huh," Maya said, seeming only now to get the significance of her statement.

"Do the two of you look alike?" Jessie asked as she pulled out her phone and called Susannah. "Comparable size? Hair color?"

"We both have brown hair," Maya confirmed, "which we styled and tied back like this. And we're about the same size, yeah."

"What's up?" Susannah asked, picking up the phone.

"I think we've got the wrong victim at the wrong house," Jessie said quickly. "Maya says she was attacked next door at her neighbor's party, which has the same Roaring Twenties theme. The neighbor, Lola Dorman, is dressed in a matching outfit and has the same build and hair color."

"I'm heading over there now," Susannah said.

"I'll meet you," Jessie said before hanging up and turning to Maya. "Text us Lola's cell number and a recent photo of her. And lock the door again after I leave. There's still a chance that you were the target."

She darted for the door.

"All this time you've been watching me," Maya said, "what if he's already been over there? What if you're too late to help her?"

"Lock the door!" Jessie shouted as she left the bedroom and ran down the hall to the stairs.

It was all she could say because she didn't have a good answer to Maya's question. In fact, she was asking herself the same one: what if they *were* too late?

CHAPTER THIRTY THREE

The party was still going strong.

When Jessie rushed through the front door, she had to shove her way past tightly packed pockets of people to find an open space where she could get a decent view of the living room. She looked down at her phone at the photo of Lola that Maya had sent and compared it to the faces in the room. No one was an obvious match but there were so many people littering the area that she wasn't confident that she hadn't missed her.

A text popped up from Susannah: *Music too loud to call. Let's just text. Checking the kitchen and first floor back rooms. SO many people!*

Going up the stairs to get a better view of the living room, Jessie texted back.

She ascended the stairwell and stood on the second-story landing, where she could look out on the entire crowd. Even though it was almost midnight—11:53 to be exact—there were still easily a hundred people spread out in the room below her. That didn't account for the additional fifty-odd people milling about in front of the house and however many were in the kitchen and the other areas that Susannah was searching down below. Even with Lola's photo, it would take forever to find and warn her.

And in that moment, staring down at an unending multitude of revelers trying to recreate the looks of people from a century ago, she realized she was going about this all wrong. If Lola Dorman was among all those partiers, she was safe, because the killer only choked his victims in public for effect. He did his kills in private.

Jessie turned around and looked down the hall of the second floor, which was much quieter than the first. In fact, other than two women in the open-doored bathroom in the middle of the hall, giggling as they reapplied makeup, there was no one around. If he was going to kill Lola, it would be up here, in a bedroom, just like the previous victims. She was right where she needed to be.

Jessie shot off a quick text to the chain that included Susannah, Sergeant Breem, and Officers Shaw, Timms, and Oldmeyer, which read: *Believe real target tonight is Maya Easton's next-door neighbor, Lola Dorman. Checking upstairs bedrooms. Assist when possible.*

Then she did something she could never have done downstairs: as she walked along the hallway away from the stairs, she called Lola's phone. While the music from downstairs was still audible up here, it was quiet enough that she hoped she might hear it ringing.

Sure enough, a loud trill began to call out from a room off to her left. She pulled out her gun and reached for the door handle. It was locked. That could be completely innocent—a homeowner locking their bedroom door to keep people out during a party. But most homeowners kept their phones with them during parties.

Jessie had a bad feeling and decided to risk whatever blowback might come her way if the decision she was about to make went south. She took two steps back, then rushed forward and kicked the door in. The home may have been expensive, but the lock wasn't, and the door shot straight open.

Framed in front of her in the darkened bedroom, with the moonlit balcony behind them, were Lola Dorman and the man who'd been killing women like her. His hands were tight around her neck as they stood in front of the bedroom's long, glass balcony doors. They were both facing Jessie. Lola's back was to him, and she was desperately flailing, trying to knock his hands away, without success.

The man, of medium height and well built, was wearing a striped, short-sleeved shirt and matching striped shorts. A straw hat was on the floor at his feet. He was standing mostly behind Lola, making it impossible to take a shot without risking hitting her.

Jessie stepped into the bedroom and prepared to order him to release Lola. But it only took a second to realize that wasn't going to happen. The man barely seemed to have noticed that anyone had broken into the room. His eyes were filled with frenzied, murderous glee and they were fixed intently on the muscles of Lola's neck.

Because the woman's back was to him, he couldn't see her face, but Jessie could, and it was clear that she was in bad shape. Jessie didn't know how long Lola had been without oxygen, but it was clear that she couldn't go much longer. Her eyes were bulging, and her face was bright red.

Unable to shoot, Jessie did the only thing she could think of—she charged at them. She focused attention on the man as she sprinted hard, hoping that she could make more physical contact with him than with his victim. At the last moment, he seemed to sense her presence and looked up, registering that a woman was running at him with a gun in her hand. He released his grip on Lola and shoved her toward Jessie.

Unfortunately for him, it turned out that his grip on her neck was largely what was holding Lola up. When he let go, she collapsed to the ground rather than into Jessie, leaving a clear path for the profiler to launch herself at him. She slammed into him shoulder-first and felt him careen backward a fraction of a second before she heard the glass balcony door shatter as he smashed through it.

His back hit the balcony floor and Jessie landed on his chest before shooting past him and banging hard into the metal balcony railing with the back of her head. Ignoring the sharp twinge of pain, she shot to her feet, feeling the crunch of broken glass under her shoes. She glanced back into the bedroom, where Lola was clutching at her throat. At least she was conscious.

"Run!" Jessie shouted at the woman before returning her attention to the man on the balcony with her who had rolled over into the fetal position, moaning. She didn't see her gun, which had popped out of her hand during the collision, so she pulled out her handcuffs and snapped one on his left wrist. She was just snapping the other cuff to the railing when he suddenly spun around toward her.

In the moonlight, she saw a flash of something in his right hand and jumped back just in time to avoid getting slashed by a thick chunk of glass he was gripping in his right hand. But the sudden backward motion threw her off balance and she fell. She scrambled to slide backward away from him into the corner of the balcony as he got to his feet and prepared to advance on her.

She glanced behind her and realized that the balcony wasn't long enough for her to evade him, even with one of his hands cuffed to the decorative railing. She was trapped. He was directly in front of her, bloody and wild-eyed. There was a wall behind her, along with more thick glass to her left, and a twenty-five-foot drop into a crowded courtyard below on her right.

For half a second, she panicked. But almost immediately, as it always did, the fear gave way to anger. She stood up.

"I guess the only way out is through you, asshole," she said, "so bring it."

The man smiled at her, and she saw that his teeth were covered in blood.

"I'm the plumber," he hissed.

"I don't care," she shot back, getting into fighting position.

He lunged at her. Before he got close, a gunshot rang out. The man slammed against the railing and toppled over the side of it. But instead of falling to the ground, he came to an abrupt stop. He remained dangling there by his wrist, which was still handcuffed to the metal bar. Down below, people looked up, saw him, began to scream, and started running.

Jessie turned back into the bedroom to see where the shot had come from and saw Susannah Valentine standing in the doorway, re-holstering her weapon. Then her partner rushed over, stepped out on the balcony, and walked over to her.

"Are you okay?" she asked.

"We smashed through the glass," Jessie said. "I bumped my head a little bit. And then, after I thought I had him in custody, he almost gutted me. I think I'm a little bit in shock."

"I can understand that," Susannah said. "Well, the good news is that looking at him, I don't think the guy's going to be causing anybody else any problems, ever. The bad news is that your encounter with the door has you bleeding a bit here and there. I don't think tennis uniforms were designed to repel glass that well. We're also going to get that bump on your head checked out, okay?"

"I think that's a good idea," Jessie said. "Ryan will be mad at me if we don't. How's Lola?"

"She was running down the stairs as I was running up them, so she's alive, which I think she has you to thank for," Susannah said. "I'm sure the MBPD folks are here by now. We'll get her looked at too. Why don't you sit down on her bed, and I'll reach out to them now."

"That sounds like a good plan," Jessie said, letting the detective guide her inside and ease her onto the bed. "And please tell Ryan what's going on too. But not Hannah. It's late. I don't want to worry her. We can fill her in tomorrow."

CHAPTER THIRTY FOUR

The Santa Monica Pier was starting to shut down.

The rest of the gang had gone back to the beach house for the night, but Hannah and Chris had made an excuse after they all finished their gelatos and managed to sneak away for one last wander around the shops.

That was just the official excuse, of course, and Hannah knew they weren't fooling anyone when they said were hoping to find some late-night bargains. But that was okay. They weren't really trying to hide things from the others anymore anyway.

So, as the rides started to turn off their lights and the eateries shooed their final customers out, Hannah and Chris lingered at those last few shops that still had open signs. They found a gift shop, where he bought her an overtly cheesy necklace that had the Pacific Wheel, the pier's Ferris wheel, on it. She thanked him profusely, as if it was the Hope Diamond, and then planted a wet kiss on him. Finally, noting that it was almost midnight by pointing at the clock on the wall, even the shopkeeper at that place kicked them out.

"I just have to run to the restroom," Chris said as they stepped out of the shop into the steamy night again. "Then do we want to head back?"

"Sure," she agreed.

He headed off and she waited, leaning on the rickety pier railing, listening to the waves slosh against the dock pilings as she watched the gift shop lights flicker off. She wondered if she and Chris were the last people left on the pier tonight who didn't work here.

"Nice night," someone said from behind her, startling her so badly that she physically jumped.

She turned around and saw, emerging from the shadows, the gangly guy with glasses who had been hovering by the ice cream stand, staring at them. She was almost certain that it was also the same guy she'd seen by the sand dune earlier tonight, though she couldn't be absolutely sure. Either way, his presence here, when she thought that she and Chris were essentially alone, was truly unnerving.

"Sure," she said noncommittally, gripping the purse that held the pepper gel and stun gun, "I guess."

"Pretty hot though," he said. "Part of me wishes it was autumn already. There's nothing like seeing the leaves start to change and feeling them crunch under your feet when you're walking across the quad trying to get to class on a fall morning. You know the feeling, right? What are you? A sophomore? A junior maybe?"

"Yeah, I wouldn't know about that, sorry," she said, not about to give this guy any personal information.

She looked around, trying to determine how best to extricate her and Chris from this situation once he returned. She wasn't sure if this guy was just awkward and creepy or something more, but she wanted to be prepared for all contingencies.

"Of course," he said, blathering on, "that whole crunching leaves thing is a very specific sense memory. I know this one guy who's really big on that sort of concept, always talking about how current experiences evoke past memories. He's a little touchy-feely like that, but a really good guy. I was actually just visiting him at a beach house up the way a little earlier tonight. Anyway, that's neither here nor there. I guess I'm kind of rambling because I'm a little nervous. The reason I came over to say hi was that I noticed you around the area this weekend. I thought you were cute, and I wanted to know if you wanted to maybe go out sometime."

Hannah felt the tension in her chest release slightly. Apparently the guy wasn't a total psycho so much as an incredibly awkward, borderline creepy human gawk-fest in search of a date. She did her best to handle the situation diplomatically.

"That's very sweet of you," she said, "but I'm actually seeing someone."

"Yeah, I saw you with that guy," he said, his shoulders slumping briefly before he seemed to quickly rebound and regain his confidence, "but I've got to tell you, I just don't think he's right for you, Hannah."

A shiver went up her spine as she heard those last words.

"I don't remember telling you my name," she said, as she began to unzip her purse.

"Do we have a problem here?" asked Chris, who was walking out of the men's restroom with a frown on his face, only steps away from the gangly guy.

"Not if you walk away," replied the interloper, who Hannah noticed hadn't taken his eyes off her. In fact, his attention was fixed on the bag she was slowly opening.

"I couldn't help but overhear you as I was coming out," Chris said, not walking away but rather moving around the guy and toward Hannah, "and it seems like the lady isn't interested in what you're offering."

The gangly guy nodded, a thin, nasty smile on his face.

"It seems like you should mind your own business, friend," he said, with a self-assurance that Hannah found disconcerting.

"Let's just go, Chris," she said, reaching out her hand for him to grab, even as her other hand felt in the purse for the Taser.

"Yeah, Chris, you should go," the gangly guy said, now with a bit of venom in his voice.

Chris reached out to take her hand. But as he did, the gangly guy leapt forward and shoved him hard to the pier's wooden plank flooring. Hannah let go of the purse, bending over in the hope of helping break his fall. But almost immediately, she realized that she'd made a mistake.

There was no way she could prevent him from falling and by trying, she had let go of her purse and along with it, the weapon inside it, while the threat they were facing was only feet away. She quickly abandoned her attempt to help Chris.

Instead, she dipped low into a crouch. The gangly guy, having shoved Chris, was still moving forward, his momentum sending him straight toward her. Without hesitation, she pushed hard off the balls of her feet and flung herself at the advancing guy, aiming for his knees.

She made contact with her shoulder and felt him topple over her as she hit the planks. Ignoring the pain as the wood scraped her skin, she popped up, darted back over to her purse, pulled out the Taser, and began shouting, "Help! I need help! I'm a teenage girl and I'm being attacked by a man that I don't know. He's very tall with curly blond hair and glasses. Call the police. Please help!"

Meanwhile, the gangly guy rolled over like a log several times and got near the pier railing. It looked for a moment like he might tumble off the side into the water below. But he managed to come to a stop before the edge and pushed himself to his feet. Hannah moved over so that she was standing next to Chris, who was still on the ground with what appeared to be an injured ankle. She held out the Taser and pointed it directly at the guy.

"You still want that date?" she snarled.

The guy took a step toward her, then winced when he tried to put pressure on the knee that she'd slammed into. He seemed torn as to how to proceed. His face was twisted with rage but something in his eyes suggested he knew he couldn't act on it in his current condition.

Suddenly the light from the gift shop flicked back on. A voice inside called out unintelligibly. Another voice from somewhere a little ways down the pier shouted, "Hold on, I'm coming!" A second shop light about fifty feet away turned on. The gangly guy looked around, then back at her.

"This isn't over, Hannah," he growled, then turned and limped off as quickly as his long legs could carry him. Hannah wanted to go after him, but there were no lights in the direction he went. Even with her Taser, she would lose her advantage quickly in the dark. Besides, she couldn't leave Chris. Within seconds, the guy had disappeared into the night.

"How are you doing?" Hannah asked, kneeling down beside Chris, though she still kept her eyes fixed on the impenetrable darkness up ahead.

"I think I twisted it," he said through gritted teeth. "You were pretty amazing there."

She shrugged.

"I've had a bit of experience in dangerous situations."

More lights turned on and the voices were getting closer. They heard the nearby gift shop door being unlocked.

"I guess we should call the cops, huh?" Chris said.

"Yeah, I think that's a good idea," Hannah agreed. "But the locals can call nine-one-one. I may be able to get us a more direct line."

CHAPTER THIRTY FIVE

It couldn't have been a more beautiful day.

Jessie removed her sunglasses as Ryan took the curve where the Interstate 10 Freeway ended at the ocean and curved north to become the Pacific Coast Highway. She wanted to better appreciate the view for this last stretch of sand and ocean before they arrived at the beach house to pick up Hannah at noon.

After getting the story of what happened on the pier, they'd still agreed to let her stay at the beach house. That is, once they'd coordinated with the Santa Monica Police Department to have a unit stay outside the place overnight and this morning until everyone left. SMPD, who'd benefited from HSS's investigative assistance on more than one occasion, agreed without hesitation. The other condition for letting her stay was that they keep all doors locked and the security system activated until daybreak.

That part had worked out well. Unfortunately, despite Hannah and Chris both giving detailed descriptions of the gangly guy to SMPD, no one matching it had been found in the area. The guy had simply disappeared. Hannah wasn't sure how the guy knew her name, though she suspected he'd been secretly listening in on their beach conversations before she'd first noticed his presence.

As they drove, Jessie tried not to play with the bandages covering the exposed sections of skin, where she'd had multiple small pieces of embedded glass removed. She and Ryan had been at the hospital until 9 a.m., and she'd gotten thirty-one stitches over her body. They'd agreed not to mention any of that to Hannah unless she noticed and specifically asked.

Nor would they bring up the bump on the back of her head, especially since, according to the doctors, it hadn't resulted in a concussion. Once again, she'd gotten lucky on that front. To his credit, Ryan didn't harp on it.

But she knew he was thinking the same thing that was starting to weigh on her too: how many more times could she go out on cases like this, incur a head injury, and escape without suffering a concussion that might result in permanent damage?

Any answer to that question was short-circuited by a call from the office.

"It's Jamil," she said, and put it on speaker. "Hey, I'm here with Captain Hernandez."

"Great," he said. "I'm in the research office with Beth and Detective Valentine. We have some updates for you if you'd like."

"I hope nothing you tell us is going to prevent you from attending that makeup survivors' guilt group session this afternoon?" Jessie said by way of reminding him. "We both missed yesterday but that doesn't mean we can't go today."

"I don't think this will prevent attendance," Jamil responded. "I'll go if you do. Will Hannah be able to make it?"

"I'll have to see if she's up for it," Jessie said. "She had kind of a rough night, but I'll let you know."

"*She* had a rough night?" Jamil countered. "You smashed through a glass door and nearly got stabbed with a chunk of the stuff!"

"Yes, but I'll have you know that one of the EMTs on the scene last night thought I was a professional tennis player, so apparently I can handle it," Jessie said wryly. "What's the update? How's Lola Dorman doing?"

"She's recovering well," Beth volunteered. "The hospital is going to keep her at least one more night. She still can't really speak. They think there may be some minor vocal cord damage but nothing permanent. Otherwise they expect a full recovery."

"There's more good news," Jamil added. "You'll be happy to know that those music star clients of Shasta Mallory who raised a stink in the press conference at police headquarters yesterday have changed their tune. They held another press event today and this time they were full of praise for HSS, the department in general, and Chief Decker."

"That's good to hear," Ryan said.

Jessie noted the relief on his face.

"In addition," Susannah said, speaking up for the first time, "I saw an interview with Nicole Boyce's husband, Lachlan Restrepo, on a local station this morning. He looked pretty devastated, but he talked about being glad that her killer was brought to justice and hopefully being able to get some closure. I was worried that when we eventually heard from him, he was going to be irate, but he seemed more hollowed out than anything. As for the killer, we've gotten some new details on him since we talked last."

"Let's hear them," Jessie requested.

"You already know the basics—that his name is Wade Cronin, that he moved here from Bakersfield three months ago, and has been living at the Gardena apartment of a high school friend, but our friends here in research learned some more about his work history."

"Let me guess," Jessie said. "He was a plumber?"

"How did you know that?" Jamil asked.

"That's what he told me just before he tried to cut me open on that balcony."

"Well, you're right," Jamil said. "He worked for three different South Bay area plumbing companies since he moved here. That was the reason we couldn't track him to any of the victims. It turns out that he did do work on each of their homes, but only once. And in each case, he was either a last-minute fill-in or a one-day worker. He was never a full-time employee for any of the companies and was never formally on a work roster, so there was no record of him for any of the jobs. He was like a ghost when it came to the databases."

"It turns out he was a bit of a ghost in his own life back in Bakersfield too," Susannah said. "I called around this morning. He didn't have many friends. Apparently he was pretty messed up. Multiple people told me that both his mother *and* his older sister were verbally and physically abusive to him, maybe sexually too according to at least one person. Then his mom died of pneumonia just a couple of weeks ago and his sister got him cut out of the will. I'm guessing that didn't do a ton for his mental well-being."

"One last thing," Beth added. "This isn't confirmed yet, but the Bakersfield police were looking to interview him in relation to a recent murder-suicide. A local man killed his wife, then himself. The man left a note claiming she was cheating with someone he couldn't identify. They had three kids, all of whom were found sleeping in the house, unharmed. Physical evidence in the home suggests that Cronin might have been the other man. If he was aware of what happened, I can't imagine that would have put him in a great headspace."

"Who knows?" Susannah said. "Maybe one or all of those events made him crack. Maybe these ladies on the Strand just said the wrong thing to him. Maybe it was a combination of the two. His apartment in Gardena is cordoned off and I'm heading over when we hang up. Maybe we'll find something there that explains his motive. Whatever his reason, he won't be choking anyone else."

"I'll try to join you once Hannah is all squared away," Jessie said.

"Don't worry about it," Susannah said. "You just got out of the hospital. Take care of yourself and your sister. Go to your group meeting. I'll call you if I find anything."

"Sounds good," Jessie said. "If we're all done, I want to take this call off speaker so I can finish up with Detective Valentine privately if that's cool?"

Everyone said their goodbyes. Once they were all off the line, Susannah asked, "What's so special secret that we had to talk privately about it?"

Jessie took a deep breath before what she said next, hoping that it would be received in the spirit that it was intended.

"I just wondered if you'd given any more thought to what we'd talked about earlier," she asked, "in regard to a certain surfing silver fox law enforcement officer who expressed interest in getting to know you better and who didn't start drooling the minute you walked in the room?"

There was a long moment of silence on the other end of the line.

"I might have," Susannah finally said, sounding as close to shy as Jessie had ever heard her.

"Okay, well I just happen to know that Drake Breem likes to hang out at the Tortoise Tavern when he has Sunday evenings off, which he does tonight, starting at six. So if you were to stop by to buy him a beer and update him on the case, he'd be around. Just an idea."

"Just an idea, huh?" Susannah asked.

"Just an idea."

"I'll think about it. Goodbye, Jessie."

"Bye."

She hung up, confident about where Susannah Valentine would be spending her evening. She was slightly jealous, imagining what it might be like for the potential couple, as they made their first hesitant steps toward each other. She remembered that stage with Ryan and what a different place they were in now.

She thought about the emotional weight that still hung over them, mainly a result of him keeping Zoe Bradway's threat from her. He'd thought he was protecting her by not burdening her with Bradway's claim that she intended to have him, Hannah, and Kat killed. But when Bradway followed through on the threat by hiring a hitwoman, and Hannah and Kat nearly died as a result, it opened a wound in the bond of trust between them that had yet to heal. She still doubted him. He still blamed himself. And it still ate at both of them. Yet they never spoke of it.

It was time that changed. Dr. Lemmon had repeatedly suggested that Jessie bring up the issue with Ryan directly and she still hadn't. If they couldn't address it on their own, perhaps they could do it together, with Dr. Lemmon's help.

The psychiatrist had been a beacon of light for Jessie individually, as well as for Hannah. Why couldn't she do the same for Jessie and Ryan as a couple? Maybe she could help guide them back to a path of trust they couldn't find on their own.

As they pulled into the driveway of the beach house, she decided to broach the idea with Ryan and was just opening her mouth to do so when she saw something that made her jaw drop wide open.

CHAPTER THIRTY SIX

There, on the small porch behind the house, Hannah was engaged in a passionate kiss with Chris Balfour.

Jessie wasn't exactly surprised to see it, but the intensity of what was going on in front of her was difficult to process. The two officers in the SMPD squad car, parked next to them, were deliberately looking away.

"You ready for that?" Ryan asked, sounding as gobsmacked as she felt.

"I guess I have to be," she replied, hoping that saying the words out loud might help get her there.

The kids heard the tires on the sandy gravel, instinctively stopped what they were doing, and came over from the porch, now more chastely holding hands. Jessie and Ryan got out. Hannah came over and gave them both hugs.

"You guys remember Chris from up in Wildpines, right?" she said.

They said that they did and reintroduced themselves, shaking hands. Chris's cheeks were deeply flushed.

"Why don't I go grab your backpack?" he offered quickly. "I'll be right back."

He limped inside, reminding Jessie how Hannah said he'd been injured in the altercation with the attacker. Ryan quickly moved over to confer with the SMPD officers, leaving Jessie and Hannah alone.

"He seems nice," Jessie said.

"He is," Hannah said.

"Nice tongue too?" Jessie asked, before quickly adding, "I'm sorry, I had to. I swear, that's the only teasing I'll do."

Hannah blushed but didn't scold her for it.

"He's pretty great," she said. "Really easygoing. Even after what happened last night, he just kind of went with the flow, didn't get all tensed up over it. I thought he might suddenly get distant or something, but no."

"That's good, right?" Jessie said, sensing that her sister was conflicted.

"It is, of course," Hannah answered hesitantly, before releasing the floodgates, "but it got me thinking—he didn't freak out, but maybe he should have. It wouldn't be unreasonable for him to be asking himself if it's safe to get involved with me. I mean, I'm asking *myself* that. Let's be real: will it ever truly be possible for me to have a genuine romantic relationship without the threat of danger hovering over me or the person I'm involved with? Won't I always be putting them at risk because people might use them to get to me? Might another assassin try to use them as bait to take me out like Ash Pierce did? And setting Chris aside, will I ever be able to trust a guy I meet without doing a full background check on him first? Long term, what kind of romantic future does someone like me really have? And short term, can I *ever* just go on a normal date?"

With each word Hannah spoke, the lump in Jessie's chest got larger and larger until she thought it might burst out of her like an alien in a horror film. She was speaking aloud the very fears that Jessie had been carrying for her sister ever since she assumed guardianship of her, even before that.

She knew how hard it would be for Hannah because remembered how difficult it had been for herself. She recalled how poorly she had chosen the first time she got married. After all, that man ended up trying to kill her.

"That's *a lot*," she said with a bittersweet smile, then reached out and pulled her sister in for a hug.

"That's all you've got for me?" Hannah asked in a meek voice, muffled by being pressed against Jessie's shoulder.

"I don't have the answers, sweetie," she whispered into her ear as she squeezed her tight. "I wish I did. But I think you're doing a pretty good job so far. Chris seems like a great guy. And I'm happy to do a background check on him to make sure."

She heard Hannah giggle and sighed happily at the sound of it. Releasing her from the hug, she grabbed her by the shoulders and looked her in the eyes.

"No matter what, I'll be here to help you navigate your way through the mess, okay?"

"Okay," Hannah said.

For the briefest of seconds, she considered mentioning assassin Ash Pierce's imminent transfer from Lompoc Penitentiary to Twin Towers in L.A. for her earlier trial date but decided that they'd dealt with enough heavy stuff for now. That piece of bad news could wait until later.

"How's Kat?" her sister asked, switching subjects before it became an issue. "Is she still coming back to town tomorrow?"

"Yes," Jessie assured her. "And she's still planning to reopen the detective agency the next day. She wants you to know she'd love to have her intern back if you're up for it. But considering the unexpected excitement last night, you should feel free to press pause."

"No way," Hannah said. "I wouldn't want to let her down, especially since I only have two weeks left before college starts. Besides, with everything she's been through, she'll need all the help she can get."

Jessie couldn't handle any more talk of the future, particularly how, imminently now, her sister would be leaving the nest. Feeling the lump in her chest from earlier migrating to her stomach, she quickly tried to shut it down.

"Now did anything else noteworthy happen this weekend," she asked abruptly, "I mean other than being attacked by a tall, creepy guy on the pier?"

"Actually, kind of," Hannah said. "At lunch yesterday, there was a *different* creepy guy staring at me, but when I confronted him, he apologized and said it was because he recognized me as your sister. He asked me to say 'hi' and 'thank you' to you."

"Oh, who was that?"

"I think his name was something Gelman."

"Andy Gelman?" Jessie asked, surprised.

"That's it!" Hannah said. "So you *do* know him then? He wasn't full of it?"

"No, I know him," Jessie said, that uncomfortable tingle she knew so well starting to percolate in her gut. "I just thought he was out of the country."

"He said that he was," Hannah explained. "It was kind of weird, now that I think about it. He said he moved away because he was messed up or something. But he's back—said he has a beach house around here now. He also said that you helped him out of a jam and that he wanted you to know that he really appreciated it. What exactly happened with him?"

"Did I hear you mention Andy Gelman?" Ryan said, coming back over.

"Okay, what is the deal with this guy?" Hannah said. "You guys both look super serious all of a sudden."

Jessie looked at Ryan, unsure how forthright to be, then decided that there was no point in keeping this story from Hannah. She'd heard worse. Hell, she'd been through worse.

"Do you remember eighteen months ago, when we investigated the case of that escort who was killing johns?" Jessie said. "Well, Andy was going to be one of her victims. But he wasn't actually a john. He was just a sweet guy in his mid-twenties who also happened to be a multi-millionaire app designer. He was in a bar with his friends one night and met this beautiful girl. He thought they hit it off and she went back to his place. But it turned out that she intended to kill him. She drugged him and was about to slice his throat with a shard of glass from a broken tumbler. Luckily, we got there just in time to stop her and convinced her to let him go."

Jessie stopped talking and Ryan picked up the story but as he spoke she was only half-listening.

"The whole experience really did a number on him," Ryan said. "He ended up getting a villa in the south of France and sort of checked out of the daily grind completely. I thought he was still there."

"So did I," Jessie said, pulling out her phone and calling Jamil. "I think everyone did."

"It's only been a few minutes," Jamil said when he answered the phone. "I haven't forgotten the survivors' meeting."

"When you were reaching out to potential future victims of the Clone Killer," she asked, ignoring his comment and putting him on speaker, "did you include Andy Gelman on the list?"

After a moment of stunned silence, he responded.

"No. We only contacted locals and he's living in France."

"Apparently not anymore," Jessie said. "According to Hannah, he's living in a beach house not far from our current location. Can you do a search to see if he's purchased or renting anything nearby?"

"Hold on," Jamil said, typing furiously. It took less than fifteen seconds for him to come back on the line. "He moved back here two weeks ago. He bought a beach house just over the border from Santa Monica in Malibu. I'm texting you the address now."

When it arrived, Ryan pulled it up on the map on his phone.

"That's less than a quarter of a mile from here," he said. "I think we should stop by and check in on him."

Jessie nodded, already heading for the car. She looked back at her sister, who was staring at her with a stunned but unsurprised expression on her face.

"I'm sorry, but it looks like you're going to be hanging out with your friends a little bit longer."

"I figured," Hannah said.

Jessie turned to Ryan and, filled with a combination of anticipation and dread, said, "Let's hurry."

EPILOGUE

Mark Haddonfield was furious with himself.

As he sat on his bed in his tiny apartment, he turned the events of the weekend over in his mind for the hundredth time.

The Andy Gelman murder had gone perfectly, just like all the others had, just like The Strategy had dictated. He had used a long shard of glass to slice the man's neck open, just as the prostitute, Alexis Cutter, would have done if Jessie hadn't talked her down. He had left a yellow highlighter by the body as a calling card, more proof that he was now the teacher and Jessie was the student. Eventually she would make that connection.

If he had just left it at that, everything would have been fine. But then he had to go and talk to Hannah Dorsey afterwards.

In retrospect, it was a mistake to engage with her at all. At first, it seemed like a happy coincidence that she was staying within walking distance of Gelman's beach house. And he had told himself that it was actually an unexpected blessing that he would get to watch her this weekend, to learn details about her that could be used later against her sister. He could determine just how much losing Hannah would hurt Jessie.

But then he'd lost sight of the plan. He'd become smitten with Hannah Dorsey. He'd gotten overwhelmed by her beauty and her charm and her tough "don't give a damn" spirit. Somehow, despite seeing her making out with another guy—an *artist* no less—he'd convinced himself that he could win her over, that she would somehow see that they were connected to each other and meant to be together.

Instead, she'd not only rejected him, but humiliated him and even injured him, forcing him to hobble away into the night. He'd been defeated by a teenage girl who didn't even know what she was up against until seconds before the threat revealed itself. It was shameful. And it would not stand.

He hadn't just lost sight of the plan. For a while there, he'd lost his way entirely. He'd allowed himself to think that he could let her live, that there might be a fairy tale ending for her instead of a box in the dirt.

"I won't be tempted again," he whispered quietly to himself.

He wouldn't be tempted again. It was clear to him what had to happen now. He hadn't been certain before because the evidence wasn't all in. But now it was overwhelming. And now The Strategy would play out without any pitstops for silly romanticism.

It would be a double whammy. Yes, there would be Jessie's ongoing shame: the shame of failing those she had tried to save. And of course, the city would soon turn on her as the beloved Angel of the City of Angels would be viewed as L.A.'s Angel of Death.

"You're the Angel of Death, Jessie," he mumbled. "When they see you, they'll run the other way in terror."

But the best was yet to come. Mark had decided that when the time came, his ultimate victim would, of course, be none other than Hannah Dorsey. It would be so delicious. He would get to punish the girl who denied him, who degraded him.

Degraded.

And at the same time, the person whom Jessie had saved in both body and soul would be taken from her forever, destroying whatever semblance of normalcy and humanity kept her sane in an insane world.

"When I'm done with you, you'll beg me to kill you, Jessie," he muttered under his breath. "You'll plead for me to end your suffering. But you should know better than that. Seeing you suffer is my peace. Destroying your hope is my duty. I will do my duty, Jessie."

He would destroy both women, and a whole family, with just one kill. It might not be his next kill, but it would be his last one, his greatest one.

Mark felt better now. Everything was going to work out for the best.

NOW AVAILABLE!

THE PERFECT WITNESS
(A Jessie Hunt Psychological Suspense Thriller—Book Twenty-Eight)

When multiple women are found dead, fitting a pattern, yet there is seemingly no connection between them. Jessie knows they are hiding secrets deep in their past, and unlocking them will be the key to stopping this killer before he strikes again. But can she figure it out in time?

"A masterpiece of thriller and mystery."
—Books and Movie Reviews, Roberto Mattos (re Once Gone)

THE PERFECT WITNESS is book #28 in a new psychological suspense series by bestselling author Blake Pierce, which begins with *The Perfect Wife*, a #1 bestseller (and free download) with over 5,000 five-star ratings and 1,000 five-star reviews.

A fast-paced psychological suspense thriller with unforgettable characters and heart-pounding suspense, the JESSIE HUNT series is a riveting new series that will leave you turning pages late into the night.

Future books in the series will soon be available.

"An edge of your seat thriller in a new series that keeps you turning pages! ...So many twists, turns and red herrings… I can't wait to see what happens next."
—Reader review (Her Last Wish)

"A strong, complex story about two FBI agents trying to stop a serial killer. If you want an author to capture your attention and have you guessing, yet trying to put the pieces together, Pierce is your author!"
—Reader review (Her Last Wish)

"A typical Blake Pierce twisting, turning, roller coaster ride suspense thriller. Will have you turning the pages to the last sentence of the last chapter!!!"
—Reader review (City of Prey)

"Right from the start we have an unusual protagonist that I haven't seen done in this genre before. The action is nonstop… A very atmospheric novel that will keep you turning pages well into the wee hours."
—Reader review (City of Prey)

"Everything that I look for in a book… a great plot, interesting characters, and grabs your interest right away. The book moves along at a breakneck pace and stays that way until the end. Now on go I to book two!"
—Reader review (Girl, Alone)

"Exciting, heart pounding, edge of your seat book… a must read for mystery and suspense readers!"
—Reader review (Girl, Alone)

Blake Pierce

Blake Pierce is the USA Today bestselling author of the RILEY PAGE mystery series, which includes seventeen books. Blake Pierce is also the author of the MACKENZIE WHITE mystery series, comprising fourteen books; of the AVERY BLACK mystery series, comprising six books; of the KERI LOCKE mystery series, comprising five books; of the MAKING OF RILEY PAIGE mystery series, comprising six books; of the KATE WISE mystery series, comprising seven books; of the CHLOE FINE psychological suspense mystery, comprising six books; of the JESSIE HUNT psychological suspense thriller series, comprising twenty-eight books; of the AU PAIR psychological suspense thriller series, comprising three books; of the ZOE PRIME mystery series, comprising six books; of the ADELE SHARP mystery series, comprising sixteen books, of the EUROPEAN VOYAGE cozy mystery series, comprising six books; of the LAURA FROST FBI suspense thriller, comprising eleven books; of the ELLA DARK FBI suspense thriller, comprising fourteen books (and counting); of the A YEAR IN EUROPE cozy mystery series, comprising nine books, of the AVA GOLD mystery series, comprising six books; of the RACHEL GIFT mystery series, comprising ten books (and counting); of the VALERIE LAW mystery series, comprising nine books (and counting); of the PAIGE KING mystery series, comprising eight books (and counting); of the MAY MOORE mystery series, comprising eleven books; of the CORA SHIELDS mystery series, comprising eight books (and counting); of the NICKY LYONS mystery series, comprising eight books (and counting), of the CAMI LARK mystery series, comprising eight books (and counting), of the AMBER YOUNG mystery series, comprising five books (and counting), of the DAISY FORTUNE mystery series, comprising five books (and counting), of the FIONA RED mystery series, comprising eight books (and counting), of the FAITH BOLD mystery series, comprising eight books (and counting), of the JULIETTE HART mystery series, comprising five books (and counting), of the MORGAN CROSS mystery series, comprising five books (and counting), and of the new FINN WRIGHT mystery series, comprising five books (and counting).

An avid reader and lifelong fan of the mystery and thriller genres,

Blake loves to hear from you, so please feel free to visit www.blakepierceauthor.com to learn more and stay in touch.

BOOKS BY BLAKE PIERCE

FINN WRIGHT MYSTERY SERIES
WHEN YOU'RE MINE (Book #1)
WHEN YOU'RE SAFE (Book #2)
WHEN YOU'RE CLOSE (Book #3)
WHEN YOU'RE SLEEPING (Book #4)
WHEN YOU'RE SANE (Book #5)

MORGAN CROSS MYSTERY SERIES
FOR YOU (Book #1)
FOR RAGE (Book #2)
FOR LUST (Book #3)
FOR WRATH (Book #4)
FOREVER (Book #5)

JULIETTE HART MYSTERY SERIES
NOTHING TO FEAR (Book #1)
NOTHING THERE (Book #2)
NOTHING WATCHING (Book #3)
NOTHING HIDING (Book #4)
NOTHING LEFT (Book #5)

FAITH BOLD MYSTERY SERIES
SO LONG (Book #1)
SO COLD (Book #2)
SO SCARED (Book #3)
SO NORMAL (Book #4)
SO FAR GONE (Book #5)
SO LOST (Book #6)
SO ALONE (Book #7)
SO FORGOTTEN (Book #8)

FIONA RED MYSTERY SERIES
LET HER GO (Book #1)
LET HER BE (Book #2)
LET HER HOPE (Book #3)

LET HER WISH (Book #4)
LET HER LIVE (Book #5)
LET HER RUN (Book #6)
LET HER HIDE (Book #7)
LET HER BELIEVE (Book #8)

DAISY FORTUNE MYSTERY SERIES
NEED YOU (Book #1)
CLAIM YOU (Book #2)
CRAVE YOU (Book #3)
CHOOSE YOU (Book #4)
CHASE YOU (Book #5)

AMBER YOUNG MYSTERY SERIES
ABSENT PITY (Book #1)
ABSENT REMORSE (Book #2)
ABSENT FEELING (Book #3)
ABSENT MERCY (Book #4)
ABSENT REASON (Book #5)

CAMI LARK MYSTERY SERIES
JUST ME (Book #1)
JUST OUTSIDE (Book #2)
JUST RIGHT (Book #3)
JUST FORGET (Book #4)
JUST ONCE (Book #5)
JUST HIDE (Book #6)
JUST NOW (Book #7)
JUST HOPE (Book #8)

NICKY LYONS MYSTERY SERIES
ALL MINE (Book #1)
ALL HIS (Book #2)
ALL HE SEES (Book #3)
ALL ALONE (Book #4)
ALL FOR ONE (Book #5)
ALL HE TAKES (Book #6)
ALL FOR ME (Book #7)
ALL IN (Book #8)

CORA SHIELDS MYSTERY SERIES

UNDONE (Book #1)

UNWANTED (Book #2)

UNHINGED (Book #3)

UNSAID (Book #4)

UNGLUED (Book #5)

UNSTABLE (Book #6)

UNKNOWN (Book #7)

UNAWARE (Book #8)

MAY MOORE SUSPENSE THRILLER

NEVER RUN (Book #1)

NEVER TELL (Book #2)

NEVER LIVE (Book #3)

NEVER HIDE (Book #4)

NEVER FORGIVE (Book #5)

NEVER AGAIN (Book #6)

NEVER LOOK BACK (Book #7)

NEVER FORGET (Book #8)

NEVER LET GO (Book #9)

NEVER PRETEND (Book #10)

NEVER HESITATE (Book #11)

PAIGE KING MYSTERY SERIES

THE GIRL HE PINED (Book #1)

THE GIRL HE CHOSE (Book #2)

THE GIRL HE TOOK (Book #3)

THE GIRL HE WISHED (Book #4)

THE GIRL HE CROWNED (Book #5)

THE GIRL HE WATCHED (Book #6)

THE GIRL HE WANTED (Book #7)

THE GIRL HE CLAIMED (Book #8)

VALERIE LAW MYSTERY SERIES

NO MERCY (Book #1)

NO PITY (Book #2)

NO FEAR (Book #3)

NO SLEEP (Book #4)

NO QUARTER (Book #5)

NO CHANCE (Book #6)

NO REFUGE (Book #7)
NO GRACE (Book #8)
NO ESCAPE (Book #9)

RACHEL GIFT MYSTERY SERIES
HER LAST WISH (Book #1)
HER LAST CHANCE (Book #2)
HER LAST HOPE (Book #3)
HER LAST FEAR (Book #4)
HER LAST CHOICE (Book #5)
HER LAST BREATH (Book #6)
HER LAST MISTAKE (Book #7)
HER LAST DESIRE (Book #8)
HER LAST REGRET (Book #9)
HER LAST HOUR (Book #10)

AVA GOLD MYSTERY SERIES
CITY OF PREY (Book #1)
CITY OF FEAR (Book #2)
CITY OF BONES (Book #3)
CITY OF GHOSTS (Book #4)
CITY OF DEATH (Book #5)
CITY OF VICE (Book #6)

A YEAR IN EUROPE
A MURDER IN PARIS (Book #1)
DEATH IN FLORENCE (Book #2)
VENGEANCE IN VIENNA (Book #3)
A FATALITY IN SPAIN (Book #4)

ELLA DARK FBI SUSPENSE THRILLER
GIRL, ALONE (Book #1)
GIRL, TAKEN (Book #2)
GIRL, HUNTED (Book #3)
GIRL, SILENCED (Book #4)
GIRL, VANISHED (Book 5)
GIRL ERASED (Book #6)
GIRL, FORSAKEN (Book #7)
GIRL, TRAPPED (Book #8)
GIRL, EXPENDABLE (Book #9)

GIRL, ESCAPED (Book #10)
GIRL, HIS (Book #11)
GIRL, LURED (Book #12)
GIRL, MISSING (Book #13)
GIRL, UNKNOWN (Book #14)

LAURA FROST FBI SUSPENSE THRILLER

ALREADY GONE (Book #1)
ALREADY SEEN (Book #2)
ALREADY TRAPPED (Book #3)
ALREADY MISSING (Book #4)
ALREADY DEAD (Book #5)
ALREADY TAKEN (Book #6)
ALREADY CHOSEN (Book #7)
ALREADY LOST (Book #8)
ALREADY HIS (Book #9)
ALREADY LURED (Book #10)
ALREADY COLD (Book #11)

EUROPEAN VOYAGE COZY MYSTERY SERIES

MURDER (AND BAKLAVA) (Book #1)
DEATH (AND APPLE STRUDEL) (Book #2)
CRIME (AND LAGER) (Book #3)
MISFORTUNE (AND GOUDA) (Book #4)
CALAMITY (AND A DANISH) (Book #5)
MAYHEM (AND HERRING) (Book #6)

ADELE SHARP MYSTERY SERIES

LEFT TO DIE (Book #1)
LEFT TO RUN (Book #2)
LEFT TO HIDE (Book #3)
LEFT TO KILL (Book #4)
LEFT TO MURDER (Book #5)
LEFT TO ENVY (Book #6)
LEFT TO LAPSE (Book #7)
LEFT TO VANISH (Book #8)
LEFT TO HUNT (Book #9)
LEFT TO FEAR (Book #10)
LEFT TO PREY (Book #11)
LEFT TO LURE (Book #12)

LEFT TO CRAVE (Book #13)
LEFT TO LOATHE (Book #14)
LEFT TO HARM (Book #15)
LEFT TO RUIN (Book #16)

THE AU PAIR SERIES
ALMOST GONE (Book#1)
ALMOST LOST (Book #2)
ALMOST DEAD (Book #3)

ZOE PRIME MYSTERY SERIES
FACE OF DEATH (Book#1)
FACE OF MURDER (Book #2)
FACE OF FEAR (Book #3)
FACE OF MADNESS (Book #4)
FACE OF FURY (Book #5)
FACE OF DARKNESS (Book #6)

A JESSIE HUNT PSYCHOLOGICAL SUSPENSE SERIES
THE PERFECT WIFE (Book #1)
THE PERFECT BLOCK (Book #2)
THE PERFECT HOUSE (Book #3)
THE PERFECT SMILE (Book #4)
THE PERFECT LIE (Book #5)
THE PERFECT LOOK (Book #6)
THE PERFECT AFFAIR (Book #7)
THE PERFECT ALIBI (Book #8)
THE PERFECT NEIGHBOR (Book #9)
THE PERFECT DISGUISE (Book #10)
THE PERFECT SECRET (Book #11)
THE PERFECT FAÇADE (Book #12)
THE PERFECT IMPRESSION (Book #13)
THE PERFECT DECEIT (Book #14)
THE PERFECT MISTRESS (Book #15)
THE PERFECT IMAGE (Book #16)
THE PERFECT VEIL (Book #17)
THE PERFECT INDISCRETION (Book #18)
THE PERFECT RUMOR (Book #19)
THE PERFECT COUPLE (Book #20)
THE PERFECT MURDER (Book #21)

THE PERFECT HUSBAND (Book #22)
THE PERFECT SCANDAL (Book #23)
THE PERFECT MASK (Book #24)
THE PERFECT RUSE (Book #25)
THE PERFECT VENEER (Book #26)
THE PERFECT PEOPLE (Book #27)
THE PERFECT WITNESS (Book #28)

CHLOE FINE PSYCHOLOGICAL SUSPENSE SERIES
NEXT DOOR (Book #1)
A NEIGHBOR'S LIE (Book #2)
CUL DE SAC (Book #3)
SILENT NEIGHBOR (Book #4)
HOMECOMING (Book #5)
TINTED WINDOWS (Book #6)

KATE WISE MYSTERY SERIES
IF SHE KNEW (Book #1)
IF SHE SAW (Book #2)
IF SHE RAN (Book #3)
IF SHE HID (Book #4)
IF SHE FLED (Book #5)
IF SHE FEARED (Book #6)
IF SHE HEARD (Book #7)

THE MAKING OF RILEY PAIGE SERIES
WATCHING (Book #1)
WAITING (Book #2)
LURING (Book #3)
TAKING (Book #4)
STALKING (Book #5)
KILLING (Book #6)

RILEY PAIGE MYSTERY SERIES
ONCE GONE (Book #1)
ONCE TAKEN (Book #2)
ONCE CRAVED (Book #3)
ONCE LURED (Book #4)
ONCE HUNTED (Book #5)
ONCE PINED (Book #6)

ONCE FORSAKEN (Book #7)
ONCE COLD (Book #8)
ONCE STALKED (Book #9)
ONCE LOST (Book #10)
ONCE BURIED (Book #11)
ONCE BOUND (Book #12)
ONCE TRAPPED (Book #13)
ONCE DORMANT (Book #14)
ONCE SHUNNED (Book #15)
ONCE MISSED (Book #16)
ONCE CHOSEN (Book #17)

MACKENZIE WHITE MYSTERY SERIES
BEFORE HE KILLS (Book #1)
BEFORE HE SEES (Book #2)
BEFORE HE COVETS (Book #3)
BEFORE HE TAKES (Book #4)
BEFORE HE NEEDS (Book #5)
BEFORE HE FEELS (Book #6)
BEFORE HE SINS (Book #7)
BEFORE HE HUNTS (Book #8)
BEFORE HE PREYS (Book #9)
BEFORE HE LONGS (Book #10)
BEFORE HE LAPSES (Book #11)
BEFORE HE ENVIES (Book #12)
BEFORE HE STALKS (Book #13)
BEFORE HE HARMS (Book #14)

AVERY BLACK MYSTERY SERIES
CAUSE TO KILL (Book #1)
CAUSE TO RUN (Book #2)
CAUSE TO HIDE (Book #3)
CAUSE TO FEAR (Book #4)
CAUSE TO SAVE (Book #5)
CAUSE TO DREAD (Book #6)

KERI LOCKE MYSTERY SERIES
A TRACE OF DEATH (Book #1)
A TRACE OF MURDER (Book #2)
A TRACE OF VICE (Book #3)

A TRACE OF CRIME (Book #4)
A TRACE OF HOPE (Book #5)

appleTV + google
210 Bar 36 L

29 Oct
777 523 0576
7354526 booking

Made in the USA
Monee, IL
11 June 2023